BEN

Matthew Gilbert

First published 2016
by Rowanvale Books Ltd
Imperial House
Trade Street Lane
Cardiff
CF10 5DT
www.rowanvalebooks.com

A CIP catalogue record for this book is available from the British Library.
ISBN: 978-1-911240-15-0

For my wife Laura. I love you.
'Petrol tastes revolting.' I had to do the rest myself!

Introduction

I first started writing this story ten years ago when I was travelling with some friends. I had recently been to the bookstore in Bondi Junction, Sydney, and was not that interested in anything that I saw there. Being on quite a tight budget meant that my choice of books were bargain bin novels, second-hand books or books I found in hostels as we moved around. So I decided to write my own story. However, time progressed — along with my life and career. A decade later, the story is complete. It has undergone a number of plot and character changes over the years. So here it is...ten years in the making. I hope you enjoy it!

Chapter 1

There it was again. That sound. Or had he imagined it? It was a sound that he remembered well. One that used to haunt his dreams — or rather, his nightmares. It was a short, high-pitched sound, like a fork scratching on a china plate; only it seemed to reverberate inside his head for hours as if it were a rubber ball trapped inside a box. Ben lay there, in his aging single bed, in complete darkness. His headboard was metal and looked almost like a railing attached to the bed. He had lost a pillow, sacrificed to the gap between the headboard and the wall. This was a nightly occurrence. He was now awake, and had convinced himself that he had imagined the sound, or dreamt it. Either way, it had not been real; it was in his head and he had to forget about it and get back to sleep. He looked at his bedside clock. It read 2:25; he had been awake now for twenty minutes, but the more he tried to get to sleep, the more awake he seemed to become. He couldn't get that sound out of his head. He hoped it didn't mean the start of his childhood nightmares again.

The nightmares had haunted him for nearly a year when he was eleven. His parents had put it down to him joining a new school, and the beginning of his adolescence. 'A cry for attention,' he had overheard his father say one evening when he couldn't sleep; he hadn't had a nightmare but the fear of having one had kept him awake. He would always deny the fact that it was a cry for attention because it wasn't. However, he *had* joined a new school, one which was about ten times larger than his previous school (or at least it had seemed it at the time). True, he had been scared, but he knew that this wasn't the cause of his nightmares. Nonetheless, he didn't know what the cause was.

And then, not long before his twelfth birthday, the nightmares had stopped suddenly. He had eventually forgotten about them; that is, until a week ago — or maybe two weeks ago, he couldn't remember.

He looked at the clock again. The small, bright red numbers of the digital display gleamed in the darkness; it was 2:40. Ben still didn't feel tired, but he had become remarkably thirsty. Slowly, he sat up and swivelled around so that his feet were on the floor. His eyes still couldn't make out any shapes in the darkness. It did seem unusually dark, almost as if a thick blanket had enveloped him, and his senses were trapped within a cocoon of pitch. The light switch was on the opposite wall to the bed. Ben's bedroom was relatively basic with nothing remarkable about it except for a picture, which his grandmother had given him when she came back from Belarus. It was around ten inches square and had a faded sepia tone due to its age. The picture was of a woman and a man, who both had an eastern European look about them. The man had a bristly black moustache and a side parting in his dark, thick hair, which was greased down into place. He wore a suit and tie, which looked not quite black, but more of a colour that you couldn't put your finger on due to the discolouring of the picture. The woman had curly hair that was possibly dark blonde or a light red colour and a bonnet that went well with her dress. Neither one was smiling in the photograph. The woman was sitting and on her knee was a child, a young boy of about three. He was dressed in dark colours, quite possibly navy. It was possible to see that he was not wearing the same colour as the man that was probably his father (although there was no resemblance) because the shades were noticeably different. The child was the most fascinating subject of the picture, for no other reason than his facial expression. Or, more specifically, his smile. Not only was he the only person smiling in the picture, but the smile was not one of happiness or joy but rather one of menace. Many people had remarked on the smiling boy but had never decided what the smile meant. When asked why she had bought the picture, Ben's grandmother said that she just liked it.

Next to the photograph was a mirror, and below the mirror was a desk covered in sheets of paper, rubbish and the remains of last night's dinner, which had been chips and fish (battered, not breaded; Ben hated breadcrumbs on food, especially fish) with tartar sauce. Opposite the desk stood an old wardrobe that his mother had given him when he moved into the flat earlier that year. It had an old musty smell that reminded him of his parents' house: a mixture of pot pourri and cigar smoke. His father loved cigars; he went to specialty shops and bought boxes that were often priced at as much as ten pounds per cigar. Ben had often thought that it was an incredible waste of money.

Ben stood up, took two steps forward and then gave out a loud scream as a horrific pain shot through his foot and started throbbing. He had stood on something that instantly cut through the flesh and deep into the sole of his foot. The pain at first felt more like a burn but then the deep cut started to pulsate. He staggered sideways and put his hand in the now-congealed tartar sauce as he steadied himself. He leant there for several moments, grimacing and gritting his teeth through the pain, and a tear came to his eye. Ben raised himself up and, slowly, half-limped and half-hopped his way over to the bedroom door. He felt for the light switch, found it and flicked it on. Nothing. He flicked it again — *click* — nothing. He flicked it up and down several times to no avail; he would have to get to the kitchen in complete darkness with a right foot that was now in a mixture of agony and numbness. He started to sweat. Walking on his right heel, the only part of his foot that didn't seem cut or in pain, he felt the cut stretch under the strain. He winced again. Making his way through the small lounge and into the kitchen, Ben wondered what the heck he could've stood on to cause him this much pain. His thoughts temporarily replaced the reverberating sound inside his head, but not for long. His mind was now a dense cocktail of confusion, pain and that sound. He had a headache. Once again, he felt for a light switch, and he found it. Once again, the light did not come on; the kitchen remained shrouded in thick, dark silence.

'Must be the fuse,' Ben mused out loud to himself; his voice seemed to trumpet in the silent darkness. *The fridge…* he thought. *The light inside the fridge should be enough.* Ben leant over towards it, just to the left of the light switch and the doorway. He opened the fridge door, and out came a smell of fruit and cooked meats, along with the faint smell of pizza left over from the night before. He had been too tired to cook, so had ordered a takeaway. The pizza was a spicy one with jalapenos and chillies and pepperoni — his regular choice. However, there was no light to accompany the smell that met him from the fridge. He shut the door and then reopened it to see if that would set the light off — again, to no avail.

'Dammit!' Ben cursed and slammed the fridge door shut. He stood in the doorway of the kitchen for a few minutes, thinking of what he could do. He winced again at the pain in his foot. It was excruciating. Suddenly, an idea came to him: the digital clock by his bed! It had a red light, which could be enough for him to see the cuts in his foot and clean them up. Again, he crossed the lounge and entered his bedroom. He could feel the blood running down the sole of his cold, sweaty foot; it felt almost hot. He reached the clock, picked it up and went back to the kitchen. The red light, which read 3:32, was surprisingly bright amidst the night's dense shadows.

Where has the time gone? Ben thought as he

walked over to the sink. Gritting his teeth, he lifted his foot up to the tap and rested the clock on the draining board. It shone onto his foot; there was one large, deep cut and several smaller cuts, just as deep, scattered around the bloodied sole of his right foot. The blood seemed very dark, almost a gleaming black shadow seeping out through the slits in his skin. It was dripping into the sink, where it pooled, glistening darkly under the red light of the clock. Ben examined the cuts as best he could, and found that there were glass fragments in the larger cut and in one of the smaller cuts. He gently brushed his fingers over one of the fragments; pain instantly shot up his foot like a lightning bolt. The glass was wedged deep into his flesh. Slowly, Ben eased one of the pieces of glass out. The pain was almost unbearable — more dark blood poured out over his fingers. Tears now ran down his cheeks and mixed with the blood in the sink, forming a pattern similar to the tie-dye patterns on t-shirts. Finally he pulled the piece of glass out of his foot and threw it into the metal sink; it clanked as it hit the bottom. Ben turned his attention to the second piece of glass, slightly bigger than the first. Feeling slightly faint, he pulled the glass out of the arch of his foot. The blood, which now seemed even darker than before, still ran from the cuts and into the sink. He threw the glass into the sink with the first piece.

Ben turned on the tap and ran cold water over his foot. The pain hit a new level — he could almost feel the water rush into each individual wound. Gritting his teeth, he put his foot down and moved toward the cupboard where all the medicines and the first aid kit were kept. He opened the cupboard and felt around for a bandage. After knocking over several bottles of aspirin and other tablets, which were rarely used, he found a bandage. With his foot up on the sink again, Ben tried to secure the bandage and, at the third attempt, he managed a relatively loose, makeshift job.

That will have to do, he thought. He struggled back to the bedroom and lay down again. Feeling completely drained and aching all over his body, suffering through the agonising pain, it did not take him long to fall asleep.

Chapter 2

It was going to be another one of those nights. A night when every single tiny noise kept her awake. They weren't the usual sorts of noises that kept one awake, like the tap dripping into the sink or the ticking of the clock; her room was far enough away from the kitchen or bathroom for the tap not to be a problem even if it *was* dripping, and her clock was digital, so it didn't tick. The noises that kept her awake would seem to anyone else (if she had told them) somewhat psychosomatic. Although, on some level, she knew that her mind was not playing tricks on her; these noises were actually occurring, but she couldn't put her finger on where they were coming from.

'It's just stress from work, Kim,' her mother had said when she told her that she was having trouble sleeping. 'Try and take up yoga or something, that's supposed to be good to combat stress.'

Kim Coombes was a primary school teacher who loved her job; she adored children and took great joy in seeing them grow through the school. Her job did not stress her out at all. She was twenty-eight, with shoulder-length blonde hair, green eyes and an athletic physique. She went to the gym twice, sometimes three times a week and had recently started seeing a man whom even her mother liked. This was a rare occurrence, and she had caught herself thinking that he was 'the one' on more than one occasion. This hadn't happened before, and once it would have scared her. Not this time — not with Ben. They had been dating for four months now and the relationship excited her. He was about six feet tall — or maybe more, she wasn't sure. Not too tall and not too short, anyway. He had thick black hair and dark brown eyes, and his smile showed a lot of teeth. But this was fine, because his teeth were perfect. He was fit — not overly muscular, but toned — and he went to the same gym she did. This was where they had met. He had a good job; he was a buyer for an electronics manufacturing company, which paid well but did mean a lot of travelling up and down the country. He had also told her that soon he may have to travel in Europe but hoped he could take her along on those excursions, if it didn't interfere with her teaching. The thought of going through Europe with him made her tingle; she had already thought about Paris and Rome and hoped his job would take him (and her) there.

She looked at the clock. It was 2:30. She wanted to call Ben; she was wide awake and could do with a chat. She thought better of it and rolled over, giving a sigh as she did so. Thinking of Ben, she tried to fall asleep, but the more she tried, the harder it became. She rolled back over and reached for her glass of water. She took a sip. It seemed unusually cold, as if it had ice cubes in it, but it hadn't. Neither was it a cold night. However, the water was refreshing, and so she took another sip before placing the glass back on the bedside table. Again, she looked at the clock; it now read 3:32. She had to look twice. She could not believe that somewhere she had lost an hour. Had she fallen asleep? She didn't think so, but that was the only explanation. And now she really wanted to call Ben. Kim leant further over the bedside table to the phone, knocking the glass of water to the floor as she did so.

'Shit!' she cursed, and the sound almost seemed to echo in her quiet room. She picked up the receiver and started to dial Ben's number. She had dialed four digits when she laughed to herself and put the phone down.

What am I doing? she thought. *It's nearly four in the morning; he'll think I am mad, calling him.* Suddenly, she felt drowsy again. She turned over and closed her eyes. She was out within moments, as if she had been deprived of sleep for days.

The alarm on her clock woke her up at seven o'clock with a pulsating, droning noise. She groaned and switched it off. At 7:15, she sat up, rubbed her eyes and yawned. Kim looked over to the phone, and decided to call Ben.

He'll have to get up soon anyway, if he's not up already, she reasoned. As she reached over to the phone something caught her eye on the floor. A little glint. It was the glass; it had smashed and shards were glistening in the morning sun that was forcing its way between the drawn curtains. The fragments were very small and the way they were sparkling made them look almost like diamonds. Kim couldn't believe the glass had broken; she didn't remember it smashing last night. Still, she picked up the phone, dialed Ben's number and waited for him to answer. She was still gazing at the pieces of glass. Whilst the phone was ringing, she leant down and touched where the water must have spilt onto the carpet. It was bone dry. Could it have dried that quickly? She wasn't sure. She continued to look at the floor, confused. She didn't even notice when Ben answered the phone in a weary tone.

'Hello?'

Chapter 3

Ben held the phone in his left hand, his eyes still closed. When there was no answer, he shifted himself, opened his eyes and sat up.

'Hello?' he said more coherently. 'Who's there?' He was about to put the phone down when a voice on the other end said, 'Oh — Ben — sorry, I must have spaced out there for a second. I didn't sleep too well last night.'

'Kim? You sound a bit shaken — everything all right?'

'Yes, fine. I broke a glass last night and forgot about it when I went back to sleep,' she answered. 'I was just a bit shocked to see it there on the floor just now, but there's no problem.'

'Good,' Ben replied. 'Actually, I had a bit of a difficult night too, I must have broken a glass in the night and when...' He stopped suddenly as he looked to where the broken glass had been, only to find no traces of glass anywhere on his bedroom floor. *Did I clear it up?*

'Ben? Ben?!' Kim was calling him down the phone.

'Yes? Oh, actually, Kim, I think I must have dreamt it...' Ben said, confused.

'Dreamt what?'

'Nothing, it's silly. So, are you ready for a day of school?' he said, changing the subject.

'Yes, I'm raring to go. In fact, I think I'd better go and get ready now. I will see you later tonight, yeah?'

'Yes, you will. I'll come round to yours around six.'

'That's fine. Ok, I have to go now. Ben, you sure everything is ok?' Kim asked, sounding concerned.

'Yes, everything is fine — just a bad dream, I guess. I will let you go now, Kim. Speak to you soon. Love you.'

'Love you too. Bye!'

'Bye.'

Kim hung up.

Ben looked down at the floor, phone still in his hand; there was no blood anywhere, no glass anywhere. He couldn't understand it. Then he realised there was no pain either. He looked at his right foot; there was no blood on it, so he looked at the sole of his foot, where he expected the lacerations to be — or that's where they were last night. There was nothing on the sole of his foot now — no marks, no blood, nothing. He ran his finger slowly across the foot. He couldn't feel any difference at all. There was no sign that anything had happened. Had it been a bad dream? Maybe, but the pain... It had been so intense; he couldn't have dreamed that, surely? Almost in a daze of confusion, Ben got up and turned around, back towards the bed. The sheets were clean, not a trace of blood anywhere.

He shook out the duvet in a vain attempt at making his bed. As he did so, the bottom end of the duvet flicked up. Something red flashed in his eyes, and he went to the end of the bed and lifted up the duvet. There, lying on the mattress, as real as the duvet itself, was a bandage. A bandage smothered in blood. He staggered backwards at what he saw. Disbelief. He looked away and then back again, in the hope that it was his imagination. The bandage was still there. Ben walked forward, bent down and picked it up. The blood was cold and damp and was definitely real. This was no dream; no image created by a tired, and maybe frightened, mind. This bandage was in his hand — proof. He walked to the kitchen, holding the bandage out in front of him. He was looking at it almost in a trance, hypnotised by it. Ben walked up to the sink and dropped the bandage into it. There was a slight grating noise as the damp bandage hit the sink.

What was that? he wondered. Peering into the sink, Ben couldn't believe his eyes for the third time that morning. In the sink, as three-dimensional and physical as the bandage, were two pieces of broken glass, one lying on the bottom of the sink and the other resting in the plughole. He picked up one of the pieces and drew it close to his face, examining it as if it were some fantastic jewel, or a microchip that he was supposed to be purchasing for the company. He shook his head, gave a short sigh and tossed the piece into the bin. He was starting to sweat. He left the kitchen and headed for the shower. It was going to be one hell of a Friday.

Chapter 4

Ben's shower room was cold. The floor was tiled with black ceramic slabs of what seemed to be ice. The walls were also tiled with a black and white design that complemented the floor rather well. The room, although quite small, managed to squeeze a large rectangular shower, a toilet and a basin in it, all of which were white and stood out against the black floor. Above the basin was a cabinet with a mirror on the front. Inside was a toothbrush and toothpaste, hair gel, shampoo and shower gel. The shower room had been newly installed shortly before he moved into the flat; it was a major selling point and probably, he reflected, the most valuable part of the whole flat, since the kitchen, living room and bedroom were rather aged. This was also the cleanest and neatest room in the flat; the flat itself was not exactly a mess — more unkempt — but his shower room was immaculate.

Ben stood barefoot on the cold tiles and looked at himself in the mirror. He was pale and his eyes were quite bloodshot; he looked as if he was hungover from a heavy night of drinking. *A long shower would help me out,* he thought, rubbing his eyes and yawning. Ben got into the shower and washed. He stepped out feeling a lot more refreshed, wrapped a towel around his waist and went to the kitchen to make a cup of tea. He picked up the kettle, walked over to the sink and dropped the kettle; it hit the sink with a crash. Ben looked into the sink for a second time, picking up the kettle. He couldn't believe his eyes; the blood-soaked bandage had vanished, along with the second piece of glass that had been lying in the sink. With the kettle still in his hand, he looked around the kitchen for the bandage, even in cupboards, in the hope that he had for some unknown reason put it into one. The search was in vain; the bandage was nowhere to be found.

Ben filled the kettle with water and switched it on to boil. Then he collapsed onto the kitchen floor.

He awoke a few moments later with the kettle clicking off. He got up — naked, as the towel had slipped off when he fell — and ran into the bedroom to get changed. He needed to leave the flat. Things had gotten a little too weird for his liking and a change of scenery, even if it was his office, would be a welcome break. It would hopefully allow him to clear his head — for a while, at least. Ben finished changing and left the flat earlier than usual, his hair wet and his stomach growling. He got into his car, turned on the engine and, before leaving the garage, looked in the mirror. He still looked pale and his hair was still dishevelled. He didn't care. He needed to get away.

Ben turned on the stereo and put the volume up high to drown out his thoughts. He reversed out and drove up the road, the music booming from the speakers. His car was a metallic navy blue; he had bought it second-hand only a year ago. It had a fuel-injection engine of some sort — not that Ben had paid much attention to the technical details; he just about knew where the spare tyre was, let alone how to change one. All that mattered to him was that it was fast, and that excited him. The car had black leather upholstery, which still smelled new, and a CD player stereo with speakers that any boy racer would be proud of. The stereo now pumped out music for the whole town to hear (and probably the neighbouring town if he opened the windows or sunroof). The car was also fitted with alloy wheels and a spoiler, which Ben didn't really like too much, but it wasn't enough to put him off buying it.

He and Kim had had their first kiss in this car. After taking her to dinner in a pricey Italian restaurant, Ben had driven her home and, instead of a goodnight peck on the cheek, she had given him a proper kiss. He had enjoyed it. As he drove along the dual carriageway to work, he remembered that night and smiled. The thought had temporarily taken his mind off the morning's incidents.

On a good day it took twenty-five minutes to drive to work, and during this time he would usually go over his agenda for the day, what he was going to have for lunch, etc. — but not today. Today he thought about Kim, that date and how happy she made him feel. When he was with her, nothing else seemed to matter. If they were together, it almost felt as if only they had existed in that place at that moment in time. No previous relationship had ever made him feel the way she did. What amazed him most about her was the fact that he couldn't put his finger on why he was so happy — it seemed to be a number of things. She always took an interest in his job. She never seemed bored by his buyer stories, which sometimes seemed dull even to him, and he loved listening to her talk. It didn't matter what the subject was, he just loved listening to her voice, watching her smile, hearing about her life and the way the right side of her mouth sometimes lifted up when she spoke. He couldn't wait to see her tonight. Suddenly, he realised that he had already pulled up into the car park of FanCorp, the electrical company for which he worked. The company originated from China and the owner was a Mr Fan Zhiyi, whom they rarely saw. Ben looked at his watch. It was 8:55; he must have been sitting in the car for half an hour at least, just thinking about Kim. He looked at himself in the rearview mirror. The colour had returned to his face and his eyes, though still slightly bloodshot, were not as bad as they had been earlier. Ben looked at his watch again. 8:57. He was going to be late! He picked up his jacket, which was strewn across the passenger seat, and got out of the car. He pressed a lock and alarm button on the car's key ring and the car made a *beep, beep* sound. He then turned around and walked towards the main reception area of FanCorp.

Chapter 5

After hanging up the phone, Kim's mind turned back to the fragments on the floor. She still couldn't understand how the glass had broken. She bent down and gently patted the carpet again to see if it was definitely dry, and it was. She shook her head as if in attempt to clear her mind and stood up. She went to the shower room, dropped her light blue dressing gown, which she had absentmindedly put on, and got into the shower. What was waiting for her when she had finished showering and went back to the bedroom made her shriek in disbelief. The fragments of glass were no longer on the floor where they had been when she went into the shower; in fact, there were no fragments at all. Kim ran over to where the pieces had been and knelt down next to what was now an empty space of carpet, dropping her towel as she did so. She patted the carpet once again, and smoothed her hands around the area where the glass had been only minutes earlier. Kim looked up and saw there was a glass on her bedside table. She then inspected it carefully. It was identical to the glass she had knocked over last night — and it was full of water.

Kim was still looking at the glass when the doorbell rang. She gave out a little scream, which seemed to echo even louder in the quiet apartment. Again, the doorbell rang. Kim got up, picked up the towel, wrapped it securely around her and walked to the door. She looked through the peephole even though she could see the postman's uniform through the frosted glass. She gave a long sigh of relief and opened the door.

'Package for Kim Coombes,' the postman said.

'That's me!'

'Could you sign here please, Miss Coombes?' The postman handed her a clipboard and pen, and showed her where to sign. Kim signed and took the package from the postman.

'Thank you,' she said, her brow furrowed. She slowly closed the front door and walked towards the living room with the package. Staring at it, she put it on the table. She hadn't been expecting any packages at all.

Just then, the clock on the wall of the living room made a *ding* sound to signal that it was eight o'clock. Kim looked at the clock, groaned and ran to the bedroom, where she quietly got changed. If she didn't hurry she was going to be late for her meeting with the head before the start of school. She finished getting changed and headed towards the front door, then paused and thought about opening the package. She decided against it — she was late enough already. As she closed the front door behind her, the lack of sleep hit her and she suddenly felt extremely tired.

'Strong coffee for me when I get in,' she muttered to herself as she began her twenty minute walk to school. It was 8:25.

Chapter 6

'Good morning, Ben!' called a cheery voice from under the reception desk.

'Hello, Tamzin,' Ben replied to the empty space behind the desk. 'Two questions: firstly, how did you know it was me, and secondly, what are you doing under the desk?'

Tamzin got up from under the desk and smiled at Ben. Ben felt a nervous flutter inside his stomach; he always felt it when he saw Tamzin or even spoke to her on the phone when she was putting a call through to his office. She was a beautiful woman. He guessed she was around twenty-five years of age. She was only about 5'1" — but she made up for it by wearing shoes with three-inch heels or more. She had shoulder-length blonde hair that she dyed even blonder on a regular basis. Ben could never understand why some women did this, but thought that asking a woman about her looks might come across as insulting. Tamzin's eyes were a turquoise blue, and were often enlarged by the lenses of her black-rimmed glasses. She did wear a lot of makeup — lipstick, eyeliner and some other stuff that Ben couldn't really name... foundation was probably in there somewhere, but he wasn't sure. Short skirts and white blouses were Tamzin's usual attire in reception. Even though she flirted with him every time she spoke to him, Ben had always considered her 'out of his league'. He had described the situation to his mates in the pub on more than one occasion.

'She is like a Champions League team, whereas I am more of a Championship playoff contender.'

His friend Matt would mock him every time. 'Championship playoff? More like League Two relegation battler — and that's being kind!'

He snapped back to the present moment when

Tamzin spoke.

'In response to your first question — security cameras,' she said, tapping the monitor. 'I saw you in the car park. I'm not stalking you or anything. Unless you want a stalker? I have some free time since Chris left me.' Tamzin gave Ben a wink and he blushed a little. 'And I was under the desk waiting for you!' she added flirtatiously. This time Ben's face turned a full shade of crimson and Tamzin laughed.

Ben tried to laugh off the embarrassment but could not. Tamzin could see he was uncomfortable and started to type on the computer keyboard.

'Anyway, I can't stand around all day flirting with you, I'm pretty late as it is,' Ben said after a short pause, and started to walk through the double doors at the side of the reception desk and down the corridor.

'That's the thing though, you never flirt. It's always me. This relationship is so one sided!' Tamzin called after him. Ben ignored her and carried on walking. 'TEASE!' she shouted again, but got no reply.

Chapter 7

Kim hadn't been late for the meeting — although it wouldn't have mattered if she had been. The Head's father had been taken into hospital that night; the Head was staying with him for a while and therefore could not make the meeting. The rest of the school day had been rather uneventful. A bleeding nose at lunchtime — nothing sinister, the boy had probably been picking it too much! Kim was glad when the bell went at 3:15 and all the children were given back to their parents for the evening. She didn't wait around for a chat with anyone else, especially not Joan. Joan was the school secretary/nurse/gossip. She was in her sixties, but had the energy of a teenager in heat and a story for every situation you could dream of. You name it and either Joan had seen it, done it, been there or knew someone who had. Joan meant well but she really irritated Kim, who wasn't going to hang around for a story about one of Joan's bad dreams.

Kim got home, threw her bag on the floor of the hallway and went to the kitchen to make herself a cup of tea. She found herself thinking of Ben again. She had lost count of how many times he had popped into her head during school that day. Then her thoughts drifted to this evening, making her wonder what she going to wear.

'Shit!' she shouted suddenly. 'Ben's coming round here tonight; I've got to get the place tidy.' Just as quickly as the panic had hit her, so did the thought to relax a little. The flat wasn't untidy — it would take a few minutes at most to tidy what little mess there was. Kim sighed a little. 'Relax,' she muttered to herself, and started to think about her dinner.

After finishing her tomato pasta bake, which she had microwaved whilst tidying her flat, Kim got undressed and stepped into the shower. She spent longer than usual in the shower; she wanted to wash the weight of the busy school day from her body and be completely stress-free for when Ben came over. She washed the last of the soapsuds off her now squeaky clean body, turned the shower off, pulled the towel off the rail and wrapped it around her, then wrapped a smaller towel around her head to dry her hair. Kim left the shower room and went to her bedroom, passing the package that she received earlier. She stopped for a second.

Haven't got time to open it now, she thought to herself and carried on through to her bedroom to start getting dressed. Whilst picking up the odd item of clothing during her tidying up session earlier, Kim had already chosen most of what she was going to wear, but she still needed to pick out her underwear. It needed to be carefully chosen; it needed to flatter her figure as well as go with the skirt and top combination she had planned on wearing. She finally decided on a black lace bra and frilly lace briefs. She looked at herself in her full-length mirror and smiled. 'Yep, those are the ones,' she muttered to herself. It was almost a given that Ben was going to stay over tonight. It was Friday; neither of them had to work the next day, so they could lie in until late morning, talking and making love like they had done on their first night together. It had been at Ben's flat. *Not the nicest flat in the world,* Kim had thought the first time she had been inside, but it had grown on her. It was cozy and, of course, it was the first place they had had sex.

Her mind had been drifting again! She quickly put on her black skirt — not too short and not too long; it showed enough of her slim, toned legs but was not slutty. Then she put on her royal blue V-neck top, which showed just enough cleavage without it being something a sixteen-year-old girl might wear to try to get into a nightclub.

Kim was admiring herself in the mirror again when

the doorbell went. 'Shit!' she said. 'He's here already!' Running to the door, Kim stopped at the small mirror in the hallway and flicked her hair into place, took a deep breath and opened the door.

Chapter 8

'Hey, babe!' exclaimed Ben as Kim opened the door.

She looked her boyfriend up and down and said, 'Nice to see you've dressed up for me!' He was wearing his usual blue jeans — the jeans he only took off to go to work and to go to sleep — and a yellow t-shirt that had 'Button Your Fly' written on the front in bold red letters. This was Ben's favourite t-shirt; he loved seeing the reaction of men as they read the slogan and then immediately checked their fly. It made him laugh every time he saw someone do it.

'Wow, you look awesome,' Ben said after he'd spent a second looking at Kim.

'Wish I could say the same for you,' Kim replied jokingly. In the time they had been seeing each other, Ben had never dressed up. 'Dressing up' to him meant putting on brown shoes instead of his usual white trainers. She didn't mind though; Ben could pull off the relaxed slacker look with incredible aplomb. Although she *would* like to see him in a suit at some point — she thought he would look amazing in one. However, it was more than likely that the only time she would see him in a suit of any kind would be on their wedding day. *Oh god, I am thinking of our wedding already! What's wrong with me?* Kim thought and quickly brushed the idea from her mind.

'Well, are you going to invite me in then?' Ben asked sarcastically. 'Or should I head home already?'

'Sorry, I was just thinking…' She paused. 'Nothing — doesn't matter — come on in. Let's get a drink down you.'

'Trying to get me drunk, are you?' Ben asked with a cheeky schoolboy smile on his face.

'Of course I am! Then you can't go home,' Kim winked flirtatiously at Ben as he entered the hallway.

They walked through to the lounge and Ben sat down on the sofa while Kim went to the kitchen and brought out a bottle of red wine, two glasses and a corkscrew. She handed the bottle and corkscrew to Ben and said, 'Do the honours, will you?'

'What do you do when I'm not here to do it?'

'Oh, I just get one of my other boyfriends to do it for me!' Kim replied with a wry smile on her face.

'Har har,' Ben said sarcastically, but a little thought popped into his head: *I hope she doesn't have any other boyfriends…* The thought quietly echoed around for a moment then disappeared. His last girlfriend had cheated on him with one of her coworkers, and when he had found out he'd been distraught. But Kim was not like her, not in any way. That was one of the things that he liked so much about her.

Ben opened the bottle of wine and went to pour it into the glasses, but Kim stopped him.

'It needs to breathe for a bit first,' she said. It was something her dad had told her when she was young — red wine needed time to breathe after being opened. She didn't know why, and had never thought to ask, but it was something that she always remembered and liked to adhere to.

After a little while, Kim poured the wine into their glasses. They toasted each other and drank. The wine was one of Kim's favourites. They talked about their work for a while, when suddenly Ben stopped short. 'Oh god,' he exclaimed, 'I nearly forgot — I won't be around this weekend, babe. They have sent me on this conference thing up north — Birmingham somewhere. The guy who is supposed to be going called in sick today. Well, I say called in, he was rushed into hospital late last night. Don't know what's wrong with him but he won't be going to the conference tomorrow, so they are sending me because it's very important someone from the company attends.'

'That's a bit short notice, isn't it? What if you

couldn't make it?'

'I don't know, but I do know that it's all expenses paid. Five-star hotel for the night, all food paid for — and drinks too, I'm guessing.'

'Can I come?' Kim asked.

''Fraid not, babe, just me. I already asked that when they said I had to go.'

'Oh well, I will have to get one of my other boyfriends over to keep me company then,' Kim teased.

There was that thought again... *Is there someone else?* Ben shook his head to rid himself of the thought. 'You don't mind, do you?'

'No, of course not!' She *did* mind but didn't want to be 'the controlling girlfriend'. She was disappointed that she couldn't spend the whole of tomorrow morning dozing and making love. Instead, Ben would have to be up early, which meant *she* would have to be up early — and on a Saturday, too!

Kim changed the subject and they talked for a good while longer, drinking and eating crisps that Kim brought out of the kitchen.

After some time, Kim looked at the clock; it was eleven. She was very tipsy by now. Together they had drunk nearly three bottles of wine, which was plenty for her. She stifled a yawn but Ben noticed.

'Boring you, am I?' he joked, and smiled at her.

'No! It's just been a long day and I can't wait to get my hands on you, that's all!' Kim replied flirtatiously and winked at him.

'Shall we head to bed then?' Ben asked.

'Yes, come on.' She got up, pulling Ben's arm as she did so. Ben got up off the sofa and followed her to the bedroom.

As they entered the dark bedroom Kim turned around and started to kiss Ben passionately. He held her tightly in his strong arms and slowly kissed her mouth, then moved down to her neck and shoulder. Ben then raised up her arms and slid off her top, revealing her black lace bra. The sight excited him, and he took off his t-shirt and threw it onto the floor. They both fell onto the bed, where he lay gently on top of her and kissed her toned stomach. Kim gave a deep sigh; this felt so sensual. No one touched her like he did. He looked up at her, caught her eye and smiled at her as he slid off her black skirt. He saw her lace briefs and this was almost too much for him; she looked incredible, her toned body lying on the bed. She beckoned him up to her and kissed him slowly and deeply. She slowly undid the button fly on his jeans and eased them off his muscular thighs. They lay down together and made love. It was the most passionate loving making that Kim had ever experienced; she never wanted it to end.

Chapter 9

The next morning was bright and the sun shone in through the curtains in Kim's bedroom. She woke up to find Ben already up and dressed. He was sat on the bed drinking a cup of tea, looking a little agitated.

'What's the matter?' Kim asked him.

'Huh? Oh nothing, just worried about this conference. It's my first one and I have no idea what I am supposed to do when I get there.'

'If it's like any of the conferences I have been on, you do very little and drink lots of coffee!'

Ben smiled at her. 'Right, I have to be off now, babe. I need to arrive before eleven and it takes nearly three hours to get there.'

'Three hours? Urgh what time is it now then?'

'Six o'clock,' Ben replied.

'My God, six on a Saturday!'

Ben laughed and kissed her. 'Thanks for a wonderful night.'

'Thank *you*,' she replied, and winked at him.

'Ok, you go back to sleep, I am heading off.'

'I will…speak to you later, yeah?'

'Yes, I'll text you when I get there.'

'Cool. Bye, babe — safe journey! Love you!'

'Love you too, babe.'

With that, Ben turned and left the flat. Within a minute, Kim had fallen back asleep.

The drive northwards was not as bad as Ben had anticipated. The weather was good, the sun was out and there was a warm breeze. He had made very good time on the motorway; it had only taken him two and a half hours to get there, so he had plenty of time to check into the hotel before the start of the conference instead of doing it during lunch.

The hotel was awesome — marble floored lobby,

chandeliers hanging everywhere... He was called 'sir' four times before he had reached his room, even though he was wearing his jeans and *'Button your fly'* t-shirt. The room itself was immaculate. A huge king-size bed stood in the centre of a large bedroom. It was so high off the ground Ben thought that he might need a stepladder to get onto it! Just off the bedroom was the en-suite bathroom. *Marble floor in here too,* Ben thought to himself as he looked around. The bath was huge, big enough for a football team to comfortably wash in. Ben quickly changed into his work suit and went downstairs to the conference, where there were already a large amount of people gathered around three tea urns. They were all talking about some kind of business or other that they must have been representing at the conference. Ben quickly decided that he hated conferences. He could almost smell the air; it was thick with coffee, pretentiousness and one-upmanship. He went over to the tea urns and poured himself a cup. Just as he was about to enter the conference room he remembered that he had to text Kim. Ben got out his phone and wrote a quick text to say that he had arrived safely and that he would speak to her later. He pressed send, but the message beeped at him. He looked closer at his phone and it said *'no service'* in the corner.

'Shit!' he exclaimed. 'Should have checked earlier.' The message went into the draft folder. Suddenly, a thundering, deep voice shook him like an earthquake. Ben looked up to see a man in his late thirties with a dark brown beard and short brown hair that was greying at the edges. The man was the same height as Ben but decidedly wider than he was.

'Hello!' bellowed the voice. 'Name's Chris — Chris Oakley.'

'Err, B-b-ben,' Ben stammered, somewhat taken aback by the abrupt introduction.

'On your own up here then?' Chris Oakley asked.

'Me too,' he continued, without waiting for Ben to reply. 'Come grab a seat next to me — we singletons need to stick together in this place!'

'I-I-I'm not single, I have a girlfriend,' Ben replied, not quite understanding what Chris meant.

'I'm sure you have, mate — I have a wife. I meant, we are up here on our tod. No missus and no colleagues from work with us!'

'Oh, right. Yes, of course. Sorry.'

'What you apologising for? You ain't done nothing wrong. Not yet, anyway!' Chris gave Ben a wink but Ben didn't quite know what it meant.

Chris led Ben through a set of off-white double doors with mock gold handles and a border pattern of ferns and leaves. They headed towards a table that was laid out with bottled water —both still and sparkling — mints, a plate of biscuits and a bowl of miniature chocolates.

'If you want any of the chocolates, best get to them before I do. Once I start eating 'em I don't stop!' Chris let out a roaring laugh that made everyone in the room stop what they were doing and look in their direction.

$$* * *$$

Kim had gotten up after a few extra hours of broken sleep. She had made herself a cup of tea and a couple of slices of toast. Not her regular choice of breakfast on the weekend; she much preferred to have a cooked breakfast of sausage, bacon and eggs — especially if it was cooked by Ben. She sat down with her tea and toast and saw the package again. She had forgotten about it last night.

What could it be? Kim wondered. She picked it up, tore open one of the sides and pulled out a box. A white cardboard box. She opened it and a number of small polystyrene pieces fell out onto the floor, revealing what looked like a wooden object. Kim pulled it out, forcing more polystyrene onto the floor. It was a small picture frame. She turned it over so that she could see the front. There was a picture in the frame. It was unusual; it was around ten inches square and looked aged. It depicted a woman and a man; the woman was sitting down and on her knee was a young boy. No one was smiling. Only the boy had a facial expression that sort of resembled a smile, but it was not a happy one.

What a strange picture. She tipped the box upside down and all the other polystyrene pieces fell out, but there was nothing else in the box at all. No note, no receipt. Kim couldn't think who had sent it to her or in fact whether it was intended for her at all. She looked at it again. It looked vaguely familiar but she couldn't place where she had seen it before.

***

Ben and Chris sat down and waited for the conference to begin. Ben looked around the large, bright room. At the front there was a large oak table, on top of which was a laptop with a few wires coming out of the back of it. One of the leads was linked up to a projector that was sat further back on the oak table, pointing at a huge white screen on the wall. Other wires linked up to a set of speakers either side of the projector, which faced the audience. To the right of the big white screen was a small board with paper on it and a variety of coloured board pens underneath it. The room itself was the same off-white colour as the front doors. It may have been called eggshell or magnolia, Ben didn't know. Decorating wasn't his strong point. One side of the room had huge windows all along the wall, but from where Ben was sitting he couldn't see out of them. Long, royal blue curtains hung either side of the windows. The floor was covered in a royal blue carpet that matched the curtains, although the carpet had a paisley pattern on it — a garish mix of red, yellow, black and a small amount of green. Ben thought it looked hideous; even looking at it for a short while made his mind spin.

He looked away from the carpet and turned his attention instead to a few of the other representatives in the room. The men were all wearing suits. The suits were all different sizes and styles but essentially were one of three colours: navy, black or grey. The women in the room were all dressed in trouser suits or smart A-line skirts and blouses. Again, most of these were grey, black or navy. There was one woman near the front, however, who was the exception. She wore a dark pink blouse and a black skirt that rose so high when she sat down you could almost see the cheek of her bottom. She was wearing tights, but had she been wearing suspenders Ben would have been able to see the top where the lace was. Ben imagined that she was the office slut, or at least the office tease. She craved attention so much that she would wear short skirts and low-cut tops so that the old men in the office would ogle her as she walked passed and stare at her breasts while talking to her. Ben imagined that she might even drop stationery on the floor on purpose just so she had to bend over in front of them and give the old men something else to stare at.

The conference was long and incredibly uneventful. The most exciting parts were the coffee breaks and lunch. Chris would talk and Ben would listen to whatever story he was telling. Ben tried to talk, but every time he did Chris had another story to tell him, and so he decided that it was best just to keep quiet.

At five o'clock the conference wrapped up and all the delegates left hurriedly and noisily. Most were saying how dull the conference was; others were saying that they thought it was very informative. Ben didn't know how informative it had been because he had stopped listening after the first coffee break.

Ben was just about to say goodbye to Chris when

the thunderous voice spoke again. 'Drink?'

'What?' replied Ben.

'Let's get a drink in the hotel bar.'

'Oh, I dunno. I was going to go to my room, have some dinner and get an early night.'

'Early night?! It's only just gone five o'clock!' exclaimed Chris, loud enough so that most of the hotel could hear. Then he grabbed Ben's arm and almost dragged him towards the bar.

'Ok, ok. But just one,' Ben said grudgingly.

Chris bought the first round of drinks and they sat down at a table. Ben picked the seats so that he could get a good view of the television. He could then drift in and out of the conversation that Chris was inevitably going to engage him in.

After they had finished their drinks, Chris said, 'Right, it's your round, mate. Get 'em in!'

Ben reluctantly got up and went to the bar. He bought two pints of lager and returned to the table. Chris immediately started to talk again. Ben didn't believe he had actually stopped while he had gone to the bar to get drinks!

The second drink went down a lot more comfortably than the first, and Ben started to relax. So much so that when Chris offered him another round Ben had agreed quite happily.

This went on for another hour or so, and by now it was getting close to seven o'clock. Chris looked at his watch, then at Ben, and said, 'Hey, mate, how about we go and hit a couple of bars? It *is* Saturday, after all.'

Ben was in quite a jolly mood now and rather liked the idea of going out in a strange town. 'Let's see what they've got to offer us, eh?'

'That's my boy!' Chris exclaimed, almost shouting with excitement.

They finished off their drinks, got up and made their way to the main entrance of the hotel. As they stepped outside, Ben noticed that the evening was considerably colder than the day had been. He looked up; there was not a cloud in the sky.

Chapter 10

It was nearing half past ten now. They had been to several bars, spoken to some locals and continued to get more and more drunk. By now, they were both chatting; it was not a one-way conversation anymore. Ben had started talking about his work and his life in general, while Chris had started to talk less and less the more he drank. They had moved from lager to spirits and mixers. Chris was drinking vodka and cola, whereas Ben was drinking rum and cola. They were now in an American-themed bar with number plates from various American states. One from California, one from Illinois, another from Colorado; all places that Ben had visited in the past. USA flags were strewn all over the place, and there were signs for different American beers: Budweiser, Coors, Miller and Sam Adams — two of which they had discovered the bar didn't even sell! It was as though various parts of the USA had thrown up in the bar. It was not organized at all, very haphazard. The bar staff and waitresses were dressed up like the characters from the Dukes of Hazzard, the men in lumberjack shirts and jeans, the women in short cropped lumberjack shirts and short hot pants. All the women were beautiful, Ben noticed. Well, all except one. *She must be the token antidiscrimination employee,* Ben thought. This waitress had short black hair and had a pierced lip. She was short and when she leaned over to pick up customers' glasses her rolls of fat drooped out from under her shirt. She had fat spilling out over the sides of her skirt as well, since she was not wearing hot pants, she had a long denim skirt on and the lumberjack shirt was full length, not cropped. Ben was quietly glad of this. He imagined what she would have looked like if she had forced herself into hot pants and the cropped shirt. He smiled to himself.

'What you smiling at?' asked Chris.

'Nothing, just the waitresses.'

'Ah yes — gorgeous, aren't they?' Chris paused for a second, he looked like he was thinking deeply. Ben doubted it though. 'What do you say we go to a strip club?' Chris then asked quietly, with a cheeky smile. This was the quietest he had spoken all night and Ben wasn't quite sure if he had heard him right.

'A what?'

'Strip club! Come on, it's only a bit of fun. I won't tell your girlfriend!'

'I dunno, it's not really my scene,' Ben said, slowly and reluctantly.

'Don't make me drag you there! You don't have to have a lap dance — you can just sit and drink if you are going to be a baby about it!' Chris teased.

'Alright, fine!' Ben finished his rum and cola and got up, staggering a little as he made his way to the door. Chris followed close behind with a huge grin on his face.

They wandered around the town for about twenty minutes before they found a strip club. They paid the entrance fee and made their way to the bar. Chris ordered their drinks and they sat on the barstools in silence. The music was very loud. They both stared out into the rest of the club, where beautiful women walked around in their underwear. Some were sat chatting to men; others were chatting to each other. There was one dancing on the stage. She was halfway through her routine and had already taken her bra off. Ben stared at the woman; she had fantastic breasts. He started to fantasize about her.

'Hi there!' Came a voice that made Ben jump out of his fantasy and back into the club.

'Err h-h-hi,' he stuttered. The fantasy had seemed so real that he actually thought he was there. The reality of the club and noisy dance music gave him a seismic crash back down to Earth.

'My name's Tara.' The girl said. She could only have been 18, 19 at the most. She was wearing a blood red bra and thong, with matching red stilettos that must have added four or five inches to her total height. Her body was very toned, and her breasts were almost bursting out of her bra, which was at Ben's eye level. She had blonde, shoulder-length hair and a small tattoo just below her navel.

'Do ya want to have a dance?' Tara asked Ben. But before he could reply Chris had necked his drink and jumped off his seat.

'I do!' he erupted with excitement.

'Ok, cool,' Tara replied. She took Chris's hand and led him to the room behind the black curtain. In this room there were a number of small booths; some were already occupied with other dancers with their punters, others were empty. Tara led Chris to one of the empty booths.

While Chris was getting his lap dance Ben sat on the same stool, looking out into the club. He surveyed it as though he was the king and this was his kingdom. The dancer on the stage finished her routine; there was a small amount of applause and she picked up her bra and thong and went through the curtain at the back of the stage.

Ben finished his drink. He felt uncomfortable sitting in the club on his own. He thought about leaving. Then another dancer started on stage. He watched her for a few seconds then ordered another drink. As he did so, a beautiful woman came up next to him.

'Mine's a vodka and orange, if you're buying!'

Ben looked around and, through slightly blurred vision, saw a tall brunette woman wearing just a black bra and thong standing at the bar, looking at him. He smiled and ordered her the vodka. She thanked him and sat on the stool next to him. She crossed her legs and Ben could see how trim and athletic she was. He composed himself and introduced himself.

'I'm Ben,' he said.

'Mel,' the woman answered, and took a sip of her drink.

They made small talk for a little while and then Mel asked Ben if he wanted a dance.

'Yes, ok,' Ben said. He was feeling more confident now. He got up. Mel took his hand and led him to the room behind the black curtain. He passed Chris on his way out of the room.

'Hey, hey! That's my boy!' he shouted and went to give Ben a high five, which Ben ignored.

'Friend of yours?' Mel asked him.

'Something like that, I guess,' Ben replied. Although he didn't really know what Chris was. He couldn't even remember his last name right now!

Mel sat Ben down in an empty booth. She told him that it was £20 for the dance. Ben paid his money.

Just as Mel started to dance, something happened. The music stopped. Or had it stopped? Ben wasn't sure; it had at least become muffled. Then it began. That sound. That high-pitched, plate-scratching sound. It shrieked inside his head. He shut his eyes and gritted his teeth. When he opened his eyes they were wider than before, almost like he was staring, but there was a blankness to the stare. Mel looked at him with concern but continued her dance. She had seen lots of weird men in her short career as a stripper. She had had to fulfil strange fetishes. Some men asked her to keep her shoes on; others asked her to leave her bra or thong on. Some men told her not to look at them through the whole dance. Other men tried to touch her or grab her. These men were very quickly and forcefully thrown out of the club by one or more of the huge doormen that were on duty. She assumed this was just another strange drunk man, with another strange idea of what happens in a strip club. She wondered how much money she could get out of him just for taking her clothes off.

'Another £10 and I will make it a dirty thirty,' she said, winking at Ben.

Ben looked at her with his blank stare. He managed to lip-read what she had said. He couldn't actually hear her, for the sound was now incredibly loud inside his head. He leaned forward to whisper in her ear.

'Do you do extras?' he asked. There was no emotion on his face at all.

Mel looked at him, shocked that this seemingly timid guy had suddenly asked her for extras. She had done extras for some men in the past, but not very often. The manager of the club always warned them of the dangers of going off with one of the punters. However, the money for doing so was quite an incentive. She could ask for whatever she wanted. There were no rules for extras; it was simply whatever the men were willing to pay. One man had paid her £500 to have sex with him. She had agreed. She got the money up front. They went to a local guesthouse that would rent respectable looking rooms by the hour if needed. The man was very drunk and had passed out after ten minutes, so she left him there and went home with her £500. No other job would pay her anywhere near that kind of money!

'Come with me,' Mel said quietly.

She took Ben out through a door painted black at the back of the room. It was almost impossible to see this door in the dark. On the other side of it was a large room full of lockers and cubicles. It was the changing area for the dancers. Mel went to a locker, opened it and took out her clothes. She started to change, and whilst doing so she said to him that it would be £150 for full sex, anything else would be on a sliding scale either downwards or upwards depending on what he wanted.

Ben agreed to the price — although he didn't really know what he was agreeing to. The sound in his head was pulsing through his mind. His vision was no longer blurred but foggy, like walking through the open moors near where he had grown up.

Mel finished dressing and they went outside. She was now wearing jeans and a white t-shirt, with a red sweater on top. Over the sweater she had a long black coat, which she did up most of the way. She had the same underwear on that she was dancing in; she no longer had stilettos on but white trainers instead. She looked a lot more casual now than when in the club.

The back door of the club was by no means as elegant as the front. This door led out into a quiet, dark alleyway, with large bins lining either side of the narrow cobbled street. There were delivery entrances to the local bars and clubs. The place stank of stale alcohol, food and urine. This seemed to make the sound in Ben's head worse than ever. They half-walked, half-ran to a small guesthouse. On the way, Ben stopped to take money out of the cash machine so he could pay Mel the £150 for 'the night of his life', as she called it. As they walked through the front door of the guesthouse, Ben didn't manage to catch the name of it.

The lobby was dark and unwelcoming. The tiled entrance hall gave way to a carpet that was fraying at the edges and looked like it hadn't been cleaned since it had been laid. The walls were an off-white colour that had been caused by years of cigarette smoke. There was a coat rail on the wall opposite the lobby desk with one stained, shabby coat hanging on it. The lobby desk was in a small cubby-hole. The cash register looked as though it dated back to decimalisation. The back wall was covered in keys with large wooden keyrings hanging off them. There were papers, envelopes and letters strewn all over the desk and floor. It smelled of stale smoke and burgers. The door to the lobby was dark mock wood panelling which was in need of painting or varnishing. It was scratched and riddled with holes. Just to the right of the lobby was a staircase. It had the same carpet as the lobby and was equally as worn and frayed. There were five or six steps and then the staircase became a small landing that turned to the left and out of sight.

Mel went up to the night porter, who was a massive man in a navy shirt and black trousers. He looked at Ben as Mel whispered in the porter's ear. The porter nodded, picked a key from off the wall and handed it to her.

'It's £10 for the hour room hire,' Mel said to Ben.

Ben took out £10 from his wallet; he seemed to Mel to be in some kind of dream state. Not really very coherent at all.

This will be an easy one, she thought to herself as she showed the way up to the 'mirror room'.

Chapter 11

The stairway was dark and dirty. The smell of stale smoke crept up the stairs with them. At the top of the stairs was another landing with a small corridor of doors leading off it. Mel took Ben to the door at the end of the corridor and unlocked it. As they walked down the corridor Ben noticed a bright red fire axe encased in a glass box. 'In case of fire, break glass' the sign on the case read. It was on its own on the wall; there was no fire alarm or extinguisher. It looked very odd placed there. They went inside and Mel switched on a small light next to the large double bed that took up most of the room. Ben looked around through the fog that was still in front of his eyes. One wall had a window on it, but the curtain was closed so he could not see anything outside. The wall opposite the window was a big mirror; it made the room look twice the size that it actually was. There was also a small bathroom off the bedroom; he could see a toilet, sink and large bath all in white. They stuck out against the darkness of the rest of the room. Next to the door that they had come in through was a huge grandfather clock. It was made out of a solid dark wood with a silver face and black hands. The clock was taller than Ben, probably about six and a half feet. It was very impressive, but was very much out of place in the room.

Being in the room seemed to make the sound echo inside his head. Up to now it had been a single sound — the high-pitched, piercing sound —but it was now more than one. Was it two, three, four? Ben couldn't work it out. For a second, he put his hands over his ears and shut his eyes. It was no use; the noise continued.

Mel looked at Ben with his hands over his ears and eyes shut. She went over to him and put her hands on his arms. Slowly she moved his arms down and he opened his eyes. She looked at him, but was met with the same absent stare as before. It was almost like he wasn't there with her; his body was but his mind was not. She smiled at him and led him over to the bed without saying a word. Ben sat on the bed and Mel lay him down on his back. Ben looked up at the ceiling and saw another mirror that he hadn't noticed when he had first entered the room. He could see the whole bed from where he was. He could see himself looking up at himself through the fog. He could also see Mel undoing his shirt.

As she undid Ben's trousers, Mel looked up at him and smiled. Ben did not smile back. His face was expressionless. The sound in his head was becoming unbearable. His head ached; his body was starting to ache too. Suddenly, the high-pitched sound became too much and he let out an almighty cry, shut his eyes in agony and sat upright. He grabbed Mel roughly and turned around so that she was lying on her back on the bed.

'Wow!' Mel exclaimed. She was shocked at this sudden energy from Ben. 'That's more like it!'

Ben still said nothing. He had opened his eyes but winced again at the noise. Mel's voice seemed to make the noise pierce his whole body now. He ripped off her top and tore down her jeans. She let out a fake moan. She was used to making noises like this to keep her punters happy and interested. The more she seemed into it, the more she could get out of the men she slept with. Ben let out another cry from the pain of the noise. He took the belt from his suit trousers and put it around one of Mel's arms, tying it to one of the bed posts.

'Ahh, kinky — that's how I like it,' said Mel in a husky, seductive voice. She was starting to work her act now.

Ben still said nothing. He took Mel's jeans and tied her other arm to the bedpost. She let out a little scream of pain.

'Not too rough though, eh!'

Ben seemed to ignore her and looked around the

room. He sat on top on Mel with his legs either side of her slim, tanned body. He looked down at her but didn't really see her. The fog had grown denser now, the noise still reverberating inside his head and body. He bent towards her and kissed her chest; she let out a quiet moan. It seemed like a clap of thunder inside his head. Ben shut his eyes again.

Just then, the grandfather clock started to boom. Ben looked at it and screamed.

'Don't worry about that,' Mel said. 'It will stop in a second.'

The noise of each chime felt like someone hitting his head with a sledgehammer. Ben screamed again. The chimes continued inside his head, even though there had only been the introductory chime and three full chimes. It was 3 o'clock.

Ben got up with his hands over his ears.

'Where you going?' Mel asked, a little concerned. She tried to get up but Ben had tied her down too tightly for her to move.

Ben ran out of the room in his underwear, his hands covering his ears. He ran to the fire axe, looked around for a split second and threw his elbow into the glass. It smashed with a loud crash that was agony to Ben. He grabbed the axe and ran back to the bedroom with it where in his mind the grandfather clock was still delivering its sledgehammer chimes.

Ben stopped next to the clock, he looked at the clock then at Mel and then back to the clock again. He lifted the axe with both hands so the head was resting on his shoulder.

'What are you doing?' Mel shrieked in panic at the sight of the axe.

Ben did not reply but took a deep breath and slammed the axe hard into the body of the grandfather clock. The noise was deafening inside his head. He forced the axe out of the clock and lifted it up again. He struck another powerful blow into the heart of the clock. The wood cracked and splintered around the room. Mel screamed. The noise inside his head and the room was deafening now. Ben's screams turned to roars now as he continued to drive the fire axe harder and harder into the clock. He aimed higher now. He drove the axe into the clock face and parts of it flew around the room. Ben roared again and again. Mel watched him, terrified.

'STOP!' she screamed at him. 'What's wrong with you?!'

Ben didn't hear her; he only heard the sound, the high-pitched screech that had completely overtaken his body. He stopped and lowered the axe. He looked at the devastation he had created. The clock was split in half and thousands of splinters and shards of wood were all around him. He kicked the remaining standing piece of clock over and it crashed onto the floor. He shut his eyes again with the pain of the sound.

'You are a freak!' Mel screamed at him. 'Untie me now!'

Ben heard a noise from Mel but didn't know what she was saying. It was just a horrendous screeching sound. He gritted his teeth and shut his eyes again. Mel could see all the sinews in his neck strain.

'Untie me!' she screamed again.

He looked over at her. The expressionless face terrified her as she stared at him. Ben walked over to Mel and stared almost through her. He let out another huge roar and raised the fire axe again.

Mel looked up at him. She tried to scream but no noise came out this time. She was suddenly aware that the bed around her legs had become wet and was getting colder. She looked down and started to cry.

'No — please!' She managed to get the words out before Ben slammed the axe down into her left leg. There was a sound of bone snapping and flesh tearing as the axe completely severed the limb. Dark red blood shot out in all directions. The bed was soon crimson. Mel tried to scream but there was no breath in her lungs; it had all rushed out when Ben had brought the axe down onto her leg. Her breath was coming back to her now but it was only coming in short tiny bursts. She could not move. Every muscle in her body seemed to be paralysed. Ben ripped the axe out of the bed and raised it up again. The noise inside his head was deafening. It now seemed to be all around him. It was coming from the woman in front of him. He had to shut the noise up. He had to shut her up. He brought the axe down again but his vision was still foggy and so he didn't get a clean strike. Instead, the top of the axe sliced through her waist, just above her hip bone. Mel managed a tiny scream but nothing else. She looked down at her hip in terror. Blood was pouring out in thick dark streams and soaking into the bed. She shut her eyes and winced against the pain. It was excruciating. She opened her eyes to see the blood-stained fire axe coming down on her head. It split the left side of her skull clean off from the rest. The severed skull fragment fell onto the floor; the eye that was left in the fragment remained open in a state of shock. On the bed, dark red blood was now mixed with the white brain matter that had poured from Mel's head. Her right eye was shut. It almost looked peaceful. Mel's body did not move. Not a twitch. She was dead.

Ben winced. The noise was still there — it was coming out of Mel's body. How could that be? He lifted the axe again and brought it down on her chest. He forced the axe back out of the chest, since it had got stuck, then smashed it into her limp body again, causing her corpse to split in two. Ben continued to hack at Mel's mutilated corpse again and again. The room was covered in blood, bone, flesh and brain. The surrounding mirrors on the wall and ceiling were also smeared with scarlet. The mirrors that made the room look twice as big made the devastation twice as catastrophic. What was left of Mel's body could hardly be recognised as human by the time Ben laid the axe down. The noise had now become a small background screech. He breathed heavily. His arms ached. He looked around the room. He went to the bathroom and washed the blood off his body. It trickled down the plughole, a bright red hue to it now. Ben picked up his clothes, got dressed and looked out of the window. The window opened onto a black metal fire escape which came out from the next room along. It would be a small jump down from the window onto it and down the steps into the back alley behind the guesthouse.

The window opened quite easily. Just as he was about to climb out, Ben caught a glimpse of a little picture in a frame that was hung on the wall. The wall around it was covered in blood but the picture itself did not have a speck on it. He squinted to see what it was. The picture was of a woman and a man who both had an eastern European look about them. The man had a thick black moustache and wore a suit and tie. The woman had curly hair and a bonnet. She was sitting and on her knee sat a child. The child was smiling a menacing smile.

'Huh,' said Ben. 'I have a picture just like that.' With that, he climbed out of the window and jumped down onto the fire escape, which clanged. Ben walked down the fire escape and into the alleyway. He pulled the phone out of his pocket and looked at the time. It was 3:32.

'My God it's late,' Ben thought out loud to himself. 'I've got to get some sleep; I have to drive home in the morning.' He trotted his way back to his hotel. The high-pitched noise had completely disappeared.

Chapter 12

Ben was woken by a cleaner knocking on his door, telling him that he should have checked out by now. His head throbbed and every sound he heard was like a pneumatic drill driving into his skull. He got up as quickly as he could and threw on his clothes from the previous night. They had been strewn across the floor in an almost timeline of how he had taken them off. His shoes were nearest the door, followed by his shirt two steps into the room, next were his trousers about five steps further in. These were not in line with the shirt and shoes; Ben thought he must have fallen over while taking them off and messed up what was otherwise a perfect path to the bed. Completing the path was a sock, and after a short search he found the other sock under the bed. He had slept in his pants and so was already wearing them. His head hurt. It seemed to erupt every time he bent down to pick up his clothes. He thought it might explode.

Ben had missed breakfast so he thought he would stop in a service station and grab a sandwich on the way home. He handed his key into a very miserable teenage concierge and went to the car park, got into his car and started the drive home.

He managed to find his way to the motorway easily enough but had only been driving on it for about ten minutes when he began to feel very ill. He felt a stale taste of saliva rise and suddenly his mouth was very moist. He was going to vomit. He gagged and felt a convulsion come from his stomach but held it down for now. He didn't want to mess up his car. The smell of vomit stayed in a car no matter how much you cleaned it or sprayed it with air freshener. He had learnt that in university. Ben hadn't been the one who had vomited in his car; it had been his girlfriend at the time, Claire. They had been at a house party the night before and had slept there. On the way home, Claire had given him no warning that she would throw up all over the car dashboard and into the footwell. It had been a mixture of purple, from the cider and blackcurrant, black from the vodka and cola and half-digested sausages, pizza and crisps. Her side of the windscreen was a real mess, and the footwell became a lake of purple and black with the sausages looking like drowning crew members from the HMS Night Before. It was disgusting and the car never fully recovered. Ben had no idea what he had drunk last night; what he did know was that he needed to pull over and throw up somewhere. A little way ahead was a blue sign saying, 'Services one mile.'

Perfect, Ben thought. All he had to do was hold it in for about a minute or so and then he could pull into the services car park and be sick in a bush. Or maybe he could actually make it to the toilets if he was lucky.

Ben turned off at the next turning, drove up the ramp and took the second exit to the services car park. He parked into a space away from the actual service building, turned off the engine and got out. He stood upright for a few seconds, taking in the fresh air. The early afternoon sun was bright and warm, and the air was sweet with a hint of coffee coming from the service building. There was a slight breeze. The whole sensation was very refreshing to Ben and he suddenly felt a little better. Standing in the sunshine and the fresh air, a thought entered his head.

'Kim!' Ben muttered to himself. 'My God, I haven't spoken to her at all today!' Ben actually hadn't spoken to Kim since he had said goodbye yesterday. He looked at his phone. It was off. He turned it on. After a few seconds of it loading up and finding a signal it erupted in a cacophony of noises. Text messages, missed calls, answerphone messages and emails were all being retrieved at the same time. Most of them had been from Kim! They ranged from calm messages asking if he had got to the hotel safely, then annoyance at not having any replies or phone calls and finally worried messages hoping that he was alright. Ben took a few deep breaths and pressed Kim's number on his touchscreen phone. It started ringing.

Chapter 13

Kim was sitting on her sofa. Her mind had been spinning out all night and she had slept very little. Now it was two o'clock in the afternoon and she still hadn't heard anything from Ben. Was he alright? Where was he? Had he crashed somewhere? Had he left her? This last thought only jumped in her mind for a second or two but it was enough to have planted a small seed that was growing every minute. How long should she leave it before calling the police? Kim's mind was like a cyclone and it hurt. She had called him yesterday and texted him. There had been no answer to either. When she called she only got the answerphone message 'Hi! You've reached Ben. Please leave a message!' Ben had made the message whilst being in a bar after a few drinks and she had kept telling him to change it because it sounded awful, but he never did. Reaching the answerphone every time she had called him suggested to her that his phone was off, or out of signal, so she decided not to text or phone anymore but to send him an email instead. That way he could get it if he was using a computer or his phone even if there was no signal. Ben hadn't replied to the email either. As a last resort Kim had sent him a message on Facebook, just in case he might see that instead, to no avail. That was when she really started to worry. Her disappointment, annoyance and anger had subsided and turned into fear. He had never gone away and not called or texted her. He would even text during the meetings he often had to attend, telling her that he was bored. He would send her raunchy messages about what would happen when he got back — what he was going to do to her or what she should do to him. These messages got her quite excited and she would write messages back to him even though she was not very good at dirty talk. But where was he now?

Kim got up off the sofa and went to her house phone, she was about to call her mother when her mobile started playing 'Livin' on a prayer' by Bon Jovi. She ran over to where she had left her phone, bumping the coffee table as she went and knocking over her mug of tea.

'Shit!' she cursed. Kim looked at her phone. It was Ben. She pressed the green button and answered. 'Where the hell have you been?!' she demanded, half shouting and half crying. 'I've been worried sick!'

'I'm so sorry, babe,' replied Ben timidly. 'There was no signal in that place; I did try to text you when I arrived but it was already too late. I am sorry.'

'I thought something might have happened to you!' Kim had started to sob now, partly because she was angry at Ben but mostly because she was relieved to hear his voice.

'I'll make it up to you, I promise. Whatever you want you shall have,' Ben said.

Kim realised that he was diverting her anger and trying to flirt his way out of trouble. She did not bite. 'I want you back safe and sound! And you aren't getting anything until I see you face to face and you get on your knees and grovel!' She was trying to remain angry, but the relief at hearing his voice had now sunk in and she smiled a little. The smile must have come through in her voice because Ben continued his flirting.

'I will definitely get down on my knees and grovel —'

'Enough!' Kim cut him off mid-sentence. 'Just please hurry up and get back here, will you?'

'I am at a service station — need a sandwich or something. Won't be too long, babe.'

'OK. I'll see you in a bit then.'

'You will. See you later. Love you!'

'Love you too,' Kim replied, and hung up.

Ben put his phone in his pocket and sighed. Got away with that one, he thought. He was feeling better now. The fresh air had cleared his head and the talk with Kim had gone better than expected. Ben pressed the remote locking button on his keys; the car beeped twice, the indicator lights flashed in unison and he walked towards to service station.

The building was light and airy, and despite the small amount of cars in the car park the whole place was bustling with people. There were families with what seemed like hundreds of children each. There were men in suits, drinking coffee alone, some with laptops on the tables, some speaking on mobile phones and others deep in thought. Ben wondered if any of these men had just had a row from their partners for neglecting to call them whilst on a conference trip. He headed for the toilets, he could smell them a few steps before he reached the door. The smell wasn't the kind of smell that greeted you in toilets in bars. That smell was vile, the stench of urine that emanated from some bar toilets would make him wretch when he was out with his mates. This smell was not unpleasant but it was very artificial, like a cross between bleach and air freshener. The air freshener was probably called 'summer breeze' or something similar. No matter where Ben had been in summer he had never smelt a 'summer breeze' that smelt like the air fresheners of their namesakes.

Ben went into one of the cubicles; he couldn't face standing next to someone when he was urinating. Not today, in any case; today, he was unwell and the thought of another man's penis being out in the open only inches away from his made him gag. He stayed in the cubicle a few minutes after he had finished urinating, taking some deep breaths to recompose himself. Not too deep though; he didn't want to breathe in too much bleachy air freshener. He felt a lot better than he had in the car. He no longer needed to vomit.

Ben left the cubicle and went to the sinks to wash his hands. He pressed the button for some soap but it was empty; he moved to the next one and pressed the button again but this was empty too. *Just water it is then*, Ben thought to himself whist giving his hands a brisk scrub. He held his hands under the hand dryer for a few seconds then decided to finish the job by wiping his hands on his jeans. He walked to the door and stopped for a second to look at the cleaning rota on the back of it. Apparently it had been cleaned and checked only five minutes ago. Ben doubted that. He left the toilets and decided that he could use a coffee and a sandwich of some sort. He was feeling hungry now.

The coffee shop had a huge sign at the entrance that read: 'COFFEE PALACE — HAVE YOU HAD YOURS TODAY?'

'No I haven't,' Ben answered aloud as he walked inside.

The coffee shop was not a palace; it was more of a hovel that smelt of coffee. There were tables and chairs spread around the room in no real order. Some of the tables had coffee cups and plates of half eaten sandwiches left over from the previous customers — possibly the previous few customers. Some of the people who had been sitting at tables when Ben had gone to the toilet had left. One or two remained, but generally the coffee shop seemed quite quiet. Ben walked up to the counter where a seventeen-year-old boy looked at him and smiled expectantly. His face showed the signs of having had bad acne when he was younger and his ginger hair seemed to clash with the red of the uniform t-shirt he had on.

'Can I help you?' The boy said.

Ben felt a little pressured; he wasn't ready to order yet. He only just finished reading the 'ESPRESSOS' menu, let alone the other three sections on the back wall of the coffee shop. He picked up a prawn mayonnaise sandwich and put it on the counter, thinking that would buy him some time.

'Anything else?' the boy asked. The sandwich hadn't

bought him any time at all. If anything it had stopped him thinking about what coffee he wanted.

'Errrr...just a regular white coffee please,' Ben finally answered, feeling slightly ashamed that he didn't want some extravagant coffee with a pretentious name.

'Would you like — uno, doplo, treblo?' the boy asked. Ben didn't even know what that meant.

'What? Errr the middle one.'

'Doplo, cool. Do you want an extra shot in it?'

'Umm, no thanks, just a normal coffee.'

'One doplo americano, no extra shot… Any flavours in it, like vanilla or caramel?'

Ben felt like he was facing a police interrogation. 'No flavours — just a normal coffee, please. What's American got to do with it?'

'That's what we call regular coffee — an Americano,' the boy replied.

'Why Americano?'

'Don't ask me, I just serve the stuff. Right, so we have one doplo Americano, no extra shot, no flavours, regular blend?

'Oh my god, yes. I don't care what blend it is! I could have made the stuff myself by now.' Ben was getting irritated.

'Don't get aggressive, sir. I am only doing my job,' the red haired boy replied without any emotion whatsoever.

'Sorry — just been a long week that's all.'

'No worries,' replied the boy. 'That'll be £7.05.'

'What? I didn't want a meal,' exclaimed Ben.

'The coffee and the sandwich together cost seven pounds and five pence, sir.'

Ben reluctantly handed the boy a ten pound note and took his £2.95 change.

'Pick up your coffee at the end of the counter. Milk and anything else you may need are on the side. Thank you — have a good day,' the boy said almost robotically.

Ben picked up his sandwich and collected his coffee. He poured some milk into the mug and went over to a clean table by the window. He couldn't believe how stressed he felt. All he wanted was a normal coffee.

'The TV show *Friends* has a lot to answer for,' Ben muttered as he sipped the hot coffee and started unwrapping his sandwich.

Chapter 14

Ben finally arrived at Kim's house at around four in the afternoon. He was tired and sweaty from the car journey. He parked on the street outside the house, got out of the car and walked up the steps to Kim's front door. Ben waited a few seconds, took a few deep breaths and then knocked.

He could hear Kim's footsteps coming down the hall to the door; she was running. She threw open the door, looked at him and slung her arms around his neck with such force that Ben nearly fell over backwards.

'Whoa! Steady!' he said, smiling at her excitement.

'Shut up! Don't say a word! I just want a hug.' Kim held him tightly for a few minutes and then let go. She took a step back and looked him up and down. 'You look like shit!' she said with disgust. 'What have you been doing?'

'I didn't sleep well; I am a bit hungover and haven't eaten properly all day. I really need a shower.'

'Damn right you need a shower!' Kim said with a smile. 'You stink! Right, in you go. You know where the towels are. When you get out we can start thinking about some dinner. But first you need a wash!!'

'Thanks, babe,' Ben said, and leaned forward to give Kim a kiss.

She backed away a little. 'Not until you have had a shower, sonny. I bet you haven't even cleaned your teeth, have you?'

Ben thought for a moment. He couldn't remember whether he had cleaned his teeth or not. 'Yes, I did — of course I did,' he replied.

'Either way, you aren't getting any until you have had a good wash!'

Ben went inside and headed towards Kim's bedroom to get undressed. Kim closed the front door, walked to the living room and sat down on the sofa.

Ben had undressed as far as his boxers and went to the airing cupboard to get a towel. He picked up a fresh, light blue bath towel and went into the bathroom. He shut the door, took off his boxers and turned on the shower.

Ben had been in the shower for a few minutes when he felt something run down his back. He jumped and nearly slipped over on the wet floor of the shower cubicle. He turned around to see Kim standing in front of him, completely naked and smiling her sweet smile.

'Oh my God! You scared me to death!' Ben exclaimed.

Kim put a finger to his lips. She moved closer to him and kissed him passionately on the lips. 'Don't say a word,' she whispered into his ear.

She kissed him again and he kissed her back, hard. Then he started kissing her shoulders and caressed her warm, wet breasts. Slowly and gently, Ben's hand snaked down her body. He stroked her thighs and he could hear Kim's breathing getting heavier. He moved his hand inside her thigh and with his fingers lightly touched between her legs. He slid his fingers inside her. She felt warm. Kim moaned as he did so. Ben smiled; he liked hearing her moan. He teased her. Before long, Kim's legs felt numb. She took Ben's hand away from between her thighs and without another word to each other they made love in the mist under the warm rainfall of the shower.

'I thought I wasn't getting any until I had showered,' Ben said as they washed each other down.

'I couldn't wait that long,' Kim replied, a smile on her face. 'Just make sure you wash yourself properly and then come into the lounge.'

'Ok, babe,' he replied.

Kim got out of the shower, wrapped a large yellow towel around her shiny, steaming body and left the bathroom to get changed.

Ben finished washing himself down, got out of the

shower and dried himself off with the towel he had picked out of the airing cupboard. He went to the sink, where he had a spare toothbrush for when he stayed the night, and brushed his teeth thoroughly before heading into Kim's bedroom. He realised that he didn't have any clean clothes with him so he looked in some of Kim's drawers. He found some female boxers and put them on, along with some black and pink spotted socks. In her wardrobe he found some casual trousers and a white t-shirt that had the words 'Lifeguard Championships 1997' splashed across the chest. He put them on and went into the lounge, where Kim was sitting on the sofa in her lounge pyjamas. They were bright yellow.

Kim looked at Ben and laughed. 'Everybody wants to be like me! How's it feel to be a girl?' she taunted.

Ben smiled and sat down next to her on the sofa. He kissed her on the forehead and said, 'I'm starving — what are we going to do for tea?'

'I can't be bothered to cook,' Kim replied. 'Let's just order in a pizza, eh?'

'Sounds good to me, it's been a long week. Where's the menu?'

Chapter 15

Ben really didn't want to go to work on Monday morning. He woke up alone in his own bed, having taken a taxi home last night. Kim had said she needed an early night, so he hadn't slept at hers. Ben's head hurt. He didn't remember drinking that much last night but obviously it must have been more than he realised. The morning was uneventful and he managed to zombie his way through until lunchtime. He had spent the morning doing the bare minimum amount of work and was thankful when lunch came around. He walked down the corridor to the large office canteen. This was quite a rare occurrence; he was often out visiting clients or prospective clients and ate his lunch on the run. Even when he was in the office for lunch he avoided the canteen, preferring to eat sandwiches or pasties at his desk. Today, however, he had neither sandwiches nor pasties. His mind was not where it should have been and so he hadn't thought to make any sandwiches or stop to buy anything on the way to work.

Ben pushed open the large swing door to the canteen, but not before glancing in through the round window in the middle of the white glossy door. He could see that it was already quite busy and that there was a queue forming at the counter. That was another reason why he avoided the canteen: queues. Ben hated queues. He let out a heavy sigh and pushed open the door. The noise inside the canteen hit him like a punch from Mike Tyson. It almost floored him — he hadn't expected it to be so loud. Ben took a second or two to steady himself and then walked over to the counter. The menu was on top of the counter; there were three hot main meals on offer today or he could have a salad. A memory suddenly hit him of his father turning his nose up at a bowl of salad that his mum had made as a side dish once.

'What's this stuff?' his dad had asked, knowing exactly what it was.

'Salad,' Ben's mum replied softly. 'It's good for you.'

'Don't care how good it is — I'm not a rabbit and I'm not eating salad.'

The menu options were basically the same meal but with different meat products: ham, egg and chips; sausage, egg and chips; chicken nuggets, egg and chips. He decided reluctantly that he would have sausage, egg and chips. This was dumped on his plate rather inelegantly and with very little enthusiasm. He picked up his tray, went over to the coffee machine and helped himself to a large latte before going to the cashier to pay.

After paying, Ben looked out into the expanse of tables and chairs that now lay before him. All the staff seemed to melt into one generic face. He recognised no one and felt all the eyes staring at him. Then he heard a voice. A high-pitched voice calling his name.

'Beeeennnn!' the voice almost screamed again.

He looked around to see if he could locate where this voice was coming from. Then the body that the voice belonged to stood up and waved. It was Tamzin. She was beckoning him over to her. Grudgingly, he smiled at her and traipsed over to her, feeling a little like a schoolboy who had just been caught doing something wrong and now had to face his punishment from the head teacher. He really didn't fancy having a conversation with anyone, let alone Tamzin, the gossip-monger and maneater. Maybe maneater was a bit harsh — she didn't flirt outrageously with every guy she met, just him. Maybe Beneater was more apt.

'Hey, Tam!' Ben said as he put his tray down on the table. He sat down opposite her.

'Alright, Ben?' she replied. 'Hey, have you heard the news? The Christmas party is going to be in the Marriot this year! A week before Christmas Eve. The email came through this morning. They have done a deal or something so it's dinner, a disco, a casino and a room for the night — all for £50! Sounds awesome to me. I have already replied letting them know that I will be there.'

Ben was thinking that he didn't really have to be here for this conversation. She wouldn't let him get a word in edgeways. Tamzin could have had this conversation on her own.

'I haven't read the email yet,' Ben replied when he had a chance. 'I guess I will go, though — should be good fun.'

'There are no partners allowed though — something to do with company staff only, so we will all get to know each other better. I think they are trying to make it a bondage session.'

Ben suddenly looked up at her; he hadn't really been listening but had caught the 'bondage' bit.

Tamzin saw his reaction and laughed. 'Only kidding — I think they are trying to make it a staff *bonding* session as well as a party. So shall I book us a double room?' she winked at Ben.

'No, I don't think so,' Ben replied nervously. 'I will have a single room.'

'Worth a try, eh?' she smiled at him.

Why did she keep making these inappropriate comments and flirtations? Every now and then would be ok, but it was every time she spoke to him. Ben started to wolf down his food. Tamzin was still talking about something but Ben wasn't listening. He needed to get out of the canteen and back to his office. He felt uncomfortable.

He finished his food and started to get up.

'Not leaving already, are you?' Tamzin asked, disappointed.

'Have to. I've got so much work to do by this afternoon, better get it done.'

'I know your sort — always leave them wanting more!' she replied and winked at him again.

Ben faked a laugh and left the table. 'See you later, Tam,' he said.

'You can count on it!'

Ben walked out of the canteen and breathed a deep sigh of relief as the cooler air of the corridor hit his face.

SCREECH!

Ben stopped suddenly on his way to his office. What was that? The sound smashed through his head like someone driving a truck into a store window during a ram raid. It stopped him in his tracks. He felt his breathing get very heavy and loud. His pulse seemed to be beating too fast. Something else had happened when the sound had hit him this time. He saw something. What was it? He tried to recall it but couldn't. It had only been in his mind for a split second. Not long enough for him to capture it and record it. He steadied himself and continued the walk to his office. He opened the door, walked in closing the door behind him and sat down at his desk. He was still breathing quickly and his heart was still trying to batter its way out of his chest. He shut his eyes, trying desperately to recall what had shot through his mind when the screech occurred.

It was dark. Wherever, whatever it had been, it was dark. His head started to ache because he was trying so hard to remember what it was. Slowly, something appeared. Something Ben soon began to wish hadn't appeared.

It was a room. A bedroom. Not his and not Kim's. It wasn't one that he recognised. It was a hotel bedroom. Not the one he stayed in while at the conference, either. As he tried harder to see what else was in the room, there was a scream. A horrific, blood-curdling scream of agony. Ben jumped up from his chair. The scene disappeared from his mind. He couldn't see anymore. He didn't want to see anymore. The scream was enough. It was so real. Whoever had made the scream was in pain, a lot of pain. It was terrifying.

Chapter 16

Kim was in the staffroom. There was a lot going on around her as it was lunchtime. Then again, there always seemed to be a lot going on in the staffroom because it was so small. Not that it needed to be big; the school was not very big and there was only one class per year group. That meant there were eight classes in all. Thus, there were only eight teachers, the head teacher, administrators and a few support staff. The whole staff amounted to twenty, including the secretary and the caretaker. They were never all in the staffroom at the same time, but there were always people coming in and out of the staffroom and this made it look busier and smaller than it actually was. There were ten chairs against two of the walls, a fridge, a sink and a microwave. There were a load of cupboards full of crockery that never got used. Everyone tended to bring their own in and each staff member had their own mug for tea. This was taken very seriously; if you were caught using someone else's mug you would get the speech from someone. The speech went something along the lines of:

'I wouldn't use that mug if I were you, that's [insert name]'s mug. If he/she catches you using their mug you'll be in trouble!'

'Trouble' ranged from a steely glare to a public confrontation, depending on whose mug you used. Kim remembered a poor student teacher using Mrs Jones's mug once; she had regretted it for the duration of her time at the school. Mrs Jones taught year five and she was what the children called 'a strict teacher'. However, she wasn't just strict with the children, she was strict with the staff too. Most of the staff in the school were afraid of her.

Kim had absentmindedly switched off from the busy staffroom and found herself thinking about Ben.

She must spend most of her time thinking of him these days. Maybe it was because he wasn't like other boyfriends she had had in the past. He was different. Special. Was he going to be the one? If he asked her to marry him today she would probably agree in a heartbeat, even though they had only been going out for a short while. Her mother had told her after she had broken up with an earlier boyfriend that when you know, you know. Up until now, Kim didn't quite know what her mother had meant. She couldn't quite put her finger on why she knew it was right with Ben, but she just did.

Her last serious boyfriend was about a year ago. They had met in a nightclub, got talking and had taken each other's numbers. The next day, Dan had called her and they arranged to meet the following night. They had gone to a Mexican restaurant. She couldn't remember what food she had ordered but she did remember that it had gotten cold because they had talked for so long. The food almost got in the way! They'd had a lot in common. He was a secondary school teacher. Maths. He was very intelligent. They went to a bar afterwards for a drink — a soft drink, because they were both driving, but that was ok because the conversation kept flowing. She couldn't remember exactly what they had talked about for so long but there had never been an awkward silence. At the end of the night they shared a kiss by her car as they said goodbye. She went home full of excitement. He was a nice guy. They had dated for about a year-ish. They had a few arguments along the way, but nothing major. They moved into a flat together and it all seemed quite nice. Her friends kept asking her when she was going to get married and she would laugh it off but underneath somewhere there was a feeling that it might happen. But she didn't know. This was the difference with Ben. She already knew with Ben. Just before Christmas, she and Dan had gone on an awesome holiday to India. They saw all the sights. They stayed at an incredible Hilton resort. She remembered thinking that real Indian food is nothing like Indian food at home. It was delicious though. When they got back they had spent Christmas with each other's families and New Year with her friends. A few weeks later, Dan said that he wanted to move out. Not to break up but to move out. Kim thought this was weird but let it happen because she didn't want to break up. Not too long after Dan had moved out he kept getting messages from his ex-girlfriend. They had remained friends after they had broken up and she often texted him. This had made Kim feel uneasy throughout their relationship but she let it go. She was of the opinion that if you broke up with someone then that was it — you just broke up. You didn't keep texting each other, reminiscing and upsetting each other.

A few weeks later after moving out, Dan told her that he wanted to break up. Kim had been devastated. She thought about how much time she had spent on this relationship and how much of it was wasted now that it was over. Her mates and family had been very supportive, but her emotions were all over the place. However, now she was happy. She had Ben. He was incredible. She knew life was so much better with Ben than it ever would have been with Dan. What made her laugh was that she heard that Dan was now back together with his ex-girlfriend. The one he had claimed was a bitch that he hated throughout most of their relationship. He now had a child. Something that Kim would never do. She was pretty old fashioned; she believed in sex before marriage but would never have a child before she got married. She had Ben — she had won. Dan had lost, big time.

'Kim?' a voice said out of the blue. 'Earth to Kim?!'

Kim snapped back to reality suddenly. The staffroom was empty except for the head teacher, Mrs Williams.

'Lunchtime's just about to finish, Kim.'

'Oh, wow, I was miles away! Sorry,' Kim replied, a little dreamily.

'I have been calling you for ages! What were you thinking about?'

Kim thought for a second and then said, 'Ben.'

The head smiled at her. 'Ahh, true love. But you have to get to your class now; they will be waiting for you.'

'Ok, on my way.' Kim got up from her seat, left the staffroom and headed upstairs to her classroom.

Chapter 17

Ben left the office early. He needed to clear his head. Ever since he'd managed to recall part of the vision he couldn't get the scream out of his head. It would just jump in and out every so often like a jack-in-the-box being constantly wound up. He wanted some fresh air and a change of scenery. He also didn't want to bump into Tamzin again today — once a day was more than enough.

Ben reached the car park without seeing anyone. He was relieved because he couldn't have explained why he was in such a hurry or why he was sweating.

Breathing in the fresh air in the car park was like taking a first breath of air after being underwater for a long time. He gasped and sucked in the air through his nose, but he couldn't get the air in quick enough so he opened his mouth to breath in more. The air was cool in his mouth and sent a small tingle down his throat. There was a slight breeze, which felt very cold on his neck due to the amount that he had been sweating. Ben stood still for a few minutes and closed his eyes. It was fantastic.

Walking over to his car, Ben dropped some of the papers he had been carrying. They fluttered away in the breeze and he chased them around for a while but managed to collect them all up again. When he stood up he felt dizzy. He saw a number of little flashes in front of his eyes that looked like stars. This must be where cartoons get the idea of stars flying around a characters head when they get hit by a frying pan or something hard. He blinked a couple of times and the stars disappeared. He walked back over to his car. After dumping the papers in the boot, he got in the front seat and started the engine. A song blasted out on the radio, making him jump and press hard on the accelerator. The car gave a loud growl.

Good job it wasn't in gear, Ben thought as he turned down the radio and reversed out of the parking space.

The drive home passed quickly and, after a light dinner, Ben spoke to Kim on the phone. They were both quite emotional about their working days. Ben thought often during the conversation that he should tell Kim about the vision in his head and the noise that had accompanied it, but decided not to. Kim had seemed upset on the phone but assured him that everything was alright.

Kim told Ben about her daydream in the staffroom at lunchtime. He laughed when she told him that she had been thinking of him. It was an uneasy laugh. He didn't quite know what to say to her. He did think about her during his day but never really thought it was newsworthy, so he never told her that he had been thinking of her. He told Kim about the Christmas party.

'Oh, it would have been nice to spend the night in the Marriot together,' Kim said when he told her that no partners were allowed.

Ben explained what Tamzin had said about it possibly being a staff bonding session as well.

'I suppose they couldn't have made it such a big deal if there were going to be partners as well as the regular staff,' Kim said, sounding disappointed.

'Never mind,' Ben replied, 'I will take you out for a meal in the Marriot to make up for it. Have our own Christmas party. We could even book a room there as well, if you like?'

'You are a sweetie! Sounds good to me.'

'Cool, I will look into it tomorrow. I am going to head to bed now, babe, I am shattered.'

'Ok, Ben, sleep well! Love you.' Kim blew him a kiss down the phone.

'Love you too,' Ben replied and blew her a kiss in return.

Chapter 18

Monday afternoon came by rather quickly for Kim. School finished and she decided not to stay and do work after school. It was a balmy winter's day, unseasonably warm, and she was looking forward to the walk home. Normally at this time of year she was driving the short distance to the school with the heaters on full blast. As she reached her driveway she was surprised to see Ben sitting on the front lawn. A pang of excitement shot through her body.

'What a nice surprise!' Kim exclaimed with a huge smile on her face.

'Hi, sweetie, I took the afternoon off in the hope you would be home straight after school. I thought we could take advantage of this beautiful day and go for a walk somewhere nice. I was thinking about the forest by the old castle — what do you say?' Ben was almost stumbling over his words.

'I say can I get a kiss first?'

'Oh yes, sorry, of course,' Ben replied and picked Kim up and kissed her passionately on the mouth.

Kim smiled. 'I say yes! Let's go! You can drive.'

They got into Ben's car and drove the ten minute journey to Old Crag Castle. The castle had once been a hospital — more specifically, a hospital for people who had contracted tuberculosis. Many patients who went into that hospital never came out. Patients were treated poorly, sometimes left out on the terrace throughout the wintertime or left inside with windows open. Many of those who didn't die of tuberculosis died of exposure to the elements. It was not all about death though; many patients did survive and lived through the illness. There were many stories about the castle being haunted by various old patients and the old woman who owned the castle in the 1800s. The castle itself was set in a huge forest with trees of all sorts of sizes and colours. Parts of the forest were very dense and dark, even on sunny days. There was a small river that ran from its source in the mountain, through the forest and out into the town and the sea beyond.

Ben parked the car and they both got out. There was a slight breeze in the car park that made Kim shiver as they walked around the old castle and down the steps into what was essentially the castle's back garden. There were a few other walkers slowly wandering around the forest edges, along the paths. Kim took Ben's hand in hers and he smiled at her. They walked across a small stone bridge that didn't actually arch over anything; it was more ornamental than functional. The path meandered gently into the forest and before long Ben and Kim were alone. It was suddenly very quiet. The other walkers were around somewhere but the density of the forest was such that their voices did not travel very far. The silence was a welcome break from the noise of the primary school children that Kim faced every day. After a few minutes, however, Kim felt the quiet getting too much and had to find something to say.

'We are having our school play in the theatre in the castle this year.'

'What? In that castle?' Ben asked, pointing in the direction of the castle that was now lost behind the thick trunks of the trees.

'Yes, one of the new teachers knows the manager of the place and so we have it for two nights coming up to Christmas.'

'Wow! That's awesome. So it's like a real play then,' Ben said with excitement.

'Well, as real as a school play can be, I guess,' Kim replied with some scepticism.

They continued talking for a few minutes more, until suddenly Ben noticed that they had drifted off the path that had become covered with fallen leaves.

'Kim, do you know where we are?' he asked, looking around.

Kim stopped walking and looked around her. She couldn't see the actual path but did have an idea of where they had come from. It was noticeably colder now than it had been earlier. She shivered. Ben hugged her closer to him and kissed her head. Kim looked up at him and smiled.

'I think I remember the way we came in,' Kim said, and looked behind her as if to show the way.

'Ok then, shall we head back? It's getting quite cold now and I'm also getting hungry,' Ben said.

'Yes, let's go.' Kim turned around as she spoke and led Ben back toward the path. In a few minutes they were back on the edge of the forest where they could once again hear the voices of the other walkers and the faint trickle of the river. The light had ebbed away from the sky and the afternoon was now giving way to the evening. The lights had come on in the castle — or at least they were now more noticeable because it was darker outside. They climbed the steps and made their way back to the car park. They got into Ben's car and he started the engine. Despite the heaters being on full blast, there was a definite chill in the air as they headed back to Kim's house.

Chapter 19

Over the next few days the weather got increasingly colder. Thick knitted jumpers had replaced the light sweaters people were wearing as they went about their daily business. Some people had already started wearing their winter coats. The weather-orientated small talk had returned to 'winter is coming', or 'there's a real nip in the air', or 'isn't it cold today?'

It was late November and up until now the weather had been quite mild; a mix of late autumn sun and rain. However, the drop in temperature was signalling the end of the autumn and the start of winter. It would soon be Christmas. The shops around where Kim lived had had Christmas decorations up since just after Halloween. Some of the larger supermarkets had displayed Christmas decorations and Halloween decorations at the same time. Kim thought this quite a strange situation, considering Halloween was very anti-Christian in origin and Christmas was obviously the biggest Christian celebration. It amazed her that there would be pictures of skeletons and witches and ghosts next to pictures of angels and Jesus and Santa. Not that Kim was overly religious; she simply thought that the supermarkets and marketing companies had made both Halloween and Christmas far too commercial and were trying to get as much money out of the public as they possibly could. Ben, who was far more business-minded, would have said that it was 'just good business'. It was supply and demand; give people what they want and make money doing it, and if the people don't know what they want then tell them what they want and make even more money.

Kim loved Christmas. It was her favourite time of year. She heard about people hating Christmas because a loved one had died around the festive period, and selfishly hoped that no one she knew would ever die around Christmas because she wanted to continue loving it each year. She got annoyed at people who hated Christmas for no reason other than it was Christmas. People would say that they didn't like how commercial it was or how expensive it was. She privately thought these people were sad, miserable people who just liked to moan about anything they could. Christmas, for Kim, was a fantastic time where most people were happy and the air around the streets was that little bit sweeter.

Ben shared her passion for Christmas. They were both like children. They got very excited whenever they talked about Christmas or whenever they heard Christmas songs in the shops. They both liked the Christmas songs that they heard when they were growing up, but more and more recently the shops had started playing newer stuff with raps halfway through 'Jingle Bells' or 'White Christmas', much to the couple's distaste. 'If it isn't broken, don't fix it,' was their motto when it came to Christmas songs.

School was strange around Christmas. There was a lot of excitement from both the children and the teachers. The decorations would go up in the first week of December. The older children would help with putting up the decorations and the younger children would be allowed to help decorate one of the Christmas trees. The school bought in two fresh Christmas trees every year. One was decorated by the teachers and was put in the school reception —this was the 'neat tree'. The other was decorated by the younger children and was put in the school hall — this was the 'children's tree'. This was usually decorated with a mix of brightly coloured plastic decorations and other decorations that the children had made out of either salt dough or card.

One thing that Kim didn't like about school at Christmas was the school production. Every class had to do something in the school production. This included the little ones singing a Christmas carol and the older children taking part in a small play. Two years ago, Kim had volunteered to oversee it all and be the director of the production — a move that she had regretted ever since because she was now stuck with the role of director until someone took the title from her. She couldn't see that happening for a while. At least not until a new teacher who was full of enthusiasm and zest for the job came to the school; then Kim could offer them the director's role as a way of 'developing their potential' — a buzz phrase that she hated.

The first year she directed the production, she actually wrote the play for the older children herself. What a nightmare that was. The production itself was very good but getting the children together to practice proved nearly impossible. She almost gave up on more than one occasion. Last year, she used one of the productions schools can buy in. The music was done for her, the script was done for her and all she needed was the set and costumes. It was infinitely easier than the previous year. The play itself wasn't as good as her own creation but it was far more stress-free for her.

This year, Kim had decided that she would use a new production that the school had bought in a number of years ago so that none of the parents would have seen it before. She didn't want there to be parents saying 'oh we've seen this one,' or 'they did that one when John was in the school and now James is doing the same thing.' This year's production was going to be a nativity play with a difference. It was taken from the animals' points of view. The big selling point for this show in Kim's eyes was that it was a lot easier to cast animals than humans. If you had too many children for human roles it was difficult to put them all in the show without it looking very fake. However, with animals you could just add more sheep, or cows, or pigs, etc. The play did still require a Mary and a Joseph, and Kim had to cast them as soon as possible.

The casting proved quite difficult, the reason being that everyone wanted to be Mary and Joseph even though the main parts in this play were actually a cow and a horse! No matter how hard Kim tried to explain this to the children, they all wanted to be Mary or Joseph. Eventually, she managed to convince the two children she wanted for the main parts, Tom and Hannah, to be a horse and a cow. They were probably the two children with the highest reading abilities who were actually keen to be centre stage for a large part of the show. Tom was ten and Hannah was going to be ten in February. With these main parts chosen it was full steam ahead for the rehearsals and costume design.

Chapter 20

Ben was having difficulty sleeping. It had started ever since he'd returned from his drunken exploits on his recent business trip. He kept hearing that screeching noise, high-pitched and deafening. He kept dreaming about being trapped in a dark room. There was no door and no windows and, from where he was, he could never see the ceiling — it was too dark. During the dream, shadows appeared on the wall. Human shadows. However, each one that appeared disappeared quite quickly and was then replaced by another. Each shadow looked slightly different. The first was invariably grasping a severed head by the hair. The others tended to mix their positions around. These shadows all had a limb or two missing. He could see their eyes — darker shadow-pits — staring at him, piercing through his body and causing his heart to pound violently in his chest. After the shadows had finished their macabre catwalk, Ben was able to see something in the corner of the room. It was not a shadow. The room was too dark to see what it was and he was rooted to the spot. Then he would wake up, sweating and breathing heavily, his heart trying to erupt out of his chest. The time was always 3:32 when he woke, no matter how often he had the dream during the night. This led Ben to believe that it was a dream inside a dream. How could it always be the same time?

* * *

'Morning, sweetie!'

Tamzin's voice grated inside his tired ears. He had no interest in talking to her this morning. The lack of sleep was taking its toll. Not to mention the weather. It was a cold and wet December. Depressing.

Ben groaned in Tamzin's direction, not looking at her.

'Hey, mister grumpy pants! What's wrong with you? Got out of the wrong side of the bed?!'

Ben realised that he was not going to get away with not speaking to her this morning. 'Sorry, Tam. I've not been sleeping well and my head is killing me.' Ben mumbled and rubbed his temples to emphasise the pain.

'Aw, poor lamb. You should come home with me — I'd soon have you tired out and sleeping like a baby!' she winked at Ben and smiled.

She had a nice smile — perfect teeth. It was quite infectious and Ben smiled back without saying anything.

'That's better; you're a lot sexier when you smile.' It seemed Tamzin was about to go into full flirt mode.

'Sorry, Tam, I can't stay and chat with you this morning. I've loads to do today and I want to get home early tonight.' Ben thought that would end the conversation but Tamzin had other ideas.

'Ok, I'll let you go,' she started, then remembered the party. 'Are you excited about the party on Friday? I am.'

Ben had been poised to move on to his office but stopped. 'Yes, I need to relax a little. A bit of fun and booze may help me sleep.'

'Awesome! Stick with me and you'll have plenty of fun and definitely get smashed!' she looked back at her computer.

'Sounds good, see you later.' Ben turned to leave.

'See ya.'

Ben started walking towards his office when he heard the dreaded sound scream deafeningly from behind him. He cringed and put his fingers in his ears. It stopped and he turned back to look at Tamzin. She looked up at him.

'You ok?' she asked.

'Did you hear that?'

Tamzin looked confused. 'Hear what?'

'Oh nothing — don't worry about it. Think my mind is slowly giving up on me!' Ben replied with a forced smile. He turned back towards his office and left Tamzin looking after him, shaking her head.

Chapter 21

Kim got home early. She had had enough of the children today. She always thought she had plenty of patience but during the Christmas play rehearsals she had her patience tested to the max. It was hard work trying to get the children to stand where they should, sing when they should and speak when they should. Not to mention be quiet when they were meant to be. So today she had left only a few minutes after the final bell went.

Kim put the kettle on and made herself a cup of tea, as strong as possible. Throughout the day she drank coffee, even though she preferred tea. This was because the tea in school was horrible. It was hard to make instant coffee badly so she drank that instead, but always looked forward to having a good cup of tea when she got home.

She sipped the hot drink and made her way to the lounge. On the way she passed the globe drinks cabinet. She stopped by it for a second. Kim took another sip of her tea and then opened the drinks cabinet. She took out one of the bottles of whisky that she kept for special occasions, poured herself a glass and sat down on the sofa with the tea and a large glass of whisky. After downing the tea quicker than she normally would and burning her tongue on the liquid, Kim turned her attention to the whisky. She took a long sip. The amber liquid tingled on her lips and in her mouth. It hurt her tongue where the tea had burned her only minutes earlier but she hardly noticed. It tasted and felt good. She let out a satisfied sigh and finished the rest of the glass.

She found herself thinking of Ben again. She looked at her watch. He would be home in about an hour. Kim got up and poured herself another glass of whisky, larger than the first, and returned to the sofa.

The television was on; Kim didn't remember turning it on but flicked absentmindedly through the channels anyway. She downed the whisky in three gulps. It felt fantastic! She was already feeling much better. Slowly, Kim drifted off to sleep.

* * *

Ben had been knocking on the door for a few minutes. Kim's car was in the drive so he figured she must be home. He had rung her phone but there was no answer. He decided to walk around the back and look through the window in the lounge. Kim was asleep on the sofa. Ben banged on the window and Kim sat up, looking dazed and confused. Ben smiled at her through the window. It took a few seconds for Kim to work out who it was, but then she smiled back and went to the front door to let him in. Ben came into the kitchen and Kim kissed him. Ben was about to speak when Kim kissed him again, more passionately this time. The kiss was intense. Ben let it happen.

Kim couldn't remember Ben saying that he was going to come over but she was very glad that he had. He was exactly what she needed right now. The kiss was intense. His tongue felt warm and soft in her mouth; it hurt her burnt tongue when he brushed it with his but she didn't mind. She wasn't going to stop now. She reached her hand down towards the front of his trousers and slowly massaged his rapidly growing member. Ben let out a deep sigh as she did so. Kim undid the zip of his fly and slipped her hand inside. She felt around and made her way inside his tight boxers. Ben was cupping and massaging her right breast. It felt fantastic. Kim started to kneel down and took Ben's penis out of his boxers. It was rock hard now. She put it into her mouth and worked her tongue around the tip and down the shaft. Ben leant back against a kitchen cabinet and brushed her hair back with his hands. She looked up at him and he smiled down at her. She kept the eye contact while she was sucking hard on his rigid penis. She could taste him now. Ben reached down and pulled her up towards him. He unbuttoned her blouse and undid the clasp of her bra while Kim unzipped the back of her skirt. Suddenly, she was standing in the kitchen in just her knickers. White lace but comfortable — not overly sexy. Ben started to bend down, taking the knickers down with him. He worked his mouth down her body and started to play with her clitoris. She lifted one foot onto the kitchen counter so he had more room. Ben slid a finger deep inside her and stroked her from the inside. She started to moan. This felt incredible. She started shaking; her standing leg was giving way. Was she going to collapse? Kim didn't know. She pushed Ben's head closer to her, gripping his hair tightly.

'Oh my god!' Kim whispered. It was all she could say. She felt butterflies rising in her stomach.

Ben kissed his way back up her body. He kissed her on the lips; she could taste herself on him.

He turned her around to face away from him. Kim put her leg back up on the counter to give Ben room to manoeuvre. He glided his hard penis inside her and they moaned in harmony. Slowly, Ben moved back and forth and Kim moved her hips in time with his. She looked back towards Ben and he kissed her cheek. He was cupping her breasts now, massaging them in time with their rhythm as it got faster. Kim's legs were tingling, like pins and needles. She was close. She found herself moaning louder and louder.

'Don't stop,' she cried out, louder than she had expected.

Then, suddenly, there it was — the intense orgasm that she had been waiting for. Craving. She shut her eyes hard.

Ben let out a moan and gripped her hips, hard. She felt him unleash inside her. He slowed down and held her. Their breathing was hard and fast. Kim turned around and looked at Ben. He smiled at her.

'Nice to see you too,' he said.

She smiled back at him and held him tightly. She felt much better now.

Chapter 22

Friday. Ben woke up feeling like he had a hangover, despite the fact that he hadn't drunk any alcohol the previous night. Not even a glass of wine with his dinner. He had spent the night at Kim's and he had slept fitfully, disturbed by the same dream over and over again. Each time, he would look at his phone to check the time and it would say 3:32.

As he was driving into work, Ben recalled one of the dreams from the previous night. It had been slightly different to the others. The room was the same and he was still unable to move. There were shadows as usual but one of the shadows was definitely that of a woman. It had breasts. Before there was no real definition in the shadows other than if their hair was obviously long — like the headless one. The female shadow was not headless. It had long hair and the eyes were a deeper black with a tiny speck of red in the centre. Even more fascinating than this development was the fact that he thought he could see what was in the corner. Whatever it was had shifted slightly and Ben had almost caught a glimpse of what it was. In the dream he had stared at the corner in the hope that his eyes would become more accustomed to the dark and see what was there, but they did not and he had woken up to find the time was 3:32.

Ben started to feel better when he arrived at the reception. He saw Tamzin at the front desk and smiled at her.

'Someone's looking happier,' she said.

'How can I not be happy when I get to see you every day?' Ben replied, smiling.

Tamzin blushed slightly. 'Oh, Ben, you really know how to get a girl hot under the collar!'

'Absolutely! If you play your cards right I might make you hot all over!' Ben winked at her.

'Just give me a time and a place, baby!' Tamzin said, looking back at her computer to signal that she was done flirting for the time being.

Ben laughed and headed to the office. As he did so the high-pitched noise hit him like a sledgehammer. He bent over, holding his head.

Tamzin looked up at him and rushed over to where Ben was almost curled up on the floor.

'Hey! Ben! You ok?'

The noise seemed to increase more intensely than before. Tears started to stream down Ben's cheeks. He cried out in pain. Tamzin touched his back gently. The noise erupted like a volcano inside his head. The noise lava drowned out everything else nearby. He couldn't take it anymore.

'Get away from me!' he shouted at Tamzin, but he couldn't actually hear his own voice. The volcano in his head was too loud.

Terrified, Tamzin stood up and rushed back to her desk.

The noise relented. Slowly, Ben got up. He leant against the wall. He was breathing fast and heavily. Ben wiped his eyes and ran down to his office, where he collapsed into his chair. For the next twenty minutes, he rested his head on the pile of paperwork in front of his computer.

Tamzin came into Ben's office about half an hour later with a cup of tea. Ben looked up at her and managed a smile.

'Thought you might need this,' she said as she placed the cup on his desk.

'Thanks, Tam.' Ben sighed. 'Sorry about shouting at you, my head just hurt so much all of a sudden.'

'Don't worry, sweetie. I just hope you'll be ok for this evening!'

'No problem, I will be fine. I feel much better now already.'

'Ok then, I'll see you later. Lunch date today?'

Tamzin asked.

'Yes, why not — I'll treat you.'

'Sweet! You rock my world!'

'And you blow me away!' As soon as he had said the words Ben knew what was coming next.

'And I'd blow you any day, sweetie!' Tamzin replied and left the office.

Chapter 23

Ben got home from work feeling better than he had going to work. The party was starting at 7:30. He got undressed and showered. The warm water felt great on his tired body. He got out of the shower, shaved and cleaned his teeth in the sink. Ben walked through the lounge and into his bedroom. He paused and looked at the strange picture on the wall. It seemed as if the boy had grown a little older. He squinted at it and then laughed to himself, deciding that that was a crazy thought.

With the picture of the boy still in his mind, Ben opened his wardrobe and picked out his favourite shirt: one with a blue, black and white check pattern and short sleeves. He paired this with his black smart casual trousers. Ben got dressed, looked at himself in the mirror, adjusted the collar on his shirt a little and sprayed on some aftershave. The alcohol burnt his cheeks a little. He went over to the kitchen and opened the fridge. A cold can of Coors Light was looking back at him. Ben took it out and opened it, making it hiss satisfyingly. He drank almost a third of the can in one go. It tasted fantastic.

Ben picked up his phone and called a taxi to go to the hotel. It would be about fifteen minutes. *Perfect,* he thought to himself, *just enough time to finish the beer.*

He was starting to look forward to the evening.

* * *

Ben arrived at the hotel a little after 7:30. He made his way to the large function room where the party was being held. The company had booked out the whole room. Ben remembered that when he worked for a smaller company a few years ago their Christmas party was in a similar room but it was mixed with a few other companies. That situation had been weird because everyone became very secular. No one mixed with each other. Companies stuck to their own sections and you ended up talking to people who you didn't like just so you didn't have to talk to a drunken stranger!

The room itself was massive. There were four huge chandeliers on the ceiling and a multitude of uplights all along the walls. The walls themselves were papered in a burgundy paisley-esque pattern and the carpets were also burgundy. There were fifteen round tables spread throughout the room with white tablecloths on them. There were eight place settings on each table. At the far end of the room stood the bar which already had a queue of people waiting for drinks. Britain's teenagers are not the only binge drinkers in the country. You just have to look at office Christmas parties to see that. At the other end of the room, opposite the bar and the end that Ben had entered, was the dance floor. There was a DJ hidden away in one corner already pumping out tunes, dying for the first drunken office worker to step onto the dance floor and make a fool out of themselves.

Ben spotted Tamzin in the queue for drinks. She was wearing a red blouse and a black skirt that ended just above the knee. She had very high red sparkly stilettos that must have added four inches to her height, at least. Her legs looked very slender and toned. He walked slowly towards the bar. As he got closer, Tamzin glanced around and saw him. She screamed in excitement and left the queue to give him a huge almost painful bear hug.

'Ben! You're looking sexy tonight,' Tamzin said loudly over the noise of everyone meeting and greeting each other.

'You too, Tam. Gorgeous!'

'You flatterer,' she said, winking. 'Come on, let's

get you a drink.' She took him by the hand and made her way through the ever-growing crowd to the bar.

Two pints and whole lot of small talk later, it was half past eight and the meal was served. Ben sat next to Tamzin at a table that was overcrowded with eight place settings. Six would have been comfortable, seven a little cosy, with eight on the table they spent more time apologising for bumping arms than talking about anything else.

The food was a standard Christmas dinner. Vegetable soup to start, followed by a turkey dinner, then Christmas pudding and coffee to finish. Vegetarians were allowed a nut roast. The room was full now. Ben thought that there must be at least one hundred people there, probably more. After food, the staff cleared away a few tables so that there was more room to mingle. Ben bought himself a lager and ordered Tamzin a large glass of white wine. He was feeling a bit lightheaded now.

Chapter 24

Kim was looking over the marking she had brought home with her. Had it come to this? Half past eight on a Friday night and she was marking! Ben was at his Christmas party enjoying himself and she was at home on her own. She got up from the sofa and went into the kitchen. She found a bottle of red wine next to the microwave. It was still half full. She'd had a glass last night but she was not as partial to a glass of wine as she used to be. But it was Friday night; it was almost a rule that she should have something to help her unwind after a pretty hectic school week. The head teacher had told her to put the curriculum on hold for the next week so that they could concentrate on the school play. Tomorrow was the first dress rehearsal in the theatre in Old Crag Castle and, as much as Kim was looking forward to it, she was worried that the children would be distracted by all the decor of the place. Kim poured some of the wine into a large glass that almost held half a bottle if she filled it right up, but she very rarely did. Her dad had always told her that she shouldn't fill the glass too much and it stuck in her mind. The wine was dark red and she could smell some sort of fruit in it. Possibly blackberries. She was no expert in wine, but she did know a little bit about wine regions. Most of all she knew what she liked and what she didn't like.

Kim went back to the sofa, sat down, stared at the pile of marking on the table next to her and sighed. She really didn't fancy doing it right now. She sipped her wine. It was slightly colder than she liked for red wine but it tasted good. Far better than it had tasted yesterday. Kim took a few more sips and turned the TV on. There wasn't anything on that interested her, just reality TV shows and documentaries. She glanced over to where her DVDs were stacked on the bookshelf.

'I could put a film on,' she thought out loud. She fancied watching a scary film. Not a gore fest though — something that made her jump. She decided on *The Woman in Black*. She had recently bought it and, although she saw it in the cinema and read the book as a teenager, this was the film that jumped out at her.

Kim put the disc into the player, pressed play, sat back on the sofa and sipped some more of her wine. She was starting to feel relaxed now. As the film began, Kim felt a cold shiver run down her spine. She looked around the room but there was nothing out of the ordinary. She felt a second shiver, a little more intense than the first. She pressed pause on the remote and got up to have a look to see if there was a window open.

Kim walked back to the kitchen but no windows were open. She poured the rest of the wine into her glass and walked back to the sofa. As she did so, she noticed something on the floor under the table. She bent down to pick it up. It was the photograph of the strange family. She couldn't help feeling puzzled. She remembered putting it on the bookshelf and couldn't work out how it had ended up under the table. She looked again at the picture. The little boy appeared to be grinning at her now.

That can't be — I must not have looked at it properly the first time, Kim thought to herself as she put it back on the bookshelf. She sat back on the sofa and pressed play. The people on the screen started moving again and Kim took a sip of her wine. She started to feel warm again.

Chapter 25

Ben had spent the past hour drinking, talking, dancing and flirting. He was having a fantastic time, though he was feeling a little hot and sweaty now. He went to the bar and ordered himself a vodka and cola. He had had enough beer two drinks ago. This was Ben's third vodka and he was quite drunk. His confidence was at an all-time high and he was talking to people who he had never laid eyes on before. He made his way back to the dance floor and saw Tamzin was already there.

Tamzin saw him, too. She pushed her way towards him through a few people, kissed him on the cheek and smiled. 'Where have you been?' she asked loudly. They had gradually danced their way over to where the speaker was and they had to shout to be heard over the music. 'I thought you might have left without saying goodbye.'

'No, I'm having a great time. It's a great party!' Ben shouted. He looked at his watch. It was just after eleven. 'Wow! Doesn't time fly when you're having fun!' he cried.

'It sure does, but this place is going to kick us out at half twelve so we don't have much time left. Some of the girls are going into town afterwards, if you fancy it,' Tamzin replied; her throat hurt a little as she strained to be heard over the noise.

'Yeah, sounds good.' Ben smiled.

'Let's get another drink.' Tamzin said as she led Ben by the hand away from the dance floor. They got another drink each and went to one of the tables away from the speakers and sat down. They started talking again. It was far easier to be heard now and Tamzin's throat no longer hurt her. They talked about work for a little while and then Tamzin spoke of her last boyfriend, who seemed to be a bit of a lunatic. Ben tried to talk about Kim but Tamzin kept changing the subject. It was coming up to half past twelve when Ben heard the dreaded sound. He winced and looked at Tamzin.

'You ok?' she asked.

'Yes — did you hear that?'

'Hear what?'

'Doesn't matter.' Ben dismissed the sound as something he had imagined. Then, just as he was thinking of going to look for his coat, the sound hit him again — far worse than before. He winced and shut his eyes, gritting his teeth hard. The pain inside his head was agony.

Ben opened his eyes to see Tamzin looking worriedly at him. She put her hand on his shoulder. 'What's the matter?'

Ben didn't answer her. He hadn't heard her. The sound was deafening. The screech was tearing his eardrums apart. Tamzin took Ben's arm and led him out through a door that opened out into a back street, normally used for service deliveries. The cool fresh air hit them both as they left the big, stuffy hall. Tamzin tried to get Ben to speak to her but was unsuccessful. He held his hands over his ears and kept his eyes shut. Tamzin shook him gently but nothing changed. She shook him harder and eventually Ben responded. He opened his eyes. Tears ran down his cheeks.

The noise seemed to ease and he could hear Tamzin shouting his name. He looked her straight in the eyes. She smiled at him. Without saying a word, they started to kiss. Softly at first, but then passionately. Their hands explored each other's bodies. Tamzin felt warm in his arms. She walked backwards, still embracing Ben, until she hit a huge bin that held all the empty glass bottles from the bar inside. The bang of them hitting the side of the bin caused them to break their embrace. They both smiled at each other and then continued kissing. Tamzin started to undo the buttons on Ben's shirt.

* * *

Was this it? Was she about to have sex with Ben? The guy she had been chasing for months and months was kissing her. She could feel him hard against her thigh. She was unbuttoning his shirt. She was touching his chest — his rather muscular chest. She let out a little sigh through the kiss. Ben had put his hand on her breast and was stroking it gently. He started to unbutton her blouse. Suddenly, his hand was inside her blouse, caressing her breasts. It felt amazing. Ben's hand slid slowly down her side and reached for the hem of her skirt. He started to lift it up as he pressed hard against her. Suddenly, Tamzin's mind drifted to earlier and she found herself thinking about what knickers she had put on. She couldn't remember. She was hoping they weren't the Bridget Jones style granny knickers she had thought of putting on. Then she remembered — just as Ben's hand found its way up to her bare thigh. She had put on her lacy red knickers. Her sexiest ones. She was relieved and relaxed again.

Tamzin reached down to Ben's trousers and started to undo his fly, marvelling at how hard he was. She put her hand inside the front of his trousers and stroked him. Gently. Ben let out a little moan and she smiled.

Tamzin suddenly felt herself slammed back hard against the bin. She opened her eyes in shock. What was going on? That was a little rougher than she had expected it to be! She looked at Ben. He was bright red. His teeth were gritted and there was spit starting to foam in the corner of his mouth.

'Ben?' Tamzin said quietly. She was getting scared.

* * *

Ben felt the pain inside his head again. It started as Tamzin touched his penis. His first thought was that he had ejaculated, but then the screech started to deafen him. He opened his eyes but couldn't see anything. There was a red darkness around him. The sound seemed to be coming from Tamzin. Was she taunting him? Did she know about the sound? She opened her mouth and screeched at him. A high pitched screech that he could almost see. He quickly pushed her back. She hit the bin with a crash. Some glass inside the bin shifted and smashed. The screech didn't stop. It got louder and louder. It was almost pulsing now. He felt as though his head was going to explode. He had to stop the noise. He had to shut Tamzin up.

Ben reached forward and grabbed Tamzin's throat. It was warm between his fingers. It felt soft and hard at the same time. He squeezed his hands closer together. She started shaking her head violently and grabbed his wrists. The sound was still there. It seemed to be all around him. He looked up the street. He couldn't see anything or anyone. He lifted Tamzin up by the neck. She started kicking her feet out at him and caught him in the shins. He hardly noticed. He shook her then dropped her to the floor, where she started coughing and spluttering. Ben stared down at her. Each cough was a new level of pain. It was like she was jabbing his mind with each one. He couldn't stand it anymore. It had to stop. He had to stop the noise.

Ben lifted up the hinged lid of the bin and looked inside. There were a lot of broken bottles and the bin stank of stale alcohol. Ben reached in and picked up a green bottle. He turned around to face Tamzin, who was still on her knees, trying to get the air back in her lungs. He slowly raised the bottle above his head and brought it down onto Tamzin's head with a smash. The bottle broke and she screamed. The scream cut deep into Ben's head. There was blood on his hand as he looked at the broken end of the bottle he was left holding. He looked down to Tamzin, who now had her hand on her head. Dark liquid was oozing through her fingers. The ooze seemed to bring a new level of noise that Ben didn't think was possible. Ben bent down and picked the bleeding woman up. She flopped toward him and Ben could see her face in the darkness. It was covered in the dark liquid. It was seeping into her mouth and in her eyes. Still, the sound continued.

'STOP IT! STOP IT! STOP IT!' Ben screamed at her.

He lifted Tamzin up and turned her towards to bin. He rested her neck on the rim and brought the heavy lid down with a crash. He felt Tamzin's body jump as he did so. He lifted the lid and slammed it down again. The sound eased slightly. He crashed the lid down on her neck again and again. Tamzin's body went limp. Ben lifted the lid and looked in. Tamzin's head was hanging inside the bin and her body was hanging limp on the outside. Still, the sound continued. He had to stop it. Again and again, Ben slammed the lid down onto Tamzin's broken neck. More and more blood dripped down the side of the bin. Ben then lifted the lid right up and forcibly slammed it down. Tamzin's body fell to the floor. Ben looked down. There was no head attached to the body. He lifted up the lid and looked inside again. Staring back up at him was Tamzin's lifeless face. Her eyes were looking straight into his. Ben opened the lid fully, picked up Tamzin's bloody, broken body and hauled it into the bin — on top of her head. He shut the lid on the bin one last time. The sound had completely stopped. The silence was an incredible relief. There was no pain.

Ben sighed loudly. He looked at his watch.

3:32.

'Oh my god! Is that the time?!' he exclaimed.

He started to walk down the back street and out onto the main road. He needed to find a taxi. As he walked, he noticed his shirt was undone. He did up the buttons. Then noticed his fly was undone too, and zipped it up.

'Wow! What happened in that alley?' he asked himself.

Ben saw a taxi driving towards him and stuck up

his hand. The taxi pulled over and Ben got in. He told the driver his address and the taxi pulled away. As Ben relaxed back in his seat, he looked at his fingers. He noticed on his right hand a tiny dark spot. *Is that blood?* Ben asked himself. *Where'd that come from?* He rubbed at it gently and it disappeared.

A short while later, the taxi pulled up outside his flat. Ben paid the driver and went inside. He got himself a glass of water, downed it in one go and poured another. Ben went to the bedroom and undressed. He toppled over as he pulled off his trousers. 'Shit!' he exclaimed as he picked himself back up. 'I must be drunker than I thought.'

He got into bed and quickly passed out.

Ben hadn't been asleep for long when he was woken by a sound. That high-pitched sound again. He covered his ears with his hands as a reaction to the noise even though he knew it did no good. The sound was already in his head. He stifled a scream. The sound got louder. Ben got out of bed and knocked his glass of water off the bedside table. It fell to the floor, spilling water over the carpet. He didn't notice. Ben went to the lounge and put on the television to try to drown out the sound. While waiting for the TV to warm up, he glanced at the clock on the wall. The time was 3:32. Ben shook his head in disbelief.

'What?! How can that be?' he muttered to himself. 'It must have stopped.'

He got up off the sofa and went to the kitchen to look at the clock on the cooker. It also said 3:32. Ben was confused. He ran to the bedroom to look at the bedside clock. 3:32. All the clocks said 3:32.

I must have got the wrong time earlier, Ben thought. He went back into the lounge and suddenly noticed that the sound had stopped. It was silent again.

Ben turned the TV off and decided to go back to bed. He could feel a hangover coming on. He was not looking forward to Saturday morning.

Chapter 26

Kim woke up early for a Saturday morning. The school play rehearsal was to be held in the theatre at Old Crag Castle today. The children were supposed to be there around 10:00. It was already 9:15. She got into the shower and washed herself quickly before stepping out and dressing herself in jeans and a t-shirt. Kim looked out the window and decided she would take a sweater; even though the sun was shining there was still a frost on the ground. Kim quickly made a cup of tea and poured some cereal into a bowl. She added the milk and ate her breakfast as fast as she could before running out of the door. She jumped into the car and started the drive out to the theatre. As she drove her mind drifted back to the other day when she and Ben had walked around the grounds of the castle and then almost got lost. She thought it was a weird sensation. She remembered feeling completely lost but they must have only been yards away from the castle itself. Her mind then jumped to Ben. He had been out last night at his work Christmas party. He hadn't text or rang her to say that he was home and she had been so busy this morning that she had forgotten to text him.

I hope everything is ok, she thought. *I'll text him when I get to the theatre.*

After about twenty minutes, she arrived at the castle car park. It was empty except for two cars. Kim walked up to the reception where there was a woman in her twenties waiting expectantly. Her black hair was tied up on top of her head and her face was plastered in thick makeup. She was striking to look at but Kim wondered what she would look like without any makeup on.

'Hello, how can I help you?' asked the receptionist.

'Hi, I'm Kim Coombes. I am using the theatre this morning for a school play practice.'

'Oh yes. The theatre is already open so if you know where to go you can go straight in.'

'I know where to go, thanks. Can you send the parents and children straight down as they arrive?'

'Will do,' replied the receptionist, shooting her a smile that was almost too fake.

Kim walked down a small corridor, lined by lots of paintings of hunting scenes and the countryside, down towards the theatre. Along the way, she noticed a really small picture. It stood out because it was a photograph instead of a painting. It was also unusual because it was of a woman and a man who both had an eastern European look about them. The man had a thick black moustache and a side parting in his thick black hair, which was greased down into place. He wore a suit and tie. The woman had curly hair that was possibly dark blonde or a light red colour and a bonnet. Neither was smiling. The woman was sitting and on her knee sat a child, a young boy of about three but his face seemed much older than that. The child had a strange facial expression. He was smiling, unlike the adults in the picture, but the smile was not one of happiness or joy but rather one of menace or evil. Kim stopped for a few minutes and stared at the picture. She had seen it before. But where? She racked her brain. Then, all of a sudden, she remembered. The picture was the same as the one in Ben's bedroom!

'Ben!' Kim thought out loud to herself. 'I'll give him a text now.'

Kim stopped looking at the picture on the wall and she got her phone out of her jeans pocket. She texted Ben quickly and then went into the theatre. The first child to arrive was Tom, then the others all seemed to arrive together. There were twenty-five children there in all. A good turnout for a Saturday rehearsal.

Chapter 27

Ben texted Kim back half an hour later. He told her that he was hungover but he'd had a good night. He mentioned that he would come to see her at the theatre and they could go for a late lunch after the rehearsals. That made her feel good. Ben had this knack of making her feel all warm inside.

The rehearsal was going very well — better than expected. Tom and Hannah had learned a lot of their lines and needed very little prompting. The other children needed reminding of their lines and what they had to do and when they had to do it, but as the morning went on even they started to get it right. By one o'clock the play was starting to look really good. She only had two more practices in the theatre but still had the week in school to finish off anything that wasn't quite right yet. She was pleased with how things were progressing.

Ben arrived just after one o'clock, looking a little pale. Kim went over to him and kissed him. The children made 'oohing' sounds behind her. Ben pulled away to smile at her.

'Where have you been?' Kim asked.

'I was a mess earlier but I'm much better now. It took longer than I thought to get myself together.'

'Ok, well sit in the front and watch the rest of the practice. The children are doing really well today.'

Ben went to the front row of the theatre and sat down. Kim went to the front of the stage and told the children that Ben was going to watch to see how well they were doing. The children became quite excited and seemed to look far more alert than they had been a few minutes ago.

Ben looked to his left, where a young boy was sitting.

'What's your name?' he asked.

'Tom,' replied the boy.

'Tom… You're the main boy in this, aren't you?'

'Yes, I am, but I am not in this scene now.'

Ben looked back toward the stage and saw Kim directing two children to the correct side of the stage. She looked a little red-faced and stressed. Just then, Ben heard the sound. The high-pitched sound. He looked all around him and then down at the boy sitting next to him. Tom. It was coming from Tom. The boy looked up at Ben and smiled uneasily. Ben forced a smile back and the noise stopped. Ben breathed a sigh of relief.

'You ok?' asked Tom.

'Yes, fine, thanks. I think I need some fresh air.' Ben got up and went out of the theatre. He ran to the front door and breathed in the cool, fresh air. It was a relief. He took a few more breaths and then returned to the theatre. Kim watched him as he entered. She was starting to send the children home.

'Managed as much as ten minutes, did you?' Kim asked Ben when the last child had been picked up.

'Sorry, I felt a bit funny and had to get some air. I'll come to the main show, though.'

'Great. And before that, you can buy me lunch. Come on, let's go; there's a nice pub just up the road. We can go in your car and then you can drop me off later so I can drive home.'

'Ok, no worries,' Ben replied as they walked towards the main entrance. They both said goodbye to the receptionist and got into Ben's car. Within five minutes they were inside the Old Post Inn.

The inn was a traditional pub in every sense, with a dimly lit bar and a dusty lounge area. There was a long, dark wooden bar with a number of pumps offering a range of local ales and commercial beers. Behind the bar was an array of different spirits on the back wall, seemingly multiplied by the mirrored wall. There was a variety of bar snacks available — crisps, peanuts and the like.

There was an old man sitting at the bar and he

glanced as Kim and Ben entered the bar area. Ben walked into the airy, lighter lounge area, Kim following close behind. There were larger tables and a smaller bar area. This bar had no ales but had the commercial beers. There were a few spirits on the back wall, but not many, and there were fewer pub snacks. Ben and Kim went over to one table and sat down. They hadn't yet seen a member of staff. Ben picked up a menu and studied it hard, and Kim did the same. After a few minutes, Ben asked Kim what she wanted.

'I'll have gammon, egg and chips, I think,' she replied.

'Nice. I'm going to have scampi. What do you want to drink?'

'Just a coke for me — a large one but no ice, please.'

'Cool, I'll be back in a sec.' Ben got up and headed for the bar. He peered through the door at the end of the bar and a man in a white chef's uniform saw him.

'Be there now, mate,' the chef said.

'Ok.'

The chef came out a minute later, wiping his hands on a rag. 'Right, what can I get you?'

'One gammon, egg and chips and one scampi and chips, please. Can I also get two large cokes, no ice?'

'Sure, anything else?' asked the chef.

'No, that's it, thanks.'

The chef poured the cokes into two pint glasses and handed them to Ben. Ben paid the chef and went back to the table.

'Thanks, babe,' Kim said, and then took a huge gulp of her drink.

The two of them chatted about the play and Ben's Christmas party. He told Kim about a bad dream he had about the clocks in his house. The food was brought out to them by the old man from the other side of the bar.

'Wow, that guy actually works here!' Ben whispered

to Kim after the man had given them their food and returned with their cutlery and condiments.

'I can't believe it,' Kim said, and smiled.

They both wolfed their food down. Ben couldn't believe how hungry he was, considering how bad he had felt earlier that morning. When they had both finished, Ben drove them back to the castle and Kim got out of the car and into her own.

'Your place or mine?' she asked, winking and smiling at him.

'Let's go to yours — my flat is a bit of a mess today,' Ben replied.

'Ok, see you there.'

Ben drove off and Kim started her engine and followed a few minutes behind.

Chapter 28

Ben got to Kim's house before she did and sat outside in the car waiting for her to arrive. She pulled up a few minutes later and got out. Ben got out of his car and followed her up the steps to the front door. The both went inside.

'What shall we do this afternoon?' Ben asked.

Kim looked at him and smiled. 'I have an idea,' she said, and walked over to him. Without saying anything else, Kim ran her hand up Ben's inner thigh and slowly unzipped his fly.

'Oh, I like that idea,' Ben murmured.

Kim put her hand inside Ben's fly and felt his penis. It was already hard. She pulled it out of his pants and through his open fly. She slowly went down onto her knees, looking up at him as she did so. Ben smiled and shut his eyes. Kim moved her mouth towards Ben's erect penis and then stopped suddenly.

'Oh my God, Ben!' Kim cried in disgust. 'You stink! Have you not had a shower since last night?'

Ben was incredibly embarrassed. He was usually keen to shower as soon as he got up in the morning, but this morning he had been a mess. The night before was a blur; something weird had happened at some point but he couldn't remember if it was just a dream or real. This morning he hadn't had a shower. He had just about cleaned his teeth.

'No I haven't,' Ben said, his face now bright red.

'Go upstairs and get in the shower right now. I'm not going near you until you are clean!' Kim replied crossly. 'There's a towel in the airing cupboard on the landing.'

'Sorry, Kim,' Ben muttered as he walked up the stairs to the bathroom.

Ben got undressed and stepped into the shower. Kim had a huge rain effect shower overhead and jets on the side. If you put both on together the shower cubicle became a steam room. Ben turned the heat up high and soaked in the warm water. It felt amazing. He could feel the hangover lifting. Ben washed himself thoroughly but still stayed in the shower; he couldn't face getting out yet. He wanted to stay in the shower for hours. He shut his eyes and let the water run over his face. Suddenly, Ben felt something stroke his penis. His eyes flew open and he saw Kim standing in front of him, stark naked. She had her hand on his penis.

'Now that's better,' she said, flashing him a twinkling smile. Ben smiled back.

She stroked his hard penis up and down and then got down onto her knees. She put him inside her mouth and moved her tongue around it. The warm water splashed down over her face and it felt good. She moved her tongue up and down Ben's shaft, tasting him. He gave out a quiet moan and she did the same. After a few moments, Ben pulled her up towards him and kissed her hard on the mouth. Kim felt his hand move between her thighs and she opened her legs to let him in. He moved his fingers slowly inside her. She gave another moan; it felt incredible. Ben continued to kiss her as the water cascaded over them. Ben moved his fingers onto her clitoris. She knew it wouldn't be long before she had an orgasm.

A minute later, she gave a cry of ecstasy and held Ben tight in her arms, breathing heavily. Her hand went back onto his penis. She urgently pulled him closer to her and pushed him inside her. He was warm and hard. Ben started thrusting slowly. The water was splashing up from in between them and there was a faint slapping sound as their two bodies repeatedly came together and apart. Ben started moving faster. He was moaning. Kim found herself struggling to hold back a loud cry of excitement.

'Oh, fuck!' she screamed loudly. She was shocked

by the intensity of her orgasm. She shuddered and kissed Ben's neck and he kept driving deep inside her. Harder, faster. Then he let out a loud cry as he came inside her. She grabbed his arms tightly and held him close. They were both breathing heavily. When their breathing had slowed a little, Kim let go of Ben's arms. There were small lines of blood where her nails had dug into his flesh.

'Wow,' Ben said breathlessly.

'Wow indeed,' Kim murmured. 'That was amazing.'

They gently washed each other down and got out of the shower. Ben watched Kim as she dried herself off with a towel. Her toned, wet body was glistening in the bedroom light. She dressed in some tracksuit bottoms and a casual t-shirt, and Ben did the same, borrowing some of Kim's baggy clothes. They both went downstairs and sat next to each other on the sofa. Ben turned on the TV.

'How about a quiet night in with a film and a Chinese takeaway?' Ben said.

'Sounds good to me,' Kim replied and kissed him.

The takeaway arrived an hour later. Ben and Kim ate almost all of the meal and then returned to the sofa and put on a romantic comedy. It was Kim's choice; she needed something light hearted after the scary thriller she had watched the night before.

The film finished with the sort of ending Ben expected from a romantic comedy. They both went upstairs to Kim's bed and Ben fell asleep within a few minutes. It had been a crazy day. He was shattered. It was one of the best night's sleep he had had in a while.

***

Kim woke up on Sunday morning to the sound of Ben's gentle snoring. He wasn't a heavy snorer. Not like her dad. Her dad's snoring would probably register at the high end of the Richter scale. She remembered nights growing up when she thought that the windows were going to blow out of her parents' room and onto the street below. She couldn't understand how her mother could sleep next to him with the noise he made almost every night. Ben, on the other hand, did snore but it was more like a quiet growl. It was almost like he was protecting her by growling at any intruder that may come into the room during the night. She leaned over and gave him a kiss on the forehead. He stirred a little but remained asleep. Kim got up and put her dressing gown on. She went downstairs to make herself and Ben a cup of tea. She put two slices of bread in the toaster and got the butter out of the fridge. The toast popped up and she buttered the hot bread. She put the tea and toast onto a tray and took them up to Ben. She got into bed and shook him gently. He woke up with a little groan.

'I've made you a cuppa and some toast,' Kim said quietly.

Ben sat up, smiled and kissed Kim. She handed him one of the cups and a slice of toast. Ben ate the toast in three mouthfuls and took a sip of the tea.

'Thanks, babe,' he said. He grabbed the remote and turned on the TV. A Sunday morning politics show came on.

'Urgh!' cried Kim. 'I hate these shows; they either annoy the hell out of me or bore me to death.'

'Me too,' Ben said before taking another gulp of his tea.

'I have something far more exciting we can do,' Kim whispered into Ben's ear.

The sound of her whispering in his ear made Ben hard almost instantly. He looked at her and, without saying anything, kissed her hard on the lips.

They made love while the presenter of the show took questions from the audience. The lovemaking was sleepy, sensual, and when they had finished they dozed for an hour in each other's arms. When they awoke the politics show had become a DIY show. Ben turned off the TV, and they both got up and went downstairs. It was now nearly lunchtime so Kim put together a modest meal of bacon sandwiches. After lunch, Ben helped Kim to clean up and then kissed her goodbye. Kim watched him pull out of the driveway and then went to her kitchen table. She had a lot of marking to do for Monday.

Chapter 29

It was going to be a long week. Ben woke up to the thunderous clanging of his alarm. With dreary eyes, he got up and went to the bathroom for a shower. He brushed his teeth without really concentrating, then looked in the mirror and saw that his jaw was covered in stubble. He couldn't be bothered with shaving this morning. He sorted out his hair haphazardly and went back to the bedroom to get changed.

After changing, Ben went downstairs and made a cup of tea but didn't eat any breakfast. He just didn't feel like eating this morning. He hadn't slept very well and was now feeling the consequences as he got into his car and started the journey to work. He went through his week in his mind as he drove. He had meetings with other buyers, sellers and managers of various companies, as well as a meeting with Mr Fan Zhiyi — a very rare occasion. However, Ben didn't think he would actually show. He normally sent someone to represent him. Ben couldn't remember the last time he had actually seen him. That was work; he also had to see Kim at some point. That wasn't a chore but it was still on his list of things he had to do. He also had to go and see the school play on either Wednesday or Thursday. He would probably go and see it on Thursday, so after the show he and Kim could go out for a meal somewhere. Not to the Old Post Inn though; he couldn't face going there for a Thursday night meal. The food in the pub had been pretty good but the whole ambience of the place wasn't quite what he wanted for a romantic evening with Kim.

Ben had spent his whole commute deep in thought and had driven to the company car park on autopilot. However, he was brought back into reality when he almost drove into a car that was reversing into a parking space in front of him.

'Shit!' Ben cursed. He gave an apologetic wave to the cross-looking driver of the old purple Ford Fiesta and pulled into a nearby parking space. He got out of the car and walked slowly to the main entrance. He took a quick look back at his car and saw that he had parked very poorly. He was over two spaces and on a slant. He couldn't face going back and moving it. *If there's a problem they can call me and then I'll move it,* he thought.

He walked into the reception area expecting to have to come up with some flirtatious line as a comeback to a comment Tamzin would make. Instead, he saw that there was another receptionist at the desk.

'Where's Tamzin?' he asked her.

'She hasn't come in this morning,' replied the young receptionist. 'She hasn't even bothered to ring in. The boss is not happy.' She was actually the receptionist to one of the managers upstairs. Ben thought he must have asked her to cover Tamzin today. It was odd though; Tamzin was rarely ill and she was the sort of person who would call in to let them know.

I'll give her a call later, Ben thought as he went to his office. He needed some strong coffee, and fast.

* * *

Kim had only been in work for a few hours but she was already thinking about the weekend. However, first she had to get through the school Christmas play. The rehearsals were going well but she couldn't concentrate on them today because of her excitement about the weekend. Tom and Hannah had become very comfortable in their roles and the play as a whole only needed a small amount of tweaking. Everything was going to plan, so she decided to let her teaching assistant, Amy, take over most of the rehearsals today. It was only a case of going through the songs to make sure that everyone came in on time and a few quick run-throughs of the children's lines.

Kim wasn't very hungry when the lunchtime bell sounded, but the smells of the lunch hall were wafting down the corridor and into her room and before long she was starving. All she had brought with her were some cheese sandwiches, which didn't seem too appetising. She went to the hall and was told by the lunch staff that today's meal was a sausage dinner. There was no contest. Kim paid her money and sat down with a few of the other teachers to eat her lunch. Kim usually sat in the small staffroom to eat, because she generally had a packed lunch. If she had a school dinner she would sit in the hall with the children but on the 'teachers' table'. As she ate, some of the teachers asked her how the play was going. Kim told them that it was going incredibly well. She felt that tomorrow's dress rehearsal in front of the rest of the school would be fantastic. She could feel herself getting excited about the play and a smile appeared on her face. Before she knew it, Kim was beaming. Her mind was a little more focused on the play now and less on the weekend. She was looking forward to the practice in the afternoon. It had to go right; there was a full dress rehearsal to be ready for tomorrow afternoon.

* * *

Ben's day was not going very well. He was getting worried about Tamzin. He had called her mobile a few times, as well as her house phone. He had also texted her twice just to make sure that he had made contact of some sort. There was no reply at all. This was unlike Tamzin. Normally she would have replied with some text like, 'Stop harassing me, will you?' and a little smiley face, but to have no reply at all was strange, to say the least.

He didn't have much time to deal with Tamzin's absence. His day was very busy. However, he just couldn't concentrate on his work. Ben decided to go home after lunch. He told the new receptionist to take messages and tell anyone who wanted to speak to him that he would get back to them in the morning.

Ben left work and drove home. He thought about going round to see Tamzin but instead he went home and went to bed. His head was aching. He was tired and he felt himself getting angry. A short nap would help him feel better.

Chapter 30

Kim felt shattered as she stepped through her front door. She had stayed on a little longer than she had intended to at the end of the school day; she'd had to clear up the costumes and scenery after all the children had gone home. She could have had the pupils do it but she wanted to make sure that everything was where it should be so that it would be easier to get the props and the pupils ready tomorrow evening. It had taken longer than she had envisioned and now she was tired and cold. The rehearsal had gone very well and she was optimistic about the first performance in the castle. She decided that she would have an early night tonight so that she was refreshed and ready for the long couple of days ahead of her.

She hadn't planned on seeing Ben tonight so she thought she would give him a call to see how his day was. She wasn't worried when Ben didn't answer the phone; it was about the time he drove home from work. She would cook dinner and then give him another call after she'd eaten.

Kim's dinner consisted of a ready meal warmed up in the microwave: macaroni and cheese, to which she added some ham; she didn't think it was a proper meal unless it had some meat in it. Macaroni and cheese was a new choice of food for Kim. As a child, she had eaten it but hadn't liked it at all. Then a month or so ago, a thought had hit her: she liked pasta and she liked cheese, so why wouldn't she like them both together? The next day Kim had gone to the supermarket and bought a readymade macaroni and cheese. When she tried it later that day she found that she loved it. Where had it been all her life? The meal soon became a favourite of hers for when she was just eating by herself.

When she had finished her food, Kim gave Ben

another call. This time he picked up but he sounded quiet and muffled.

'Ben?' Kim asked.

'Yep,' Ben replied in a dreary voice.

'You ok?'

Ben was disorientated, having slept for the past few hours. He slowly realised where he was and who was on the phone.

'Kim! Hi! Yes, I'm fine. I've been asleep. I had to leave work early today. I didn't feel too good.'

'Oh dear, do you want me to come round?' Kim asked, concerned.

'No, I'll be fine. Just felt strange for a bit and decided to go home and sleep it off. I feel a lot better now,' Ben said trying to put Kim at ease.

'Ok, well if you need anything let me know. I'm going to get an early night tonight because I have a hectic few days coming up.'

'Yes, of course. How did the show go today?'

'It went really well actually. Hannah and Tom are doing brilliantly in their roles. And the rest all know their lines and the songs. I'm really excited about it!'

'Cool, so what time am I to be there tomorrow?' Ben asked.

'You don't have to come tomorrow. I have a ticket for you but you can just come Friday. You don't want to see the thing twice. But make sure you are there by half six.'

'Ok, babe. I'll be there.'

'Great stuff. Right, I'm going to watch some TV in bed and then go to sleep.'

'I won't keep you any longer then — sleep well.'

'You too. Ben, are you sure you're ok?'

'Yes I'm fine, honest.'

'Ok, speak to you soon.'

'Love you.'

'Love you too.'

Kim pressed the red key on the phone and looked

at the screen. Something didn't quite feel right. Should she go round there? No. She decided to do what she had planned. It was only in her head and Ben would think she was being stupid if she did go round.

Kim went to her bedroom and got undressed. She got into bed and switched on the TV. Within a few minutes, she was fast asleep.

***

Ben stared at his phone for a few minutes after Kim had hung up. He was still feeling disorientated. It was a strange feeling. He must be coming down with something; and just before Christmas, too! What bad luck! He hated being ill over Christmas. There was enough going on over the festive period without the added stress of feeling crappy all through it. Ben really enjoyed Christmas, on the whole. What he didn't enjoy were all the crowds. Everywhere seemed to have a crowd or a queue. Nowadays, Ben did almost all his shopping online. He found it far less stressful — unless something that he ordered didn't actually arrive in time. That had happened only once, when he'd ordered a present for his mother. He had ended up having to go into town to buy her something else. The original present arrived sometime between Christmas and New Year. Instead of giving the present to his mother late, Ben saved it for her birthday a few months later.

His head still hurt. He decided to go to sleep for the night instead of dozing. He also decided that he would call in sick tomorrow morning. He hadn't had a day off in a while and maybe that was why he was feeling so rough right now. Ben put his phone on charge and lay back down on the bed. He fell straight asleep.

***

Ben woke up with a jump. His head was killing him. It felt as though something was constantly thumping on the inside of his skull, trying and failing to escape. Then it happened.

The sound.

It started slowly and quietly, almost in the distance, but then it started to get louder, more high-pitched. He looked at the clock.

3:32.

Ben wanted to get up and walk around to try to clear his head but he couldn't face moving. He just lay there with his eyes tightly shut, willing the sound and his headache to go and leave him in peace. He covered his ears with his hands, then covered his head with his pillow, but it was no use; he got no relief from the sound. Ben gave a loud groan to try to supress the noise reverberating inside his head. He rolled onto his side and curled up into the foetal position, shaking with the pain. There was nothing he could do. Tears started to roll down his cheeks from the strain he was under. He rolled onto his other side and picked up his phone. He typed in the key code and the home screen came on brightly in the dark room. Ben pressed a button to get onto a social media site and flicked through people's inane comments about their days and their children. He found some other people unable to sleep, too. Why they felt the need to tell the world that they couldn't sleep was beyond him. As if anyone in the world gave two hoots if you couldn't sleep — or if your child dribbled during their dinner, for that matter! After a while, Ben felt the noise subsiding. Then it stopped, abruptly, as if someone had switched the radio off. His headache was still there, but with the noise gone he was able to shut his eyes gently and fall asleep again.

Chapter 31

'Mum! Mum!' Tom shouted. 'We're gonna be late!'

With everything that was going on in her life at the moment, Tom's mum, Lauren, had difficulty getting Tom to school on time. Tom was growing up almost too fast and even though he wasn't as needy as when he was younger he was now having to be taken to all sorts of places: football, swimming, play rehearsals, friends' houses. She wanted to give him as much attention as possible but it was not easy with the baby around. Tom's younger brother Nathan was only a year old and was very demanding. It didn't make it any easier when Tom's father had left them for one of his research students only a few months after Nathan was born. Suddenly, she had gone from a happily married mother of two to a single mother of two. She had become depressed.

One night, she'd gone out to town with some friends. They went to a few bars and ended up in a nightclub. She hadn't been to one in years. She was enjoying herself and she was enjoying the male attention she was getting, especially from one man in particular. He was gorgeous and had taken a genuine interest in what she had to say. She had got very drunk and ended up going back to her friend's house with him. She hadn't planned on it being a one night stand but that's what it turned out to be. The worst of it was that now she was pregnant with this guy's child and she had no idea who he was or where he lived or really even what he looked like. She was so angry with herself. How could she have been so irresponsible? Now she was going to be a single mother of three.

She was constantly tired and ached all over. It was so hard getting Tom ready for school. He was quite independent these days, but until he could drive to school himself she was going to have to play taxi driver.

Tom had been so excited when he told her that he was the lead in the play. She faked her own excitement. It just meant that she would have to taxi him around to more places. Old Crag Castle was the worst place she had to take him so far. It was really creepy. She had heard numerous stories about people who had died there and were now haunting the place. She didn't really believe in ghosts but it did creep her out just being there. She would be glad when tomorrow night was over and the play had finished. Then it would be Christmas — not that it would be very joyous for her this year.

They got into the car. Lauren drove the short distance to the school and dropped Tom off. He ran from the car without even looking back to say goodbye to his mother. She gave a little smile as she watched him go into the school entrance. A little tear came to her eye. It happened quite a lot recently. It must be the hormones.

Kim was there to welcome Tom into the hall for assembly. 'Where have you been, Tom?' she asked.

'Mum was having trouble with my brother,' he lied.

'Ok, no worries.' Kim didn't want to dwell on the subject. It was common knowledge in the staff that Tom's mum was having a difficult time at home. She looked at the children in front of her. 'As long as you're here now, Tom, we can get started. We need to be ready for tonight's first performance. I'm very excited about it — I hope all of you are too!'

Chapter 32

Ben had drifted in and out of sleep for most of the day. His headache had gone but was threatening to come back. He could feel it. He needed something to take his mind off it. He was thinking about a trip to the gym. He hadn't been in a while and he was starting to feel the effects of lack of training. He thought about paying a surprise visit to Kim at the theatre. It was her first night, in any case. Even though she had said that he didn't need to be there because he was coming to the show on the second night, it might be a good thing for her to see him there. Even if he just stood at the back and didn't show his face till the end. Instead, however, Ben fell asleep again — and this time he slept through to Thursday lunchtime.

Ben had some lunch and slowly got himself ready. He found himself daydreaming about Kim, and when he eventually returned from his reverie he realised that he was late. He jumped into his car and turned the music up loud. He was feeling really happy at the thought of seeing Kim. His headache was already a distant memory. The drive to the castle seemed to take ages, even though it actually took ten minutes less than usual. He must have been speeding for most of the way. He knew his mind wasn't really on the road. Ben just hoped that he hadn't passed any speed cameras.

He arrived and found a parking space quite a distance from the front doors and reception area. He jogged up to the reception and told the receptionist who he was. She said that the show had already started but he could go through and stand near the back. There was an interval due in about ten minutes.

Ben followed the corridor down to the small theatre. He felt a weird sense of déjà vu.

He slowly opened the door at the back of the

theatre and crept in quietly. He walked to the gap in between the two sets of seats and stood looking straight up the aisle to the stage. The view was good. He leant gently against the back wall and watched the pupils on the stage sing their hearts out. It was a song that he had never heard until two weeks ago but now knew almost every word; Kim kept singing it around the kitchen while she was cooking or making a cup of tea. He found himself humming along.

At the end of the song, the curtain was drawn haphazardly across the stage and Kim came out the front and told the audience that there would now be a ten-minute interval and that they were welcome to get drinks from the bar across the corridor.

Ben went out of the door he had just come in through and found Kim talking to Hannah. She was telling the girl that she was doing brilliant and to stop worrying. Ben walked up to them and smiled.

Kim looked at Ben and then gave him a big hug. Kim suddenly realised that Hannah was looking at them. 'Hannah, this is Ben,' she said. 'He's a friend of mine. He was just saying how amazing you were in the play. Weren't you, Ben?'

'Huh?' said Ben, a little taken aback. 'Yes, I was. You were fantastic. The best in the show.'

'See? You have nothing to worry about. Go and get yourself a glass of squash before the curtain goes back up.'

Hannah smiled at Ben, turned and started to walk down the corridor a little further. She then disappeared through a door on the right.

'Those are the dressing rooms,' Kim said. 'The girls have one room and the boys have another. It's all very organised.'

'I would expect nothing less.' Ben smiled and gave her a kiss.

'Thanks for coming,' Kim said. 'But I really have to go to the toilet now. Grab yourself a drink if you want and head back in. The second half will start in about two minutes.'

'Ok,' Ben said, and kissed her again.

Kim turned and almost ran down the corridor. She vanished through a door right at the end of the corridor. Ben retreated back inside the theatre. He took his place in between the rows of seats looking down the aisle.

Two minutes later the curtain reopened with an untidy jerk. The audience started to applaud.

***

Halfway through the second half, Ben started to feel sick. His head felt thick and heavy. He was sweating and his stomach hurt. The theatre was quite stuffy. There were no open windows and there were lots of people inside. The seating area was full and there were many children on the stage. Ben needed to get some fresh air or he might just pass out.

He looked around for the nearest exit. By now, his vision was becoming blurred. He stumbled through a nearby doorway and the door shut behind him. The air instantly felt cooler. His vision returned and he looked around him. It was not the doorway that he had entered the theatre through and so he felt disorientated. He was in a small, dimly lit corridor. It may have been a corridor that led to the backstage area where equipment and props may have been stored. The corridor was littered with chairs, pieces of wood that may have been part of a stage set and dusty costumes of all colours and styles. He still needed to get some fresh air.

Ben decided to walk to the right. He guessed that this may lead outside, whereas the other way may lead back to the main corridor. Ben walked on for a few moments, hurdling the different props that had fallen to the floor over years of disuse. He eventually got to another door. A big, dark, wooden door. *This must lead outside*, Ben thought. He tried the handle. It was locked.

Ben swallowed hard. His stomach heaved and he was almost sick. He looked around once again. The corridor turned to the right and ran alongside the seating area of the theatre. The corridor was completely unused; it was full of dusty chairs, blankets and other broken props that no one had the heart to throw away. A little way down this corridor, Ben could see a window. He decided he would try to climb through it. His head was killing him now. His vision had become blurry again and his mouth was starting to fill with sour saliva. He clambered over the first few chairs without much difficulty. Then he stepped on what he thought was a pile of blankets that turned out to be just some costumes covering a gap between two chairs. He fell through the gap in the chairs with a crash. Several chairs fell either side of him and he was covered in old costumes and dust.

'Shit!' Ben swore aloud. He took a few minutes to catch his breath and slowly got up. Carefully, he climbed over the heap of chairs and blankets. He hoped he hadn't disturbed the show on the other side of the corridor wall. His foot crunched on some glass. Ben looked down and saw that he had stepped on a picture frame. He moved his foot and picked up the frame. The glass was all cracked and a small piece fell from the frame as he picked it up. He looked at the picture and smiled. The picture was of the same family that he had on his wall at home. Only, in this image, the boy was smiling brightly. He looked happier than in Ben's copy. *This must have been quite a well-known family,* Ben thought. *I'll try and look them up when I get home later.*

Ben put the picture on top of a dusty chair and looked towards the window, which was now only a short distance away. It was smaller than he had thought. Ben reached up to the window and tried the handle. It was extremely dusty. There were cobwebs all over the handle and window pane. He managed to force the handle up, then climbed onto a nearby chair and pushed at the wooden frame of the window. It didn't move. He pushed again, harder this time. It moved slightly, with a creak. Ben sighed a little and pushed again. This time the window opened with an ear-piercing screech. His head pounded at the sound and he shut his eyes in pain. Ben lifted his body up to the window ledge and forced himself through the gap. It was a tight squeeze, but with a small amount of wriggling he managed to get through. He fell head-first into the flowerbed below.

'Ah, shit!' Ben swore again. He got up and dusted himself down. He was outside, breathing fresh air at last. It felt good. The air was cool and damp. Ben started walking. He realised that he was at the edge of the forest surrounding the castle. He noticed the small stone bridge that he and Kim had walked over only the other day. Ben sat down on the bridge, took a few more deep breaths and shut his eyes. His stomach was feeling better. He no longer felt sick and the cool air dried the sweat on his head and back quickly. The only thing that was still hurting was his head. It was still pounding, and he could also hear the high-pitched screech of the window being repeated over and over again. If he could just shut that out he would feel much better.

Ben had shut his eyes and was trying to close out the noise when he felt a tap on the shoulder.

'Hello. Are you alright?'

Ben turned with a jump that also startled the boy who was looking at him curiously.

'Are you ok?' asked the boy again.

'Er, yes. I'm fine,' replied Ben. 'I was miles away.' Ben looked at the boy. 'You're Tom, aren't you?'

'Yes,' said Tom.

'I'm Ben — I'm Miss Coombes' friend.'

'Can I join you on the wall? I'm boiling after being on the stage all evening.'

'Of course. The show's finished, has it? I'll have to get back to Kim — I mean Miss Coombes.'

'She's talking to all the parents. She'll probably be ages yet.' Tom replied. 'That's why I've come out here. My mum will talk forever!'

A voice suddenly came through the darkness.

'Tom! Tom! Is that you?' It was Hannah. She came running over to where Tom and Ben were sitting. She sat down next to Tom and looked over to Ben.

'Hi,' said Ben.

Tom smiled at Hannah and said, 'This is Miss Coombes' boyfriend, Ben.'

'Hello, I'm Hannah. We met earlier.' Hannah put out her hand to Ben and he shook it gently. 'Tom, I've been looking for you for ages.'

'I had to get out of there. It was too hot. Fancy a walk in the forest?' Tom replied.

'In the dark?' Hannah asked cautiously.

'Don't be scared. It'll be exciting.' Tom smiled at her. 'Come on!' He got up and looked at Ben. 'You want to come too, Ben?'

'No thanks, Tom, I'll just stay here. I've got a bit of a headache.'

'Ok, see you later. Come on, Hannah. Get up!'

Hannah stood up slowly and followed Tom into the forest.

'Be careful in there!' Ben shouted after them. 'Don't go too far!'

The two children disappeared from sight.

Ben's headache exploded in an eruption of pain and screeching noise. He covered his ears with his hands but it did no good. The pain was like nothing he had felt before. He knew that he was becoming prone to these bouts of screeching noise but they hadn't been this bad. Not that he could remember, in any case. The noise seemed to be coming from outside his head and driving deep into the depths of his mind. The sound was coming from the forest — from the direction the children had gone. He had to stop the noise. What if the children were hearing the same noise? What if they were in the same pain that he was in? He had to go and help them. He had to see if they were ok.

Chapter 33

'Don't go so fast, Tom,' Hannah moaned. She was struggling to keep up. Tom was not running but the excitement of the dark forest was getting to him and he was walking at a quick enough pace to make Hannah out of breath. Hannah was getting a little afraid of how far and fast they were going. She looked behind her and couldn't see anything but a few dark trees. The shadows were like huge ogres hiding from view. The ogres were watching her. They were waiting for her to lose Tom and then they would pounce on her.

'Keep up, Han,' Tom called. 'I can see some kind of ruined thing in the distance, let's go up there.'

'Ok,' Hannah gasped. 'But only for a bit. We have to be back before anyone notices we're missing. And I'm getting a little cold.'

'You're getting a little scared,' Tom teased. 'We won't be long, but head back by yourself if you want.'

'No, I'll stick with you.'

They reached the ruin, which was once an old stone tower. Tom walked up to it and found a small open doorway. There was no door; just an opening in the stone. He looked inside and saw some stone steps that led upwards through the tower. He went inside and Hannah followed. They climbed the small stone steps carefully; some were very unstable and others were broken altogether. Tom got to the top of the tower, where the steps opened out onto a stone ledge that was surrounded by a few broken battlements. He went to one of the battlements and looked out over the edge of the tower. They were quite high up, but due to the darkness and the height of the trees around them Tom couldn't see anything.

'This must have been a watch tower or something....' he thought aloud.

'Maybe, but it's too dark to see anything now so let's head back.'

'Ok, you win. We'll go back now.'

Just then there was a faint noise in the distance. Tom and Hannah looked at each other and then in the direction from which the sound had come. They concentrated hard. Then the nose came again, a little clearer now. It was a voice. It sounded panicked.

Hannah grabbed Tom's arm in fear. 'Who is it?' she asked.

'No idea,' replied Tom.

The voice came again. 'Kids? Kids? Where are you? Are you ok?!'

'I think it might be Ben,' Tom said.

Then the owner of the voice came out of the darkness and stood at the foot of the tower. It was Ben. Hannah could make out his face now her eyes were used to the dark.

'Ben!' Tom shouted down. 'We're up here, in the tower.'

Ben looked up and saw the two children looking down at him in fear. 'Oh, thank God!' Ben exclaimed loudly. 'Come down from there, guys, it's dangerous in the dark!'

Hannah went down the stone steps first, closely followed by Tom. They came out of the doorway and looked at Ben. He was sweating.

'You ok, Ben?' Tom asked.

'Yeah. I'm just getting a bit of a headache, I think,' Ben replied. The noise was growing inside his head. He gritted his teeth against it but it did no good. His vision was still hazy.

Tom looked more closely at Ben. His expression had changed since they saw him at the bridge only a few minutes ago. He was looking intense — angry, almost. Tom looked back at Hannah worriedly. She saw Tom's face and looked at Ben. She was scared. Ben was staring at them both.

Suddenly, Ben walked towards them.

'That noise,' he said. 'That noise — you're making that noise! Stop it! STOP IT!'

'What noise?' Tom asked, slowly backing away from Ben.

Ben didn't hear him. He couldn't hear him. The noise in his head was more than he could stand now. Ben bent down and picked up one of the stones from the floor. He walked further towards the children.

Tom looked at Hannah. 'RUN!' he shouted.

She looked back at him and saw the fear in his eyes. She didn't need to be told twice; she was already terrified. She turned and ran away from Ben and into the forest. Tom followed.

'No, wait. Come back!' Ben shouted after them. He started running.

It didn't take long for Tom to catch up with Hannah and overtake her.

'Keep going,' he said. 'We've got to get away from him. He looks insane!'

'I'm going as fast as I can,' Hannah panted as Tom ran off into the distance. She was fit but not as fast as him.

Hannah took a quick glance behind her and saw the shadow of Ben gaining on her. As she looked back in front of her she ran straight into a low-hanging branch. It hit her square in the face and knocked her backwards. A jagged rock dug hard into the small of her back and she screamed out in pain. She couldn't move. She looked straight up at the darkness of the trees above her. Then suddenly Ben's face came into view. He looked down at her. Hannah looked up at him. The sight of Ben made her scream out again. His eyes were almost shut. His teeth were showing and there was a white foam in the corners of his mouth. He looked like a wild animal. She screamed again. Ben jumped on top of her and put his hand over her mouth. He was heavy. She couldn't move. The stone dug further into her back. She tried to scream again but nothing came out of her mouth.

'SHHH!' Ben said into her ear. 'My head hurts and your screams are making it worse.'

The noise in his head did not subside at all. It seemed to be coming from Hannah but he couldn't stop it. He shook his head to try to clear the noise but it only got worse.

Ben's mind was a fog of noise and pain. His vision was almost completely gone now. He kept his left hand over Hannah's mouth. He hated her. She was making the noise. She was causing his pain. He had to stop her. He felt almost possessed by Hannah now. He felt that she was controlling him. He could not stop the noise; he could not stop Hannah. What was she doing?

Ben put his right hand on Hannah's throat. He felt her soft skin under his palm and pressed down forcefully, feeling her Adam's apple move under the pressure. Slowly, he started to squeeze his hand closed. Through the mist of his vision, Ben could see the whites of her eyes. Suddenly, Hannah started struggling, but Ben was sat on top of her now and he was too heavy to shift. Hannah tried to shake her head but his grip was getting tighter.

Hannah began to weaken. She tried to bite his left hand but couldn't reach, so she started to struggle more and more. The pain in her lower back was excruciating, but she had to do something.

'Stop struggling,' Ben grunted through gritted teeth. 'Stop making that horrific noise!'

Ben moved his left hand onto Hannah's throat. He had to stop the noise.

Hannah tried to scream when her mouth was free but her voice failed her. She spluttered. Her throat felt like it had closed completely. She tried gasping for air but nothing could get in. She started to see small, sparkly spots in front of her eyes. Like little stars. It was almost as though she had hit her head in a cartoon. She shut her eyes tightly. Was this it? Was she about to die? Maybe if she pretended to be dead Ben might let go. Hannah stopped moving. Ben didn't let go. He held her throat tightly and pressed even harder. She thought she heard a crunch in her throat. She opened her eyes and looked at Ben, almost staring straight through him. Behind him, she could see her mother looking at her. She was smiling. A tear fell from Hannah's eye.

Suddenly, Ben felt a huge pain in his ribs.

'Get off her!' said a voice. It seemed to be coming from everywhere and nowhere at the same time to Ben. He rolled off Hannah clutching his side. Thud! Another pain in his side.

'Ah,' wailed Ben. He rolled over again and felt another thud hit him on the back of the head. He looked up and saw Tom prepare to kick him again, in the mouth this time. Hannah got up and started to run as fast as she could manage. Ben started to get up. The pain inside and outside his head was too much. He felt like he was going to pass out. He stared at Tom.

'Fuck you!' Tom shouted.

Ben walked towards him, but Tom turned and ran after Hannah. Ben picked up a rock and threw it, catching the kid square in the middle of his back and causing him to fall to his knees. Ben caught up with him, bent down and picked up the rock. Slowly, Ben raised it in his right hand and smashed it down onto the back of Tom's head. Tom collapsed instantly. The noise in Ben's head started to subside. He hit Tom again and again with the rock, feeling the kid's skull crack and crunch under the force of each blow. Small fragments of bone started to break away from the rest and soft white jelly was thrown into the air as Ben brought the rock down again. The noise had almost completely gone now. His vision was better. He dropped the rock onto the forest floor and looked down at the boy below him. The body was still. The head was a mess. It was almost flat, except for shards of bone pointing out like jagged, bloody mountains.

Ben turned away from the body and slowly started walking back to the bridge and the castle.

* * *

Hannah kept running, her lungs searing. Her back was killing her. What had happened? She didn't know. She would have thought it was a dream if she wasn't in so much pain. She ran for a few minutes more but had to stop. She was too out of breath. She thought about Tom. He was faster than she was, so he should have caught up with her by now. If he had run in the same direction, that was. Hannah leant against a large tree, panting heavily. She tried to slow her breathing because it was loud in her ears and she wanted to hear if Ben was still coming after her. She couldn't hear any noise coming from the forest. Suddenly, Hannah realised that she had no idea where she was. She had run in panic but she didn't know which direction she had run in. She was lost. Completely lost. It was getting colder.

'What am I going to do?' Hannah thought out loud. She started to cry.

Chapter 34

Ben reached the castle. His headache had gone, his vision was back and he felt fantastic. He walked into the castle to look for Kim. She was still talking to some of the parents but stopped when she saw him.

'Oh my God — you're soaking!' Kim exclaimed. 'What happened to you?'

'I got too hot in the theatre and had to get some fresh air. I was really sick, but I feel loads better now. Are you ready to go?'

'Yes. I was just saying a few goodbyes. I wanted to catch Tom and Hannah before they went but I can't see them anywhere now so maybe they've already gone.'

An image flashed in Ben's mind for a split second. He saw a boy in the forest, running. Running away from him. But no sooner had the image appeared it disappeared. Ben shook his head to clear his mind.

'You sure you're ok?' Kim asked.

'Yes, I'm fine. Just a little cold, I guess.'

'Let's go then. You go and warm the car up and I'll go and tell Amy that I don't need a lift.'

Kim walked off in the direction of the theatre and Ben watched her. He turned around and started to walk towards the car. He felt a pain in his side that wasn't there before. He lifted up his t-shirt and examined his ribs. There was a bruise starting to show.

'Where has that come from?' Ben muttered. He walked to his car, got in and started the engine. He turned the heater up; he was feeling uncomfortably cold. The car started to blow cold air into his face so he quickly closed the vents and turned the heater off. He didn't need to have cold air blown at him right now. He didn't want to catch a cold.

Ben jumped a little as Kim opened the passenger door and climbed in.

'Urgh! It's not very nice out there!' she said.

'I know, I had the heater going but I'm still waiting for it to warm up.'

Kim looked at Ben. He looked different somehow. She couldn't put her finger on it...

'You're sure you're ok?' she asked.

'Fine, absolutely fine. I did have a headache but I'm ok now.'

'Ok,' Kim replied. 'Your place or mine?' she added, with a wink.

'Let's go to mine.' Ben said, and started to drive out of the car park.

As they pulled onto the main road Kim turned up the radio.

'I love this song,' she said.

Ben tutted at her.

'What?'

'It's rubbish,' he said, smiling.

Kim ignored him and started to sing what lyrics she knew whilst rocking her head up and down overenthusiastically to the beat. Three minutes and forty-seven seconds later the song finished much to Ben's delight. The DJ introduced the news and Ben absentmindedly turned the volume up. The newsreader mentioned a few stories about the threat of war in the Middle East again and that some politician had been jailed for money laundering. Then he moved onto a story that caught Kim's attention:

'The body of a woman has been found in a small backstreet hotel in Birmingham. The body is that of a woman who worked in a local strip club. Police believe the body to have been there for a number of days and has only now been discovered. This is due to the nature of the hotel that she was found in. There are no further details as yet and the police are appealing for anyone with any information to come forward as soon as possible...'

'That's a bit scary!' Kim said as she turned the following sports news down.

'What is?' asked Ben.

'That woman. She was found dead in a hotel but was there for days before anyone found her!'

'Urgh! That's gross. Think of the smell!'

'I wasn't even thinking of that. I was just thinking of the poor girl just lying there dead for days and no one knowing anything about her or what happened! It's scary!'

'Yeah, I guess so...' Ben replied distantly.

Chapter 35

The next morning Ben woke up later than he had planned. He had booked the Friday off to plan the weekend away. Kim had gotten up early to go home to get changed for school and decided not to wake him. It was now 10:30. He had wanted to be at the travel agents by ten. Ben got up and splashed some water on his face to wake himself up properly. He got changed and went straight out of his flat and into his car. He thought that he would get something to eat somewhere near the travel agents. He drove the few miles to the town centre and found a parking space on the street. Ben got out and went into the travel agents. A young woman called him over and he sat down at the desk in front of her.

'How can I help you today?' she asked.

'I want to surprise my girlfriend with a trip to Paris this weekend,' he replied.

The agent was very enthusiastic. 'Wow, cool! Let's see what we have available for you.'

It took her a few minutes to scroll through her lists of flights.

After half an hour of planning, Ben had a short break to Paris booked. Their flight was to leave at six o'clock that evening and head to Charles-de-Gaulle airport. He had booked a room in a small hotel near the centre of Paris, just a few minutes' walk from the Trocadero. The return flight was at seven o'clock Sunday night. It was going to be a tiring weekend but Ben was extremely excited about it and couldn't wait to tell Kim. He sent her a message telling her that he had a great surprise for her. She didn't reply.

***

Ben was sitting in his living room when Kim pulled up outside. He was not very happy that she hadn't responded to his text message. He felt deflated.

Kim came through the front door. Ben could tell something was wrong from the moment he saw her face. She had been crying. Her eyes were red and there were marks on her cheeks where her mascara had run. She ran up to him and hugged him, then burst into tears. Huge sobs muffled against Ben's shirt.

'Hey, hey — what's the matter?!' Ben asked gently.

Kim said nothing at first. She continued to cry into Ben's shoulder. Ben slowly moved her away from his shoulder and looked at her face.

'What's the matter?' he asked again.

Kim looked him straight in the eyes and took a few deep, shuddering breaths, trying to compose herself slightly. 'Tom and Hannah are missing,' Kim said, almost in a whisper.

'What?' Ben asked, taken aback.

'Tom and Hannah are missing. They went missing last night after the show! No one has seen them since the show ended.'

'Oh my God! Missing? But how?'

'They left the theatre after the show but then disappeared.' Kim was speaking more clearly now.

'Have the police been called? Are they looking for them?' Ben asked worriedly.

'Yes. They were at the castle not too long after we left last night! They have been looking through the night, but they've had no luck so far!' She burst into tears again and Ben hugged her close to him.

A split-second vision appeared in his head of him standing with a rock in his hand in the forest. He shook his head to clear his mind. He was lost for words. He didn't know what to say to comfort Kim. He was desperate to tell her about their trip away.

'I'll make you a cup of tea, babe, and then I've got something to tell you,' he said cautiously.

'Oh yes, your text. Sorry. It was just a horrible place in school today. I didn't get a chance to reply or even think about anything else.'

'No worries, Kim. Sit down. I'll be back in a sec.'

Kim sat on the sofa while Ben went to the kitchen and filled the kettle. A few minutes later, he returned to the living room with two cups of tea and sat down next to her.

'Thanks,' Kim said. 'So what is this surprise?'

'Well it's not easy to say now but since you have been so stressed in school lately I have booked us a trip to Paris.'

Kim's eyes lit up. 'What?! When?!' she stammered.

'The flight is booked for tonight!'

'Tonight?!' Kim spilt some of her tea in her shock. 'Shit! Ow — that's hot.' She wiped herself down. 'Tonight? Paris? Tonight?!'

'Yes. What do you think?'

Kim thought about it for a second and said, 'I think I would love that! Thank you so much! Getting away would take my mind off everything.'

'Only if you're sure. I can cancel it if you want to go another time, what with everything that is going on today.'

'No. I'm sure. I would love to go.'

'Ok, well we need to start packing. The flight is at six.'

Kim drank what was left of the tea, kissed Ben passionately on the lips and left the flat to go and pack her bag. She had forgotten all about Tom and Hannah for the moment.

Chapter 36

Hannah woke up with a groan. She felt cold and wet but she couldn't understand why. Maybe she had wet the bed. She hoped not. That was not something a girl of her age should be doing. She moved slowly and something rustled beneath her body. A dagger of pain shot up through her back as she moved. Suddenly, she remembered what had happened last night. Ben had chased her and tried to strangle her. She recalled Tom rescuing her by kicking Ben…

Hannah opened her eyes and looked around her. Dark leaves rustled above her head and sticks, leaves and moss lay beneath her. Then she remembered more details. She had run. She had run until she could not move anymore, and then she had collapsed and tried to make herself comfortable beneath a large bush. She must have fallen asleep.

Hannah tried moving again. She had to get back home. Her parents would be going crazy. Why weren't they out looking for her? She had been out all night. They might have called the police. Then why haven't the police found her? Where was she? She had no idea. Last night she had fled in a blind panic. Painfully, Hannah crawled out from under the bush. She was covered in mud and moss. She winced as she flicked off a couple of small bugs that had made their way onto her clothes. She didn't want to think about what other creatures might be in her hair. She didn't like creepy crawlies and hated getting muddy.

Hannah managed to stand up slowly and look around her. There was nothing that she recognised. It all looked the same; there were trees and bushes everywhere and rocks on the ground. What was she going to do? Which way should she go? If she went the wrong way she would end up deeper into the unknown. Hannah started to cry. She sat down on a large rock nearby and put her head in her hands.

A few minutes later, Hannah took some deep breaths and stood up. A stab of pain hit her back again and she tried to rub the agony away. There was some swelling. She remembered the pain she had felt as she hit the floor last night.

'I have to start walking now,' she muttered to herself. She looked around for an idea of which way to go. She thought she saw a small clearing in the distance and decided to go that way. Slowly and carefully, she walked through the bushes and undergrowth. She didn't want to trip up and do more damage to her back. The clearing was a disappointment; there was nothing there, just a small gap in the trees where light was coming through from above and hitting the ground. Once again, Hannah started to cry. But she quickly stopped herself and shook her head; she didn't want to cry anymore — she had to start acting grown up. She had to be strong.

'Help! Help me, I'm lost!' Hannah shouted, but her voice was hoarse and the shout was only a croak. It hurt her throat. She was getting thirsty and her stomach had started to make noises. She had to find some water at the very least. She needed to find a stream or a river — or, even better, her mum.

Hannah walked on through the clearing and back into the thicker forest. The trees blocked out most of the light and she had no idea of the time. Was it morning? Afternoon? Her stomach was rumbling, so it could be lunchtime. She didn't have her watch on. She was still in her dress from the night before. Her shoes were soaked through and now covered in mud. Hannah started to think about what she could eat in the forest. Which berries were edible? Which would make her ill? The last thing she needed whilst being lost in the forest was to get food poisoning.

Chapter 37

Ben and Kim almost ran into the airport departure lounge. They were late. There were only a few minutes left before the gate was due to close. They only had hand luggage, so they could go straight through to passport control. They were both very excited. The queue at passport control was short, much to Ben's relief. He didn't want to miss the flight. It had been a rush from the moment Kim had gone to pack her bag. Ben had picked her up and then driven them to the airport; the journey normally took about an hour, but Ben had made it in under forty-five minutes. He hoped there weren't any speed cameras on the motorway.

After passport control, they went straight to their gate and joined the boarding queue.

Ben breathed a sigh of relief. They had made it. They were going to Paris! He looked at Kim, who was smiling. He kissed her. 'I love you,' he said.

'Love you too,' Kim replied.

The queue shortened quite quickly and before long they were sat on the plane, Kim in the window seat and Ben in the middle seat. He was hoping that the person next to him was not going to be a fat person. They always felt the need to use both armrests even though the joining one was a shared armrest. And their body went over the imaginary separation line. However, ten minutes later the doors were shut and the cabin crew were preparing the aircraft for take-off. The best possible result. There was no one sitting next to him. He had the whole space to stretch out in.

The flight was peaceful. Kim fell asleep. They landed gently and in no time Ben and Kim were on their way to the Hôtel Triomphe. The journey to the hotel took half an hour. By 8:30 they had settled into their room comfortably; they were on the second floor and their room boasted a king size bed, an en-suite bathroom and a large balcony that looked out onto a park behind the hotel. The view was not the most exciting but it was peaceful.

'Shall we go out for a drink somewhere?' Ben asked.

'I'd love that. I need a drink.'

They left the hotel and walked towards the city centre. They found somewhere which looked comfortable and homely. They went inside and Ben headed for the bar.

'*Deux bieres, s'il vous plait,*' he ordered.

The barman smiled and poured two Kronenbourgs into glasses. The beers were topped with large amounts of foam. 'Why so much head?' Ben thought to himself. 'Always so much head.'

He took the beers over to where Kim had found a sofa by the window. He sat down next to her.

'Thanks,' she said.

'No worries, you ok?'

'Getting there,' she replied.

Chapter 38

It was dark now. Hannah had been out in the wilderness for a whole day and was scared. Why had no one come for her? Was anyone looking for her? How long would it take before anyone found her? She had spent the afternoon looking for food and water. She had found a blackberry bush and eaten all the dark fruits she could find on there. She was tempted by the unripe ones but, again, she was not sure if they would make her ill or not. She hadn't found any source of water but she had found a large puddle of muddy rainwater. She had been so thirsty by then that she had drunk straight from the puddle. She had felt like a dog lapping up water on a hot day.

The day was a long way from being hot. It was the height of winter and she was only wearing a dress — and that had got damp overnight. The worst part of her experience so far was the need to go to the toilet. She had needed to wee early on in her day and that wasn't a problem. She had had to wee in a forest before when she and her mum had been on a trip to the country in the summer. It wasn't the nicest thing to do, but it was possible. No, the wee was not the worst. She needed to poo. This she was terrified about having to do in the forest. She had never done that before. She really didn't want to have to do that. So Hannah decided to hold it for as long as she could. She was sure someone would find her soon.

While she was wandering through the forest, she had been shouting out for help in the hope that someone — anyone — would hear her, but no one did. Her throat hurt a lot now and she was getting really hoarse. After a few hours of walking in the forest and not finding the way out, there was no way she could hold it any longer. It hurt.

Hannah found a large bush, climbed into the

centre of it and pulled down her knickers. When she was finished, she tore some leaves from the bush and used them to wipe herself clean. Unhappily, she pulled up her knickers and left the confines of the bush. She ran for a few minutes, wanting to get away from the toilet bush. Not long after that ordeal, it started to get dark. Hannah had resigned herself to the thought that she would have to spend another night in the forest. She had to find somewhere quickly because once it was dark she would get cold again. She wandered around until she came across a small downhill slope. At the bottom of the slope, there was a crop of trees and bushes. Hannah slowly walked down the slope and pushed her way through the branches into the centre of the bushes. There was a small space there where she curled up. There were a few broken branches that she used as a blanket. She was so tired that the sounds of the forest and the rustling of small bugs and creatures didn't worry her in the slightest. She was asleep in minutes.

***

Kim was on her third beer and could feel herself getting a little tipsy. Ben was on his fourth. He had told Kim the plan for the weekend. They were going to see the Eiffel Tower and the Arc de Triomphe the next day. It was going to be a busy day, so they would have to get up early.

They finished their drinks and then headed back to their hotel room, Kim wobbling slightly as she walked. They spent a few minutes watching a little mouse scurry to and fro outside the window. Kim wondered where its family was — was it lost? Her thoughts drifted to Tom and Hannah. She hoped they were ok. She hoped they would be found soon. She hadn't heard anything from Amy, which was probably a bad thing. Where had they gone? What had happened to them?

She was getting emotional now.

Ben glanced at her, trying to determine how drunk she was. There was a thin line of drunkenness for Kim. If she was a little tipsy, they would have sex. Not just any sex, but incredibly passionate, almost pornographic sex. It was awesome. He loved that level of drunkenness. However, if she was too drunk, she would head straight to bed and fall asleep almost instantly. This was the worst kind of drunk — especially if he really wanted to have sex.

They took the lift up to their room and started getting ready for bed. Kim went to the bathroom, changed into an old t-shirt of Ben's and climbed into bed. Ben undressed, hard with anticipation. He looked at Kim's face as he neared the bed.

She was already asleep.

'Bugger!' he muttered, then climbed into bed and lay down beside her. His mind started drifting. He thought about the missing children. Another vision hit him like a right hook to the face. He was looking down at Hannah; he could see her terrified eyes staring back at him. But no sooner was the image there it was gone.

Ben soon fell fast asleep.

Chapter 39

Hannah woke up with a jump. Her back screamed at her for moving too fast.

There was something sniffing around in the forest just outside of the bush.

She stayed quiet for a moment and strained to see through the leaves, trying desperately to get her eyes used to the dark. Whatever had made the noise was large.

A branch cracked under the thing's weight. Hannah's heart was pounding so hard that she could hear it in her ears. The thing moved again. She realised that she had been holding her breath, so she let it out in a loud gasp. The thing stopped dead, then turned and ran away.

Hannah started to breathe again. She was breathing very heavily having held her breath for so long. She sat upright for a number of minutes, waiting.

Silence.

Slowly she lay back down and tried to fall back asleep. She lay there for what seemed like an eternity. The adrenaline was running through her veins and there was no way that she could get back to sleep now. Hannah sat back up again. She rubbed the swollen area of her back. It throbbed. She thought that the swelling was worse now but couldn't be sure. She slowly and carefully got up and crawled out of the bush that had been her bed for the night.

She stood up and looked around. It made no difference however. The forest was pitch black. Hannah shivered. What should she do? She could try to find her way out of the forest, but was there any point in moving in the dark? She sat down on a nearby log. It was wet and cold to the touch. It was covered in moss which made it soft to sit on. What time was it? How long before it was daylight? She had no idea.

She hoped it wasn't long until dawn.

Hannah had been sat on the log for about an hour and found her head was drooping from drowsiness. She moved slowly from the log to the floor and lay down. Maybe she could fall asleep again until it became light. Maybe someone would find her.

***

Ben's phone alarm went off at 8am. The buzzer sounded like a drill going through Kim's head. Ben jumped out of bed and headed to the bathroom to shower. Kim was glad to have the extra few minutes to come round. She could never understand how Ben could just get up as soon as the alarm sounded. She always needed some time to become fully awake. She liked to press the snooze button on the alarm and grab every extra second she could before she actually had to get out of bed, but Ben was able to jump out if necessary.

A few minutes later (although to Kim it only seemed like seconds) Ben came back into the bedroom wearing a white towel around his waist. There was a shimmer of water on his body. He was almost glistening. Kim looked at him and felt a sudden urge. She had to have him there and then. She sat up on the edge of the bed and pulled Ben towards her. She looked him in the eyes as she made the towel fall to the floor, and then she took his penis in her hand, gently stroking it. Ben became rock hard almost immediately. She smiled up at him and put his penis in her mouth. Slowly, she worked her tongue around the end of his shaft, then licked it up and down. Ben was looking down at her. He desperately wanted to keep going. He wanted to jump on top of her now. He wanted to play with her. He wanted to hear her moan. But he knew they were on a schedule; they only had one full day in Paris.

He put his hands on Kim's cheeks and lifted her

up towards him. He kissed her and said 'we can't, we haven't got time.'

'You're stopping me? Oh my God, Ben — I can't believe it!'

'Believe me, I don't want you to stop. But we have to get going if we want to see all we can today,' he replied.

'Ok, I'll just jump in the shower.'

Kim got up and went into the bathroom.

Ben lay on the bed. He felt awful to have stopped her. He was now so horny he thought about finishing himself off just to clear his head, but he refrained. Instead, he went to the kettle and turned it on. He needed a cup of coffee. At least one. Kim didn't take too long in the shower. She came out wearing a towel around her and another one around her head. Ben had dressed himself in jeans and a yellow t-shirt. He finished his coffee and made one for Kim while she got dressed.

'I think we should get some breakfast from a patisserie on the way to the Eiffel Tower,' Ben suggested.

'Good idea,' Kim replied. 'I want a pain au chocolat or pain aux raisins, maybe.'

'Deal. We'll look for one on the way.'

They finished their coffees and picked up their coats. It was cold but the weather was bright. The sort of crisp December weather Ben loved. He didn't like wind and rain but crisp, cold weather was his favourite. They left the hotel and started to walk down the street towards the Eiffel Tower.

After about ten minutes Kim spotted a cosy patisserie down a small side street. 'How about that one?' she asked.

'Looks good to me,' Ben replied.

They went into the patisserie and were greeted with a multitude of sweet pastries. Croissants, pain au chocolat, cream cakes, Danish pastries... Ben picked a round pastry with a cherry in the middle that was covered in icing. Kim picked her pain aux raisins. They took them out onto the street instead of sitting in the shop and started their walk towards the Eiffel Tower.

The walk took about fifteen minutes. Kim loved strolling through the Parisian streets. The city still seemed very old in parts; Kim felt like she was walking through streets in the 1920s. The air was crisp but the sun was shining. It was a perfect winter's day. They reached the park in front of the Eiffel Tower. They stood at the Mur de la Paix and waited their turn to take a picture of themselves with the Tower in the background. If you get the positioning right, the Mur frames the photo perfectly. They walked through the park towards the Tower. The gardens were elegant and beautiful even though it was winter.

The Eiffel Tower was an incredible, imposing sight. Both Kim and Ben stood on the other side of Avenue Gustav Eiffel and looked at it in awe. They crossed the road and joined the back of the queue. Ben wanted to walk up the steps but Kim was having none of it. The queue for the lift was longer but she thought it would be worth waiting for. The queue went down quickly and after about forty minutes they were on their way up to the top. The lift was packed and Kim couldn't see out of the windows properly due to the condensation, but when they stepped out of the lift at the first stop the cold air hit her in the face like a sledgehammer. It was bitterly cold this high up but the view was fantastic. There were no clouds and they could see for literally miles. Paris is very flat, and they could see all the major landmarks; Kim caught sight of the Arc de Triomphe, Sacré-Cœur and the big glass pyramid of the Louvre. The plan was to see both the Arc de Triomphe and Sacré-Cœur today but Kim would be happy just to stay up here on the Tower and drink nice French coffee in the café all day. She was happy. Very, very happy.

Chapter 40

Hannah woke up with the sun shining on her face. She had managed to fall back asleep but she had no idea of the time. Her back still hurt, her neck ached and her legs were weak. The fall and the subsequent night spent sleeping on the uneven forest floor had taken their toll on her young body. However, now the sun was up she felt warmer than she had been for a while.

Hannah lay where she was for a few minutes until a spider crawled up the side of her face. She screamed and jumped to her feet. Her whole body shrieked in agony. She slapped the spider off of her face and tears rolled down her cheeks.

'Help! Help me, please!' she cried in desperation, then sat down on the log and sobbed into her hands. What was she going to do? Why had no one found her yet? How long was she going to be stuck in the forest? Would she be here forever? Was she going to die here?

Hannah shook herself and stood up slowly. She needed to wee. She was also thirsty and hungry. *What exciting foods am I going to find for breakfast today?* she thought sarcastically, then laughed to herself.

She didn't bother finding a secluded place to go to the toilet this time. There was no one around, after all. In fact, she would be quite happy if someone found her, even if she was doing her business. At least then she could go home.

She found herself thinking about Tom. Had he been found? Had he told anyone about what had happened in the forest before she had run off? She certainly hoped he had.

She started to walk on through the forest, searching for food. She would like to see a big blackberry bush again and eat her fill of the blackberries. She also hoped to find a stream or some kind of running water;

she didn't want to drink out of a muddy puddle again.

After half an hour of stumbling through the undergrowth, Hannah was starting to get really hungry. She hadn't found anything to eat and hadn't found any running water. There had been a few puddles but she had decided not to drink from them in the hope that she would find a stream. So far she hadn't.

'I'll keep looking for another hour,' she muttered to herself, 'then I'll have to drink something.'

There seemed to be plenty of puddles around so Hannah didn't think that finding a water supply later on would be a problem. Food would be the problem. On the plus side, though, she wasn't too cold today. Sunlight was bursting through the trees, and, even though it was December, it actually felt quite warm. Her clothes were starting to dry out a little.

***

After visiting the Eiffel Tower, Ben and Kim made their way to the Arc de Triomphe. They climbed to the top and looked over Paris again. Looking straight down, they had a great view of the Champs-Élysées, a very busy road famous for its shops, boutiques and restaurants.

'We'll have lunch somewhere down there,' Ben said, pointing.

After taking some photos, they came back down and started walking down the Champs-Élysées, searching for somewhere to eat. They found a restaurant with outdoor heaters and decided to eat there. They found a table by one of the heaters and the waiter came over to ask if they wanted something to drink. They both ordered a beer.

A few minutes later, the waiter came back with two beers.

'Cheers,' Ben said, lifting his glass to Kim, who picked up her glass and clinked it with Ben's.

'Cheers,' she replied.

They spent a while deciding what to eat. When the waiter came back Ben ordered steak and chips with a pepper sauce and Kim ordered mussels and chips in a garlic sauce. The waiter returned with some bread, which Kim started eating straightaway. She was really hungry now and the bread was fresh and warm.

They talked about the plan for the rest of the day until the waiter came back with their order. The portions were huge and the food smelt and tasted delicious. For a few minutes neither of them said anything; they were too busy eating. They ordered another beer each and used the map Ben had brought with him to work out which metro station they needed to get off at to see the Sacré-Cœur Basilica. They discovered they'd need to get off at Blanche station, which actually came out near the Moulin Rouge.

They finished their lunch and paid the bill, then went down the steps of the nearest metro station. They paid for a day pass ticket and got on the train. It took only a few minutes before they arrived at Blanche station. The station itself was not busy, but as Kim and Ben came up the steps and onto the street they found it was heaving with tourists taking photos of the Moulin Rouge. They stopped and took the obligatory photograph, and then made their way through the narrow backstreets and up the many steps of the Sacré-Cœur Basilica. Kim started to count the steps as they climbed, but she quickly got distracted by all the sights and sounds.

There were lots of people climbing the steps, and many others were sat on picnic blankets watching a huge big screen TV showing the history of the building. They made it to the top, and Kim was glad to see that she wasn't the only one out of breath; Ben was as well. They paid for their tickets and went down into the crypt. There were hundreds of stone tombs there. Ben was excited by the names he saw on the tombs but Kim felt uneasy. She didn't like being around all the death. She rushed her way through the crypt and made her way to the exit, then waited for Ben outside. Ten minutes later Ben came out of the crypt and saw Kim on the steps.

'Where did you go? I've been looking for you!' he said.

'I didn't like it in there. It was eerie. I came out for some fresh air.'

'Ok. I thought it was quite fascinating,' Ben replied. 'Anyway, let's get back to the hotel, get some dinner and get drunk, eh?' he asked with a smile.

Kim smiled back at him and kissed him. He held her tightly in his arms and kissed her intensely. It was already getting dark.

* * *

Hannah was getting very desperate now. She had spent the day looking for food and water. She hadn't found any running water, so she'd once again been forced to drink from a muddy puddle. She drank one puddle almost dry and ended up getting a mouthful of sloppy mud. She spat it out and retched. The dirty water she had been drinking had started to make her stomach make some funny noises, and had also given her diarrhoea.

She hadn't found any food. There were no blackberry bushes or any other kind of food. She had seen a small tree with red berries on it, which had looked tempting, but she had always been told that those berries were poisonous to humans. She remembered seeing a robin eating them in her grandparents' garden and asking why the birds could eat them and she couldn't. Her grandmother had told her that the berries were not poisonous to the birds but would make her very ill. The last thing she wanted now was to become 'very ill'. She had also seen some kind of mushroom at the bottom of a large tree. Once again, she thought that these might be poisonous. Either that or they might make her high. She had heard about mushrooms making people high. She decided against eating the mushrooms, too.

It was getting dark now. She had to start thinking about where she was going to sleep that night. Just then she thought about the creature she had heard sniffing around last night. She hadn't seen what it was but she didn't want it coming round again. It was probably a fox or a badger. She had learned in school that both were nocturnal, and both were afraid of humans. Still, she didn't fancy meeting one in the dark.

Hannah walked on for a while longer and then she came across a stone wall. Her heart hammered in excitement. Was this a house? A barn? It was quite dark now. She felt her way around the building and came to a space where there would once have been a door. Her heart sank as she stepped inside. The building was small — only a little bigger than a garden shed. She looked up and saw that the roof had fallen in. There was no chance that someone was living here now.

She stepped further inside. The ground underfoot was uneven; there was rubble from the roof and some broken glass. Old beer cans lay crumpled in a corner, and she could see the remnants of a fire in the middle of the room. Someone had been here once, but had probably left a long time ago.

Hannah decided that she would stay here for the night. It was better than a bush.

Carefully, she cleared the ground near a pile of ash and lay down. There must be civilisation somewhere close by, she reasoned. She thought about looking for a village nearby before going to sleep, but quickly dismissed the thought. It would be crazy to go wandering around in the pitch darkness. She could fall and injure herself further. That would almost certainly mean death. With that thought in her mind, Hannah drifted off to sleep.

* * *

Ben entered the hotel room, followed by Kim. He started to take off his jeans. He wanted to get changed quickly and head to a bar to get a couple of beers in him. However, Kim had other ideas.

She went over to Ben and whispered in his ear, 'Shall we do something a little naughty?'

Ben turned and looked at her. She was grinning at him. She put her hand down his Calvin Klein underpants and he instantly became hard.

'How naughty are we talking?' he replied.

'Very…'

She started stroking Ben's hard penis. He pushed her hands away and took her t-shirt off, then she took off her tight jeans so she was standing in the room in her bra and knickers. Ben in his underpants.

'The balcony… Let's do it on the balcony,' she said seductively.

'Wow! Yes. It's cold though.'

'I'll put a coat on.'

With that, Kim put her coat on over her underwear and stepped out onto the balcony. Ben followed her, dressed only in his underpants, and then Kim pushed him onto a chair. Ben looked out over the balcony. There was no one walking around on the pathway below. It was dark, and the park was empty as far as he could see. Kim sat down on top of him. The coat she was wearing pretty much covered her body completely. She moved her knickers to one side and pulled Ben's erection out of his boxers. Gently, she slid his penis inside of her. They both moaned quietly.

Kim started moving up and down as Ben held her arms tightly. This was amazing. She started to move faster. Up and down. She ground on him and Ben shut his eyes, wanting to hold on for as long as possible. Kim was moaning louder now. Ben started wondering whether anyone could actually see them. The thought that someone might spot them made the act even more exciting.

Kim moved up and down again and again. Ben's orgasm was getting close. No, he needed to hold on just a little longer. It couldn't end now. Kim moaned again. 'Yes, Ben, keep going,' she whispered. That was enough. Ben couldn't hold any longer. He exploded inside of her. Kim felt the warmth of his load and moaned loudly. They both sighed deeply.

Kim leaned back onto Ben, breathing heavily. 'That was awesome,' she whispered.

'Yes, it was,' Ben gasped. Kim then got up quickly and ran back inside the hotel. Ben got up and saw the reason for her quick departure. There was a small group of men walking on the path below them. Had they seen them? He wasn't sure. Maybe they had, but he didn't care. He had loved every minute of it.

He went inside and they both took a quick shower and got dressed. They decided to dress up a bit. Kim wore a black dress with black high heels and Ben wore his chinos and a navy shirt. They both slipped on jackets and went out onto the street. They decided to try the bar from yesterday, as the menu had looked good.

Kim went into the bar first and ordered a couple of beers. They sat at a table this time and started to look at the menu. When the waiter came over, Kim ordered a pasta dish with mushrooms and chicken and a cheesy garlic sauce; Ben ordered veal in a rich, fruity sauce with puréed potatoes. They both ordered another beer each and a bottle of Merlot to follow.

Their meals arrived with the wine. The waiter opened the bottle and poured a small amount into Ben's glass. Ben picked up the glass, sniffed the wine and took a small sip. Once he had swilled the wine around his mouth a little, he swallowed and said, '*Oui, c'est bon.*'

The waiter then filled his glass up and poured wine into Kim's glass.

'*Merci*,' Kim said.

'*Bon apetit*,' said the waiter, with a nod, and he left.

The food smelt delicious. Kim tucked into her pasta with fervour while Ben cut off a piece of his veal and tasted the sauce. It was sweet and heavy and rich.

'Wow,' Ben said. 'This is delicious — try some.' He offered a fork with a piece of veal on for Kim and she ate it without taking the fork from him.

'That is lovely. Do you want some of mine?'

'I'll have a try,' he said.

Kim gave Ben a fork with pasta curled around the tines. Ben ate the mouthful.

'Mmm — nice. It's like a chicken carbonara really, eh?'

'Yes, I guess so,' replied Kim.

They ate the rest of their food and drank the wine. Ben ordered a second bottle of Merlot. They finished their food and the waiter came to take their plates away. They both declined dessert. They talked about the day as they drank the rest of the second bottle. Kim was starting to feel a little tipsy now, and Ben noticed that she was starting to slur her words.

They finished the last of the wine and Ben paid the bill. He helped Kim to her feet, as she was now quite drunk. They walked back to the hotel, which took longer than usual because Ben was acting as a crutch for Kim, helping her to walk in a straight line. It was not an easy task.

They finally made it to the hotel and took the lift up the second floor. Ben walked Kim to the room, helped her out of her clothes and put her to bed. No sooner had he laid her down she had passed out. Ben kissed her forehead and covered her with the blanket.

'Sleep well, babe,' he whispered. 'Love you.'

Ben wasn't feeling too drunk and he wasn't very tired. He decided to go downstairs to the hotel bar for a nightcap.

To his dismay, when he reached the bar Ben found that it had closed just half an hour earlier.

He went out of the hotel. After walking down the street for a few minutes, he found a small, intimate bar that had just a few tables and a small bar area. It was enough for what he needed, so he went inside.

The bar was quiet. There were a few old men at the bar itself and one or two people sat alone on a few of the tables. Ben went to the bar and ordered a beer. He took the glass over to a table next to the window so he could look out onto the street outside. He was daydreaming when a shadow fell over him and someone sat down on the seat opposite. He jumped out of his reverie and turned.

A woman.

She had long, straight black hair and her lips were stained with dark red lipstick. She wore black, thick-rimmed glasses that framed her deep green eyes, which seemed to burrow into his thoughts. She wore a white low-cut blouse and Ben could see the tops of her breasts; her right breast seemed to have a tattoo on it — some sort of writing. Was it someone's name? Was it a phrase from a poem? She had a short skirt on and thick black tights. She was smiling at him. Then she spoke.

Ben looked at her. He hadn't understood a word of what she said. He must have looked confused, because the woman then said, '*Anglais?*'

'Yes,' Ben said.

'Sorry,' replied the woman. 'Can I sit here?' she had a strong French accent.

'Y-yes, of course.' Ben was nervous in the woman's presence. Why had she sat next to him? What did she want? 'My name's Ben.'

'Élodie,' said the woman. 'Pleased to meet you.'

'Likewise. Why did you sit here?'

'I was bored and I like talking to people. I saw you were alone and thought I would join you,' Élodie explained in her thick accent.

Ben struggled to understand it all but certainly got the gist. They talked for a while. They talked about their jobs and where they both lived. Élodie was a local to Paris. She lived just around the corner. Ben had to speak very slowly and in broken English to explain what he did and whereabouts he lived. Élodie asked him if he had seen the Eiffel Tower at night. He hadn't. She grabbed him by the hand and took him out of the bar. They walked quickly through the streets and she showed him a few shortcuts. Élodie, being a local, knew the streets well. They got to the tower in half the time it had taken Ben and Kim earlier in the day. It stood in front of them like a huge, impressive beacon that lit the whole sky around it. Ben was lost for words.

Élodie turned to face Ben and smiled. '*C'est fantastique, non?*' she said.

'Yes, it's amazing,' Ben replied.

Élodie leaned into him and kissed him. Ben pulled away for a second, shocked. This woman was really forward! He looked into her green eyes again and found himself kissing her back.

After a few minutes of passionate kissing, Élodie pulled back and turned towards the park. 'Come, this way,' she said, and started pulling Ben by the hand. She dragged him into the dark, deserted park. Ben was excited. This woman was crazy, but he liked it. They hurried even deeper into the park, then Élodie left the path and went into the wooded area. Ben followed. She reached a huge tree and stopped. She turned and kissed Ben again. Ben shut his eyes. This was incredible. Was he dreaming?

Oh God — no — not the sound.

It hit him like a bomb. For a second, he thought that Élodie had punched him. She hadn't. He shook his head to try to get rid of the shrieking sound, but it only got worse. He gritted his teeth so hard they threatened to crack. He lost track of what was happening or where he was. Élodie had undone his fly and was now rubbing her hand inside his trousers. He was hard. But, fuck, that noise was killing him!

His eyes were open again but his vision was failing; he was struggling to see the girl in front of him. What was going on? He squinted at Élodie and saw that she was hitching her skirt up.

Ignoring the noise, Ben pulled down her tights and saw through the blur that she was wearing a black thong. She pulled the thing to the side and leaned over towards the tree. Ben was throbbing with excitement as she manoeuvred his penis into her from behind. She grabbed hold of the tree for support while Ben started to thrust into her. He shut his eyes again. The noise — the pain! It got worse.

Élodie started to moan quietly. The painful noise seemed to come from the girl he was fucking. Who was she? Why was she making this noise? Why wouldn't she shut the fuck up?!

Ben grabbed Élodie's hips and thrust harder inside her, again and again. She started to moan louder but this made the noise in Ben's head worse. He had to shut her up.

His movements grew faster, more forceful. He grabbed her hair and pulled her head backwards. Élodie screamed. Not in ecstasy, but in pain. Ben forced her head forward as he continued to thrust deep inside her. Élodie's head smashed hard against the tree. Her glasses broke and fell from her face to the floor.

She struggled against him now. Ben pulled her head back again and smashed her head into the tree trunk again with his next thrust. Élodie screamed again, louder. Ben continued fucking her. He heard the thud of her head against the tree with each thrust, and the noise slowly subsided. Her head fell to one side. Ben thrust once more, smashing her head into the tree, and she fell utterly silent as her body went limp.

He pulled himself out of her and she fell to the ground in a heap. The noise had stopped. Ben looked down at the lump of dead meat below him. He saw his hard penis and hurriedly put it back in his trousers. He looked around, unsure of where he was.

Ben turned around and starting walking back to the path. He looked at his watch; it was 3:32.

'Oh my God!' Ben said. 'I have to get back to Kim.'

He started walking back to the hotel. He passed the Eiffel Tower. 'Wow,' he murmured. 'It looks awesome at night.'

Chapter 41

Hannah woke up just as it was getting light. She had actually slept really well. It hadn't been as cold inside the brick building as it had been out in the forest on the previous night. As she was coming round, she heard a flapping sound. She opened her eyes, thinking it might be a bird, but when she saw where the noise was coming from she sat up in horror. Amongst the broken, rotting beams in the roof of the building there were large black blobs. Every now and then, one of the blobs stretched its wings and then returned to its blob state.

They were bats.

Hannah counted maybe forty of them. She hadn't seen them in the dark when she went into the building last night, and she must have been asleep when they all woke up in the night — but now she could clearly see them.

She held her breath, not daring to move. Her back throbbed but she paid no attention to it. Her eyes were locked on the bats above her. She spent ten minutes watching them, but they were all clearly asleep and not going anywhere. Quietly, she got up and gently rubbed her back. It was heavily swollen now. The pain wasn't as sharp as it had been though; it was more of a dull ache. Hannah went out of the doorway and into the forest.

Away from the distraction of the bats, Hannah realised that she was starving. She hadn't eaten for over a day now and it hurt her stomach. She was thirsty as well. She stood outside the building for a few minutes, thinking of what she should do. She decided that she would use the building as her base. She would go out for a short distance in search of food and water and then turn back towards the building. If she was unsuccessful in her search, she would return to the building and then venture in a different direction for a short time and back again. If she repeated this a few times, she was bound to find food or water at some stage. She had to leave a trail of some sort, though.

Hannah looked around for something that would be useful as a marker for the path she had to take. There were rocks and sticks, but these were no good in a forest; they would just blend into the surroundings. She looked back inside the building. There were some old beer cans — blue and silver. These would stand out in amongst the greenery.

She picked up a blue can and as she did some liquid poured out. Quickly, she turned the can back upright and thought hard. How desperate was she for water? Very. She lifted the can up and poured some of the liquid into her mouth. She winced at the bitter taste. She drank another mouthful and then put the can down. She checked the other cans, and gently poured each of the cans' contents into the first one. After the last can was emptied, she had almost a full can of liquid. She put this down near the fire remnants and carried the empty cans out of the building to make the trail.

Hannah decided that she would walk ten paces between each can and see how far she got. She started from the doorway of the building. After ten paces, she put down a blue can. She walked another ten paces and put down a silver can. Keeping in a straight line as best she could, she walked another ten paces and put down another can, blue this time. She kept looking around her for some form of edible berries, her stomach growling in anticipation.

By the fifth can, she still hadn't found any food. She had one can left and wasn't holding out much hope in finding food. She walked ten paces and put the last can down. Still nothing. She had just ten paces left. It was a distance she could almost see and it wasn't looking good. She slowly walked forward and stopped at ten. Hannah looked all around her. She squinted to see if she could see further away but there was nothing to eat at all. Despondently, she walked back to the building, picking up all her cans as she went.

When she reached the building, Hannah picked another direction to walk in. She walked the seventy paces again but still found nothing. She spotted some mushrooms, but was still afraid to pick and eat them. She tried the other two directions and still found nothing.

Hannah went back inside the building and sat down. Her stomach was killing her. She really needed food now.

On the walls of the building there was some moss. Could you eat moss? Hannah didn't know, but she was starving. She scraped some off the wall and looked at it in her hand. She shut her eyes and threw it into her mouth. She tried not to chew but had to. It was moist, bitter and gritty, but it didn't taste too bad. She swallowed it with a gulp and looked around the walls for some more. She spotted some on another wall. Again, she scraped off the moss and threw it into her mouth. She did this a number of times and her stomach eventually stopped hurting. She washed down her lunch with some liquid from the cans and winced again at the disgusting taste. Hannah decided that she would try searching for food again, but extend the distance between each can to fifteen — maybe twenty — paces this time. But she would shout out as she went this time too. She had forgotten about being found in her desperation to find food.

* * *

Ben woke up to his phone alarm. His head hurt. What had happened last night? He didn't remember anything after he and Kim had left the restaurant.

He leaned over and looked at Kim. She looked

beautiful. He stroked her arm gently and she made a quiet moan.

'Kim,' he whispered. 'Kim, sweetie, we have to get up.'

'What time is it?' Kim groaned.

'It's gone nine. We have to be out by ten.'

She stirred, opened her eyes and smiled at him. She loved waking up next to him; he made her feel safe. Being with Ben was the best thing that had happened to her. Every now and then, her mind drifted back to her last boyfriend and she wondered what would have happened if they were still together. She wouldn't have been this happy with her ex, that was for sure. She had always known that something wasn't right there. But now, with Ben, she was truly happy. He turned her on by just looking at her, but it was more than that; she felt secure in his arms. She could easily be herself with him around. It had crossed her mind that he would ask her to marry him while they were in Paris, but he hadn't so far. She doubted that he would do it today, since they were heading home.

Ben got out of bed and went into the bathroom. A few seconds later, Kim heard the shower running. She sat up and thought about last night. She thought about the balcony. Wow, that had been hot! And *she* had instigated it. That was the thing with Ben; he made her do things that she would never have considered doing before.

Ben came out of the bathroom. 'Your turn,' he said. Kim smiled at him and got out of bed, kissing him as she approached the bathroom to shower.

Soon after, Kim and Ben were both packed up and ready to leave. They went down in the lift to reception and Ben asked the concierge if they could leave their bags there, because their flight wasn't until later. The concierge showed them to a baggage room and they dumped their bags.

They decided to go and have breakfast in the

patisserie they had visited yesterday. This time, they sat down and ordered coffees as well. Ben suggested going on a cruise along the Seine, since they had plenty of time before having to go to the airport.

After breakfast, they walked to the river and booked themselves onto a cruise with lunch included. Ben tried to order the tickets in French but wasn't too successful; hearing his attempt, the woman in the kiosk replied to him automatically in English. It made Ben feel quite small and embarrassed in front of Kim, but she just laughed and kissed him. She liked that he was willing to try to speak French to the locals.

They sat by the river and watched some of the other boats pass by as they waited for theirs to leave. At noon, they got onto the boat and picked a seat by a window. They were given a glass of sparkling wine as a welcome drink and then they set off. The cruise was supposed to take about two hours. After half an hour, they were served a starter of French onion soup with a chunk of crusty bread on the side. Kim ate the soup and watched the scenery of Paris drift by. This was fantastic. Somebody made announcements over the speaker system about the places they were passing — for example, a building called the Hotel Dieu, which apparently wasn't a hotel at all but a hospital.

The main course aboard the boat was beef bourguignon and gratin dauphinois. Ben ordered two beers to go with it. The food was so good it took the emphasis off of the Parisian surroundings. To finish they had a crêpe each. The boat pulled back to the side of the Seine nearly two and a half hours after setting off, but the time had flown by.

Kim and Ben went back to the hotel to pick up their bags and take a taxi to the airport. They arrived at the airport at half past four, two hours before their flight was due to depart, and Kim started walking into the terminal while Ben paid the driver. They checked in and went through to the departure lounge. Kim wandered around the shops while Ben went to the bar to kill some time. He only ordered a coke; he was due to drive home when they landed. After about half an hour, Kim joined him and he ordered her a beer. A television was turned on nearby, and they both watched the screen absentmindedly, neither of them understanding what was being said. At half past six, the flight information changed to say that they were to go to Gate 5. They finished their drinks, picked up their bags and started walking.

* * *

Hannah was sat in the stone building, hunched over in pain. Her back hurt a lot and her stomach was torturing her. The moss had eased her hunger for a short time, but now she felt worse than before. She remembered hearing about a boy trapped in rubble somewhere who survived by eating newspaper or ketchup sachets. She may have been mixing up stories but the ideas were true. She felt she would give a lot for some ketchup or even some newspaper to try... Her throat was dry even though she had been drinking the liquid from the cans and the muddy puddle water. She felt weak.

She drifted off to sleep every now and then. She had spent the day trying to find food using the cans as markers, taking twenty paces between each can. No luck. She was getting closer and closer to eating the mushrooms she had seen by some of the trees.

Why had no one found her? Were they even looking anymore? Maybe they had stopped? Maybe they thought she was already dead? What about Tom?

She found herself daydreaming. It helped keep her mind off the pain she was in. A bat stretched out and brought her back to the stone building. She realised that tears were rolling down her cheeks. She wiped her eyes with her dirty hands. She hadn't washed in days. She didn't know how long she had spent in the forest now. She had slept a number of times but it was not always dark when she slept and it was not always light when she was awake. She had once read in a book that the first thing people lose when they are lost or confused is the concept of time. Well, she certainly had.

Hannah shook herself fully awake from her daydream and looked around the building. On the opposite wall there was a small black splodge of something. She got up to have a look at it. On closer inspection, it turned out to be a slug. It was about the size of her thumb; not the biggest she had ever seen. She recoiled in disgust and retched at the idea that had just entered her head.

Birds eat them. Hedgehogs eat them. She was desperate.

She looked at the slug again and bit her lip. She shut her eyes and took a deep breath. Slowly, she reached out with her right hand and pulled the slug off the wall. It was cold and slimy, and it left a white snot mark on the wall. She retched, took another deep breath, shut her eyes again and threw the slug into her mouth. She tried her best to swallow it whole, but it got stuck at the back of her throat. She retched again. Swallow. It wasn't going down — she had to chew it.

Hannah gagged it back into her mouth and held her breath, then bit down on the soft, slimy flesh of the slug. She felt the insides squirt out into her mouth, leaving an awful, bitter taste on her tongue. It was grainy. It was chewy. It was vile. She chewed twice more and managed to swallow the mess she had made in her mouth. Once the slug mush had slipped down her throat, Hannah spat out what was left: tiny bits of orange goo. Quickly, Hannah went over to the beer can and she took a large swig. The liquid washed the taste out of her mouth with a bitter tang. She sat on the floor and started to cry.

* * *

Ben was tired, so he tried to get some sleep on the plane. Kim wasn't. She decided to read the free newspaper that the stewardess had handed her on the way into the plane. She didn't usually read tabloids — she couldn't bear reading the stories and bullshit that they sometimes made up — but she didn't have anything else to read other than the menu card.

She read through some gossip pages and then a headline caught her attention: 'Murder in Backstreet Hotel.'

She started to read through the story. The police had apparently released more details about the woman found in the hotel in Birmingham. The hotel was one in which you could rent a room by the hour. A no-questions-asked sort of place. The victim had been a stripper.

The next part made Kim feel sick. Apparently, the woman had been hacked to pieces with a fire axe. Everything inside the room had been almost completely destroyed. There were no witnesses. There were no leads. They didn't even have a real name for the woman who was murdered.

Kim sat there thinking about the poor woman. A nobody. Somebody somewhere must have been missing her, surely…

She nudged Ben to wake him up. 'Ben,' she said.

Ben woke up with a groan. 'What?' he said grumpily.

Kim showed Ben the newspaper and told him about the woman.

'Wow, that's awful,' Ben said, without much compassion. He was tired. He shut his eyes again and fell back asleep.

The plane landed on time. Kim had managed to get a little sleep and they were both a bit groggy when they touched down with a bump. They went through passport control and walked straight through the baggage reclaim area; travelling with just hand luggage definitely had its advantages. They turned their phones back on and a few emails came through, along with a 'welcome back to the UK' text. Kim had an extra text — one that made her gasp and feel sick. She burst into tears outside of the airport.

'Oh my God, what's the matter?' Ben asked, his voice full of concern.

'It's Tom. They found Tom,' Kim replied, through tears.

'That's great, isn't it?'

'No, he's….he's…'

Kim couldn't continue. She handed the phone to Ben so he could read the message himself. It was from Amy, her teaching assistant. She said that they had found Tom's body in the forest near the castle. His head had been smashed in by a rock until his body was almost unrecognisable.

The search was now a murder investigation.

They had no witnesses and no leads. They still hadn't found Hannah but they were trying to stay positive about her.

Ben took a deep breath and held Kim close to him. 'Kim, I'm so sorry, that's horrific.' He was trying to hold back his own tears. He needed to be strong for Kim. Something flashed in his mind as he held Kim.

He was looking down at Hannah. He was sitting on top of her. His hand was over her mouth.

Ben shut his eyes and shook his head to clear the image, then hugged Kim even tighter. He didn't know what to say. There was nothing to say. They stood there in each other's arms for a while.

Kim eventually broke away from Ben's hold. 'Come on, let's get to the car. I've got school in the morning. Although I don't know how anyone will make it in.'

Ben called the car park company and in ten minutes there was a minibus driving into the taxi rank to pick them up. They got in and sat in silence until they reached the car park. Ben went in to pick up the keys and fifteen minutes later they were driving home on the motorway, a thick, heavy silence hanging over them.

The journey seemed to last forever. When they finally reached Kim's road, Ben asked if she wanted to stay at his instead of spending the night alone. Kim declined; she wanted to be alone so she could get ready for what could possibly be the worst school day of her life.

Ben dropped her off with a kiss and watched her go inside. He drove off and headed home. He was tired. His head ached. Why was he having visions? What was going on? Was he just imagining things? Maybe he just needed a good night's sleep. Maybe he should call in sick tomorrow. But he had taken Friday off — there would be shit loads of work for him to do tomorrow. He decided he should probably just go in.

Ben pulled up at his flat and went inside. He thought about taking a shower but decided to go straight to bed. He fell asleep almost as soon as his head hit the pillow.

Chapter 42

Hannah woke up inside the building with rain dripping on her face. She couldn't remember actually going to sleep, but she felt quite refreshed so she figured she must have slept for a long time. She would have felt positively great if it wasn't for the huge amount of pain she was in.

The can she drank from was almost empty. A muddy puddle would have to do to refill it. But what was she going to eat today? Could she face eating another slug? It hadn't actually made her feel less hungry in the end; it had just made her feel sick. How long could she go on living like this? Was she going to live in this forest in this building forever? Not forever. She would die before then.

She got up and walked out of the doorway. She took the can with her, along with the marker cans. She paced until she found some water. She drank the dregs from the can and then bent down to fill the can from the puddle of muddy water. The puddle wasn't very deep and she had to splash the water into the small opening of the can, but after a while she had managed to fill the can halfway. There was some water left in the puddle, so she lapped up the last of it and then started to walk back to the stone building.

When she got back to the building, she sat outside. The rain had subsided and the sun was trying to break through the trees. Her stomach hurt so much. What was she going to eat? She needed to find something that would fill her up a bit more than some moss and a slug. There was a noise inside the building behind her. A bat was stretching out its wings during its sleep.

Could she eat a bat?

Hannah got up and walked slowly and quietly inside the building; she didn't want to disturb the bats. She looked up. There were loads of them. Under normal circumstances she would have been terrified of them — especially sleeping under them. But these were not normal circumstances.

She stared at the blobs in the shadows of the building. What should she do? If she was going to eat one, she would have to kill it. But how? How do you kill a bat?

She looked around her. There were rocks on the floor. She could throw one, but if she missed then it might scare the bats and they would all fly out at once in a huge swarm. She had seen bats do that in a film somewhere. No, a rock wouldn't work.

Hannah went outside again and looked around. There were branches on the floor. Some very large. That might work. If she could find one long enough and heavy enough, it would be like a baseball bat. She walked around, looking for branches. Sadly, many of them were rotten. They wouldn't be good for anything; they would break as soon as she picked them up.

She walked a little further away from the building — and then she found it.

The ideal branch.

It was almost a log. She picked it up. It was fresh, not rotten at all. She could lift it up easily enough, and she took a few practise swings at a nearby tree trunk. *Thud, thud, thud.* It held together and she could get some power behind each swing. Hannah took the branch back into the building and looked up again. Which poor bat would she go for? She felt bad about what she was going to do, but it was an emergency. Everyone would understand. It was a matter of life and death. Maybe.

Hannah took a few deep breaths. She picked the bat lowest down on the wall and raised up the branch above her head. She took a massive swing towards the sleeping bat. *Smash!* The branch struck the bat and it fell to the ground.

The noise awoke the rest of the bats and they all

flew out of the building at once — just as Hannah had predicted. She screamed loudly and ducked. She daren't move. She felt their wings in her hair and on her skin. They squeaked and squealed. Then there was silence. Hannah waited a moment and then raised her head. There were no more bats. They had all left.

She stood up and looked for the fallen bat. She spotted it injured on the floor, slowly crawling around. It was using its wings as arms to move. It was going to die sometime, but she had to finish it off now.

Hannah raised the branch again and shut her eyes. She brought the branch down onto the bats head. It made a thud. There was no other noise. She opened her eyes. The branch had crushed the bat's skull. It was definitely dead now. She bent closer to the bat and nudged it with the branch. She didn't feel too hungry now after seeing all the blood.

Hannah sat down on the floor, the branch still in her hands. She felt sorry for the bat. Just then, her stomach rumbled, reminding her why she had killed the poor creature in the first place. But how was she going to eat it? She couldn't cook it — she had no fire.

She would have to eat it raw. Raw bat for lunch. Yummy!

She picked up the bat by one of its wings. It looked bigger with its wing spread out. If she hadn't been so hungry, the stench of it would have turned her stomach. She shut her eyes and bit into the rubbery wing. Hmm — it was just like the skin of a chicken. She tore the skin off the arm and found it was very chewy.

She couldn't decide which was worse, the bat or the slug.

She shut her eyes and repeated the ordeal with the other wing, almost gagging this time. What next? The body was going to have bones and guts and other stuff in it. Could she face eating that? *How* would she eat it? She could tear it up and eat it in bits, or she could stuff it in her mouth and chew through whatever was inside it, perhaps...

Hannah decided to try to rip the furry skin off the bat. She put her fingers inside the neck and pulled downwards. The front of the bat opened up and dark red blood oozed out over her fingers. She tugged the skin off and then ripped the back of the bat skin off the body. The bat was now a dark red colour. Parts of the innards were coming out of the neck, but she didn't know which parts they were. Her hands were covered in blood. She licked a finger and discovered the blood tasted like her own when she had a cut on her finger and put it in her mouth to stop the bleeding. She squeezed the bat and the innards fell out of the neck. Hopefully the creature's body was empty now.

Again, Hannah stuck her fingers into the neck and pulled the flesh of the bat towards her. The bat was tough and she had to pull hard. Eventually, the bat ripped in half. She pulled out a few bones that were sticking out of various places and threw them on the floor. She then shut her eyes and put the front part of the carcass in her mouth. She had to chew. She had to pull small bones out of her mouth. It had a strong metallic taste; however, it wasn't the same texture as the slug and it was almost easier to eat. After a while of chewing, Hannah managed to swallow the bat flesh. There was one half of the bat to go. She had already done one half so she didn't build it up so much this time. She put the back half into her mouth and chewed again. Small, fast chews. She picked out a few more bones and then swallowed the last of the bat.

It was done.

She had eaten a bat.

When she got out of the woods, she would have one hell of a story to tell people. *If* she got out of there. For the first time in she didn't know how long, her stomach stopped hurting. How long would a bat keep her hunger at bay? She didn't know. What she did know was that there were no more bats in the building.

* * *

Kim was dreading today. She didn't know what to expect. She was quite shocked that the school wasn't shut to *everyone*, not just pupils. Normally, on a day when there were no pupils in school, it would be a good day. You often hear teachers saying that school is far better without the children. School is a very different place without children; that is true. The rooms seem empty and the halls seem huge. However, today was not going to be a normal school day.

Today was the start of the last week of term. The week was only going to be three days long and it was usually a very exciting time. Pupils would make Christmas decorations. There would be school discos and class parties. It was one of the best times to be a teacher.

Not this year. This year was now very different.

Kim pulled into the school car park in a daze. Her mind was miles away. She didn't notice the crowd of people waiting by the school entrance. Kim parked her car, gathered up her bag and got out. She walked up the tree-lined path to the school and was met by the crowd of six or seven people. She recognised one or two of the faces in the crowd.

They were parents.

She heard someone say, 'That's her there — Miss Coombes — that's her.'

Before she knew it, a woman had come right up to her, shouting something in her face. Kim was shocked and terrified. The stale smell of whisky hit her as the woman screamed. Then the woman pushed her and she fell to the floor.

Kim looked up at the woman who was now towering over her, still in shock. She had no idea what was going on. Then, her mind started to focus, and she could hear what the woman was shouting at her.

'You bitch, you fucking bitch! My son is dead because of you! You bitch!'

The woman, who Kim now recognised as Tom's mum, spat at her as she sat on the concrete. Kim was cowering now.

'What have you got to say?' the woman yelled, and then started to cry.

A member of the crowd came up and pulled Tom's mum away and back to the crowd. Another parent came up to Kim and held out her hand. She helped Kim up and took her through the crowd to the front entrance of the school.

Kim heard a shout as she passed.

'You murdering bitch!'

The parent buzzed the door bell and Kim went inside the school.

In the quiet, Kim burst into tears. She ran to her classroom and crawled into a ball on the floor. She was crying hysterically when the head teacher, Mrs Williams, came in.

'Oh my God, Kim, I'm so sorry. I've actually called the police to have them removed. They shouldn't be there at all.' She gently helped Kim up from the floor. 'Come to the staffroom, Kim. I'll get you some coffee. The police can speak to you too when they arrive. You should press charges against that woman.'

'She's just upset,' Kim replied dully. 'She needed to vent at someone, and I guess I'm the closest she has to the actual killer. I won't press any charges.'

They were in the staffroom now, where another few teachers were already sitting, drinking coffee and talking about Tom and Hannah.

'I can't believe they still haven't found Hannah,' one teacher was saying.

'I think she must have been abducted,' said another.

The conversation died down when Kim entered the

room, making the topic of conversation all the more obvious.

Kim sat down, shaking. Mrs Williams made her a cup of coffee, which Kim drank gratefully.

'While you're all here, I will tell you what is happening today and for the rest of term,' Mrs Williams said. 'I couldn't shut the school without talking to you all first, and that's why I called you in today. We need to make a decision about the rest of the term. We can either shut the school entirely for the rest of term or you can all come in for the next two days. What do you think?'

There was a lot of mumbling and discussion around the room, but the general consensus was that they should close the school entirely and start again fresh in the New Year.

'Ok, that's what I thought you would all say. Right, we have the police coming to remove the crowd outside, but once they are gone and the pathway is clear again you are free to go home.'

There was a little more discussion, but the teachers started to leave the staffroom and soon it was just Kim and Mrs Williams left.

'Are you ok now?' Mrs Williams asked.

'I'll be fine in a bit. I think I'll go and get all my stuff together so that I am ready to go as soon as the crowd have gone.'

'Good thinking — if you need any help, just give me a call.'

With that, Kim finished her coffee and washed up her mug, then left the room and headed back to her classroom. The school seemed emptier than ever. She didn't know if it would ever feel full again.

Chapter 43

Hannah had slept surprisingly well. She had decided to risk sleeping in the building again. Without the bats, it was almost comfortable. Almost. She still hurt, and her hunger had returned when she woke up. She couldn't remember waking in the night, though; she must have been so tired that she had slept right through until morning. Or afternoon. She had no idea what the time was, and since it was winter it wasn't light for very long.

It was only a few days until Christmas, if her body calendar was right, and by now it should be far colder than it was. Hannah felt very grateful that it was unseasonably warm; if it had been colder or snowy, she would almost certainly be dead by now. She shivered at the thought.

She also found herself thinking of Tom. What had happened to him? Was he still out here in the forest? Was he alive or dead? Maybe *she* was dead. Maybe this was heaven...or hell. Who knew? How could she tell? There was no one to ask or talk to.

Hannah found herself shouting his name. 'TOM!' Maybe he was close. He may hear her. 'Are you there?!'

She waited silently for a few seconds. Nothing. Just the birds. She felt herself start to cry and shut her eyes, then shook her head to clear the tears.

Hannah thought hard. She had a very difficult decision to make. Should she stay here at the building, which she knew was relatively safe but didn't have any food or water nearby, or should she wander in a chosen direction in search of food, water and people? She started to weigh up the options. If she stayed, she would struggle to find food and water. She would have to drift off slightly and drink from a puddle and hope to find something to eat nearby. Would anyone find her in the building? Did anyone ever come round here? If not, she would almost certainly die here. On the other hand, if she wandered in a single direction for long enough, she might find water, or food, or both. She might also find people. The theatre might be nearby, or a house. But if that wasn't the case then she would lose the safety of the shelter and would almost certainly die somewhere out in the forest.

It was not an easy decision to make. If either choice went wrong, she would probably die.

* * *

Kim left the school shortly after the police moved the crowd away. The group of parents didn't show too much dissent, and most moved away quickly on sight of the police cars. One or two parents stayed to make their feelings known to the police, but it wasn't too long before they too left.

Kim drove away from the school with her mind in turmoil; each new thought was like a spirt of hot lava shooting out of the volcano and scorching her brain. Her head ached. Her body ached. She was tired. Tom was constantly one of the thought eruptions, but even more so was Hannah. What had happened to her? Had she been abducted? Had she run away? Was she alive? Dead?

One after another, the thoughts shot through her mind, each one bringing more pain.

When she arrived home, Kim decided that she should go to bed. Some extra sleep might help her aches and clear her mind. However, after half an hour of lying in bed with her mind swirling, she got up again. Maybe a walk would do her some good... Yes, she would go for a walk to the shop at the end of the road. She needed some milk, in any case.

Kim walked slowly, almost drunkenly, up the road to the small shop. The shop sold all sorts of items, from newspapers to batteries and anything else you might need in an emergency. Kim smiled at the woman behind the counter and picked up a carton of milk before heading to the counter to pay. Suddenly, her eyes caught sight of a newspaper headline: 'BODY FOUND IN FOREST!'

Kim picked up the paper and put it the counter. The shop assistant scanned the milk and the paper and Kim paid with the coins in her purse. She walked back home, her hand getting cold from carrying the chilled milk. When she entered the house, she put the milk in the fridge and took the paper into the lounge to read the story.

The reporter wrote that the body of a ten-year-old boy had been found in the woods near Old Crag Castle. There was nobody else at the scene, but the police had launched a murder inquiry and were appealing for anyone with any information to come forward. The story didn't go into detail about the boy's injuries, but it did say that his death was caused by severe trauma to the head. The newspaper stated that a young girl of the same age was also missing and that there had been a search party out looking for her in the woods. Again, the police were appealing for anyone with information that might help to find the girl to come forward.

Kim started to cry. She just couldn't believe what was happening. She was just about to go and make herself a cup of tea to calm her nerves when she noticed a much smaller headline on the same page: 'MORE INFORMATION ABOUT STRIPPER DEATH'.

Kim read the article. The story was about the murder of a stripper in Birmingham — the same case she had read about on the plane. More information had been leaked about the crime scene. It seemed that, even though the room had almost been completely destroyed by the axe, there was no blood found around the room. The finding was so strange that the authorities were not sure as to whether the woman was actually murdered in the room or was moved there afterwards. They had called in blood spatter experts, but there was no more information at present.

Kim sat in her chair shaking. She was a nervous wreck. She didn't know what to do. She needed to speak to someone — she needed to be held.

She needed Ben.

* * *

Hannah had made her decision. It was almost a compromise between the two choices that she had given herself. She decided that she would stay where she was for one more night in the hope that someone would come by, either a search party or just a regular dog walker. If nobody came, which she thought was the likely outcome, then she would move on tomorrow. Today, however, she still needed to find food and water.

Hannah used the tactic that she had used before. She set off in a direction and walked for a number of steps in a straight line, then returned to the building and set off in another direction. She would keep going until she had some food of some sort, and water.

After a few attempts at finding water and failing, Hannah was starting to lose hope when she saw something shimmer in the distance. She was at the end of her twenty paces. She turned around to look at the building. She could just about see it through the trees, and so walked on a few extra steps to see if she could work out what the shiny thing was.

Hannah went about twenty-five paces and could no longer see the building when she looked backwards. If she kept walking in a straight line, she would be fine. She slowly stepped forward, placing one foot gently down in front of the other. The undergrowth was soft underfoot, like a thick, piled carpet. It felt nice.

Hannah reached the source of the shimmering.

It was a large puddle that looked relatively fresh. The water seemed clear. Hannah gasped loudly and almost dived into the puddle, scooping up handfuls of water and gulping it down; it felt amazing. She hadn't realised how thirsty she had become.

Hannah spent a number of minutes downing the water. Suddenly, something caught her eye; there was something at the base of a tree, just a short distance away.

She stopped drinking and stood up. Slowly, she walked over to the object. It was a dull white colour, almost grey, and possibly the size of a football — Hannah couldn't quite tell. When she got closer, it dawned on her that she was looking at an old skull.

Hannah screamed loudly and regurgitated some of the water she had just drunk. It dribbled down her chin, but she didn't notice. She stood looking at the skull for a few more minutes, and after she had calmed down and composed herself she walked up to the tree and bent down to get a closer look at the skull. She was surprised at herself for doing so; this experience in the forest had definitely made her tougher. A few days ago, there was no way she would have gone anywhere near a skull, or eaten a bat, but it's amazing what you can do if you think you might be on the verge of dying!

The skull was starting to turn green underneath; it had obviously been there a long time. There was no trace of flesh or any other part of the body. Hannah couldn't work out exactly what the skull was from. She thought it might have belonged to a fox or a badger, although she had no idea what a fox or badger skull would actually look like. She had seen foxes in her garden at night, but only briefly, and she had only ever seen badgers on TV. However, she reasoned that if there were foxes or badgers here, there must be something for them to eat. What did these animals eat? She didn't know.

CRACK! Something snapped behind her and made Hannah jump up with force. Her back shot a jet of pain straight through her body. She yelled in agony and then kept still. She tried to listen for where the noise had actually come from, but she only heard her heavy breathing and her intense heartbeat, thick in her ears.

Hannah ran back towards the building. Her back was stabbing her as she ran but she paid no attention to it. She had walked slightly off the straight line she had walked earlier and nearly ran straight past the building. Thankfully, she saw it off to the right as she reached a small clearing.

When she reached the building, Hannah let out a heavy sigh and sat down outside. She leant on the wall. It felt cold. She tilted her head back, looked up towards the sky and felt her eyes begin to close.

Before long, Hannah had fallen fast asleep.

***

Ben was having one of those days when the phone rang. He had arrived at work. Tamzin was still not at the front desk and there was now a man sitting there, picking his nose. He stopped picking his nose when he saw Ben. He stood up behind the reception desk and held out his hand. The one which had just been mining for gold inside his nose. Ben tried to think of a way to avoid the outstretched hand but could think of none. Reluctantly, he took the hand and shook it.

'I'm Sean,' the man said, flashing a toothy grin.

'Ben.'

'What's it…er, I'm standing in for someone for a while.' Sean kept holding Ben's hand while he spoke.

Ben broke free of the grasp, surreptitiously wiped his hand on his trouser leg and smiled at Sean. 'Nice to meet you,' he said.

'What's it…er, Ben, was it? You have some mail

here.' Sean handed Ben a pile of envelopes and sheets of paper.

'URGH! It begins!' Ben grunted.

'What's it… er, what begins?'

'Doesn't matter,' Ben said. He desperately wanted to get away from Sean. All he could think about was his hand. Was there some form of snot on it? He had to wash — fast. Ben raced down the corridor and into the men's toilets. He pushed the hot tap and added some soap, then scrubbed for a few minutes and washed the foamy lather off his hands. He did it again, just to be on the safe side.

Ben left the toilets and headed for his office. He opened the door and looked at his desk in dismay; there was a pile of papers in his in-tray. He let out a big sigh and went inside. He put the new set of envelopes and papers on top of the ones already there. Flopping into his seat, Ben turned on his computer, picked up the top piece of paper and read it briefly. It was something about a new part for some machine that he should be interested in. He wasn't. The computer was loading up, so he made himself a cup of tea. That would take the edge off.

Ben took the mug back to his desk and sat down with another flop, spilling some of the tea. 'Oh, for fuck's sake!' he exclaimed. He reached for a tissue and mopped up the tea and aimed the soaked ball at the bin. He threw and missed.

Ben checked his emails and sighed when he saw that there were fifty-four unread emails in his inbox.

That was when he got the phone call.

Chapter 44

Hannah felt disorientated. Was she dreaming? She was slumped in a forest next to a ruined building. Her head cleared a little; no, she wasn't dreaming. This was real. Too real.

Her neck was aching from the way she had been sleeping. Her back was worse. She tried to get up slowly but the pains in her neck and back were too excruciating for her to move. Was it morning or afternoon? She didn't know. It was definitely not evening — it was still light.

Food. She needed food. What could she eat? She looked around again. She used the wall of the ruined building to stand up. Hannah winced in pain. When she managed to stand upright, she looked to her left and decided to walk that way. So far, she hadn't ventured very far in this direction. Maybe she would find some berries.

Hannah walked thirty paces and looked back. She could still see the building, so she kept walking forward. She was still looking behind her when she felt some sharp, intense pain in her leg.

'Ah! What the...?' she said, and looked down at her leg. She saw the source of the pain; she seemed to have walked into some stinging nettles. She rubbed her leg. 'A dock leaf,' she muttered to herself. 'I need to find a dock leaf.'

Hannah looked around and saw a small bunch of leaves growing near the nettles. She went over and picked out the longest leaf, then wrapped it around her leg and rubbed it on the sting. After a few minutes, the pain subsided a little and Hannah threw the tattered dock leaf away.

She thought for a little while. Something was hanging in her mind. Something from her former life. The life when she hadn't been a forest dweller. The life where she had been a normal girl who lived in a house and went to school. A life that now seemed to exist ages ago and only in the dreams she had when she slept. There it was. She caught the thought more firmly this time. Something about nettles. Yes there it was. Her mother drank nettle tea. Did it sting you when you drank it? It seemed bizarre to Hannah why someone would drink these things! However she didn't have many other options. She thought she would try it.

She put her hand inside her dress and picked a nettle leaf. She brought it up to her mouth and studied it for a while. Hannah knew the hairy bit was the stinging bit. How should she eat it? She folded it in half and half again, then squeezed it hard and rolled it in her hand a little. The leaf was limper now. She shut her eyes tightly and put the leaf into her mouth. She chewed quickly and swallowed. *That's not too bad,* she thought. *I can do that. I can eat these.* It was worth a try. She didn't have anything else to eat and there were loads of nettles around.

She grabbed another leaf and did the same. She kept eating for half an hour or so. Her stomach was making a weird sound but she kept going. Slowly, she started to feel less hungry.

* * *

The phone call came from human resources upstairs. That was nothing special; Ben often got a call from someone upstairs. This call, however, stopped him dead. The woman on the end of the phone told him that Tamzin's body had been found in a landfill site a number of miles away. A member of her family had already identified her body. The woman continued to say that the police think that she must have been put into a dumpster somewhere and then the bin collectors picked up the dumpster and took it to the dump. They don't yet know exactly how long she had been there, but her body had become a festering mess. A number of different animals had been eating at her flesh. 'It would have been hard to identify her actual body if it was all complete,' the woman finished.

'What do you mean "all complete"?' Ben asked, his voice full of sadness and dread.

'Well, I don't quite know how to say this, but…they found her head separate from her body… She had been beheaded Ben.'

Ben could hear the woman start to cry on the other end of the phone.

'Oh my God!' he exclaimed. He was in total shock. His hands started shaking. Then, suddenly his mind was drawn somewhere else…to a dark alleyway somewhere. He heard a scream. He was breathing heavily. His head hurt. His eyes ached. In the darkness, Tamzin was staring up at him, her eyes lifeless.

'Hello? Ben? You still there?'

The voice on the phone brought him back to his office. He looked around. He was out of breath. What had just happened?

Ben shook himself. 'Yes, I'm here,' he said. 'Just a little shocked, that's all.'

'Did you hear what I just said?'

'A-a-about Tamzin being beheaded, yes.'

'I said that about ten minutes ago!' The woman seemed confused. 'No, I meant about the police wanting to speak to you.'

'Er, no — what did you say about that?'

'Well, the last time Tamzin was seen, as far as anyone can remember, was at the Christmas party. And she spent some time chatting to different people that night, including you. They just want to talk to you as a matter of routine, they said. I'm sure it's nothing to worry about.'

'Oh ok, I'm not sure how I can help, but let's see… When are they coming in?'

'They are coming in later this afternoon, and

possibly tomorrow, depending on how long today takes.'

'Ok, thanks for letting me know.'

Ben hung up and put his head in his hands. He thought about Tamzin and the Christmas party. He could hardly remember it. He must have been really hammered. Just then, the phone rang again and he jumped. Ben looked at it for a few seconds before answering.

It was Kim. She sounded a little distressed.

'Oh my God, Ben! I'm so glad you're there. I thought you might be snowed under or off sorting something out or whatever, I don't know but I'm so glad you're there. I needed to speak to you. I needed to hear your voice.'

'Kim, Kim, slow down. What's the matter? Is everything alright?'

'Yes — n-no — I don't know,' Kim stuttered.

'Are you still in work?'

'No, they've decided to shut the school for the time being. We've all gone home.'

'Nice for some!' Ben joked.

'No, it's not. Ben, a crowd of parents screamed at me in the yard. One woman pushed me and spat at me! The police had to be called to remove them. It was awful. I was so scared. I thought she was going to beat me up — or worse!' Kim retold the story of what had happened to her in school today. She also added what she had read in the newspaper.

Again, Ben's mind drifted. He saw the young boy in the woods. He saw a rock in his hand. He felt pain in his head. He winced. His mind moved on to the hotel in Birmingham. The axe. The clock. The picture. The picture that was in his room…it was also in the hotel room in Birmingham. And he knew he had seen it somewhere else besides there. Where? The hotel in Paris. It had been there, too. Was it anywhere else? He couldn't remember. His head started to thump. He was hoping the sound didn't start again. He couldn't face that today. He didn't have time to face that today!

'Ben?! You there?' Kim was shouting down the phone. It brought him out of the daze he was in.

'I'm here, babe, I'm here.'

'When will you be finished tonight?' Kim asked.

'I'm not sure, Kim, I have so much to do. Plus I have the police coming round soon.'

'The police?!' Kim exclaimed. 'Whatever for?'

'They are going to speak to a few of us,' Ben explained. He went on to tell Kim about the body found in the landfill site. He told her about the investigation and that the questioning was routine and nothing to worry about.

'Ok, well let me know when you are done and come round. I need to see you today. I want you to hold me.'

'I will, Kim, I will. Maybe you should get some sleep?'

'Yes, I think you are right. I'll head to bed now.'

'Ok, babe. Love you! See you tonight.'

'Love you too.'

They both hung up. Ben looked around the office. It seemed smaller than before, like it was closing in on him. He had to get out. He needed some fresh air.

* * *

Kim was still looking at the phone in her hand. Something was niggling at the back of her mind. She couldn't put her finger on it, but something wasn't right. She dismissed the idea as being something caused by the stresses of the day.

Kim got up and went to the kitchen; she really needed a cup of tea. On her way there, she caught a glimpse of the strange picture that had arrived only a few days ago. She stopped and studied it for a few seconds — and then she noticed it.

The smile. The boy's smile. It was different. Again.

The boy was looking directly at her, but he wasn't grinning. He had a menacing, evil smile on his face now, the kind a villain would have in a scary movie. She closed her eyes and shook her head to clear the image, but when she opened her eyes again the boy was still looking at her.

Kim hurried into the kitchen and prepared the tea. *Crash!* Kim jumped and almost knocked her mug off the sideboard. She turned and looked in the direction of the crash, then left the kitchen with the kettle still boiling. She looked around the lounge. Nothing seemed to be broken. She couldn't understand what it was. Then she saw it. The picture. It was on the floor. Kim went over to it and picked it up. She turned it over and gasped. The glass in the frame was broken in two places; two neat cracks were in the glass, both of them obscuring the faces of the adults in the picture. The boy had changed, too. He was grinning again. He had the look of a child who had done something to be proud of — the sort of look a young child might give a teacher when they gave them praise. This change in facial expression made Kim more uneasy than when the boy looked menacing.

She put the picture back on the shelf but laid it face-down this time. Then she went back into the kitchen and finished off making the tea. She thought of pouring some wine now, but it was only lunchtime so she decided it was too early. Tea would have to do. For now.

Chapter 45

Sergeant Matthews didn't like the case. He couldn't see any outcome other than for it to be closed without a culprit coming to justice. The body had been found almost completely decomposed. The head was found in the same dump and was in better condition, but there was no way there would be any prints or other identifying marks or information found on the body. He was shooting in the dark by going to speak to people who knew her. She was last seen, as far as he was aware, at the staff Christmas party. There would have been many people there who would have been the 'last person to see her'. He was hoping that something would be uncovered about somebody she was seeing or going to meet that evening — although he wasn't holding out much hope. Miles was a decent enough constable to accompany him — he was an enthusiastic, up-and-coming colleague — but Matthews didn't think it would make much difference.

They pulled up in the car park outside the victim's workplace. This was going to be a long and ultimately fruitless day. He just hoped that they had good coffee in the canteen.

***

It was a beautiful day. The sun was warm on Hannah's face. She looked around; she was lying in an open green clearing. She stretched and slowly got up. Suddenly, Hannah realised where she was. She was in the park at the end of her road. There were children playing on the swings and slides in the park. The warm weather had brought families into the park, so it was quite busy.

Hannah was confused. She didn't understand what was going on.

She heard a voice calling her name.

'Hannah! Hannah!'

She turned. It was her mother. Hannah smiled and ran to give her mum a hug, tears in her eyes.

'What's the matter?' her mother asked.

'Mum, I had a horrible dream. I was attacked and I was lost in a forest. I had to eat bugs and bats and weeds and drink dirty puddle water.'

'It's ok, it's ok,' her mother said comfortingly. 'How about we head home for a drink and you can come back out again later?'

'Sounds good,' Hannah said through her tears. She was starting to feel better.

They walked home holding hands. Hannah was squeezing a little harder than she normally would have. She felt like a little girl again. It felt nice.

They reached Hannah's house and went inside. Her mother got some squash out of the cupboard and poured some into a glass. She filled the glass with water and handed it to Hannah, who gulped the cool drink gratefully.

'Go and take it into the lounge,' her mother suggested. 'Your dad's in there somewhere.'

Hannah walked into the lounge and then stopped suddenly. She dropped her glass. Smash! It broke on the wooden floor, but she hardly noticed. She couldn't move. She was rooted to the spot. In the distance, she heard her mother call from the kitchen to see if she was alright. She paid no attention to her.

Standing in front of Hannah was a man she recognised — but it was not her father. It was the man who had been haunting her thoughts and dreams. It was the man who had attacked her. It was Miss Coombes' boyfriend.

It was Ben.

He looked at her and walked towards her, smiling. Hannah tried to scream but nothing came out. Ben was close enough for her to feel his rancid breath on her face. It made her feel sick.

Ben reached out and grabbed her arms. Hannah thrashed about in panic, but Ben's grip was too strong. He picked her up and stared into her eyes. Ben's eyes looked dead. They were black and lifeless like still dark lakes in the night. He breathed heavily on her face again. His smile was yellow and she could see small maggots between his teeth.

'Let's finish what we started,' Ben said to her.

Hannah leant towards Ben as he started walking to the sofa. She shut her eyes tight, opened her mouth and bit down on Ben's shoulder, hard. Some of his flesh came away in her mouth. It tasted disgusting. Spitting out the piece of meat, she opened her eyes and looked at the piece on the floor. It was black and covered with small worms. Ben screamed in pain and threw her on the sofa. She hit it with a thud as her head crashed against the arm of the sofa, and then everything went dark.

* * *

Sergeant Matthews had been right. Today had been a long and fruitless day. He had seen five or six employees who knew Tamzin and only one or two of them could give him any information about the party or if she was seeing anyone. She was not seeing anyone and she was quite quiet during the party was the general consensus. A name had come up a few times however: Ben. He was often seen flirting with her in the office and he was with her at some point during the party. Other than that, there was not a lot of information to go on. Ben was the last name on the sergeant's list and he was hoping that he would get a little more information out of him than the previous employees.

* * *

Ben opened his office door and saw two strangers looking at him. One of them introduced himself as Sergeant Matthews and the other as PC Miles. Ben invited them into his office and they sat opposite him. The desk separating them seemed like a huge chasm. The room had suddenly got bigger.

Ben sat down and smiled at the two men. 'What can I do for you?' he asked.

'I was wondering if you could tell us about Miss Locke?' Sergeant Matthews replied, getting out his notebook.

'Absolutely,' Ben said. 'It's such a tragedy. I can't believe she's gone.'

'How did you know the victim?' Matthews asked emotionlessly.

'I worked with her. Tamzin worked the front desk. I don't really know what she actually did... Answer phone calls, photocopying, that sort of thing, I guess.'

'I know what her job was, Ben — can I call you Ben?' Matthews asked. Ben nodded, and Matthews continued. 'I want to know how you knew her.'

Ben looked at the sergeant and then at the constable.

'I knew her as a work colleague, but that was it.'

'A number of employees have told me that you were known to be flirtatious together. Did you see her outside of work at all?

'I did flirt with Tamzin, and she flirted with me, but it was only a bit of fun. Never anything serious. I only ever saw her in work. The only time I saw her outside of work was at the Christmas party the other day.' There was a slight nervousness coming into Ben's voice now.

'Ah, that brings me on to the party. That was the last time, it seems, that anyone saw Tamzin. What can you tell me about that night?' Matthews was picking up some vibe from Ben. He didn't quite know what it was, but something was there. After ten years of working on the force, he was used to trusting his gut instinct, and right now his gut was telling him that Ben was different to the other employees he had interviewed earlier today.

'Well I don't remember that much, to be honest. I was pretty smashed by the end of it,' Ben admitted.

'How about you tell me what you do remember?'

'Um, ok… Well, when I arrived there were already a lot of people there. I went to the bar and got a beer. I spoke to a couple of people. Then had another drink. That's when Tamzin came over to me. She had had a fair few drinks by then. We spoke for a while at the bar and had a number of drinks together. We sat down for a bit and danced for a bit. I don't know what time she left, but she definitely left before me. She actually left quite early. I walked her outside, I think. I probably kissed her goodbye and then went back inside.'

Matthews and Miles were both making notes now. They didn't say anything when Ben finished speaking; they just kept jotting things down.

The silence hurt Ben's head. The giant room had suddenly become very small. He felt claustrophobic. The chasm that was the desk had now closed. The officers were almost sitting on top of him now. Breathing on him. Their eyes had bored holes into his head when he was speaking. He didn't like it.

'Thank you, Ben, that's all for now. We may have to ask you some more questions as the investigation moves on. We will be in touch. In the meantime, if you do remember anything else that might be useful, anything else at all, here's my card.' Sergeant Matthews handed him a small piece of white card.

Ben looked down at it and then back to the sergeant.

'I will definitely do that, thank you.'

He got up and walked round his desk. The two officers got up and shook Ben's hand. Ben opened the office door.

'Thanks again for your time,' Matthews said, and turned to leave.

Ben smiled and said, 'Thank you too.'

The officers walked down the corridor towards the exit. Ben closed the door and let out a heavy sign.

'I'm not sure about him,' Matthew said to Miles as they left the building.

'What do you mean?' asked Miles.

'I don't know, but there was something a little weird about him. I didn't like it.'

'I didn't notice anything.'

'He just seemed a little nervous.'

'Lots of people get nervous when interviewed.'

'I know but it was a different kind of nervous. Maybe I'm wrong, but I do want to speak to him again.'

'Ok, if you think there's something in it then let's do it.'

'Leave it a couple of days and we'll go back to see him. The others gave us nothing of real value.'

They got into the car. Matthews started the engine, his mind still on Ben.

Chapter 46

Ben couldn't think about doing any more work today. He felt like he had just been facing a firing squad. He spent the rest of the day pottering around his office, ignoring any phone calls that came through. Finally, it was time to go home. He packed up his stuff and switched off the lights. He had a stress headache. He rubbed his temples as he walked towards the reception.

Sean looked up from his desk. 'What's it...er, you ok, mate?'

Ben glanced over to Sean. 'Yeah, fine — I've got a bit of a headache, that's all. Been one of those days, you know?'

'Er, I do indeed. Hey, I'm finishing now, do you fancy going for a drink round the corner? What's it...er they've just done it up, so it's nice and fancy.'

'Not really, mate, I have to be back home. Not sure it's a good idea.'

'Come on, it's just a drink. It's not a date or nothing! It might help with the headache.'

Sean's voice and mannerisms were beginning to annoy Ben. However, he found himself agreeing to go for a drink with him.

Sean smiled a big, bright smile — he was almost like a child being told that he was allowed to buy anything he wanted in a toy shop. He jumped up from his seat, turned off his computer monitor and walked round his desk to Ben.

They left the building and walked out into the car park.

'Should I drive there?' Ben asked.

'What's it...er it's only a hundred metres round the corner. Just have the one drink, you'll feel better and then you can drive home.'

'Ok. It's a plan.'

They walked round the corner. There was a slight breeze that was cold on Ben's face. The cold air was clearing his stress headache already. He was starting to forget the terrible day and the police. They passed a long, fenced off car park with a grey building behind it.

'What's it...er that's where I used to work.' Sean pointed at the building as he spoke. 'I hated the fucking place! Couldn't wait to get out of there.'

Ben wasn't really listening, but he gave an acknowledging grunt in response. Absentmindedly, he turned and looked at the gloomy building. There was a light shining above the main doorway but the rest of the building was in darkness. Two small trees, possibly olive trees, bordered the main door. There were a few small steps up to the main door and then the open empty car park in front of that. The whole area was surrounded by a tall, barbed wire fence around it. The main entrance to the car park had a high gate with spikes at the top of it and there was a remote control panel on the wall next to it.

Ben thought about asking what the company actually was that warranted a barbed-wire fence and a gated main entrance but he couldn't be bothered with it. He disliked this man. He didn't even know why he had agreed to the drink. He walked on in silence.

They got to the door of the newly refurbished pub and went inside. The lights were surprisingly bright for a pub. Ben looked around. The old, dark, dingy pub had been taken over by a brewery and was now a bright, airy, trendy restaurant and bar. The tables were all different; some were metal tables with rivets as decoration, whereas others were made of thick oak. Chairs were artfully mismatched, and the lampshades were a mixture of metal and fabric. The mismatch design seemed to work. There was a fire burning in two different corners of the restaurant. The place felt inviting and Ben felt comfortable for the first time in hours.

They walked to the bar and sat on the barstools. Sean ordered two pints of beer and paid for them.

'I have to buy you one in return now,' Ben said, with a smile.

'What's it…er, next time you can get me one.'

The two men drank at the bar. The beer soothed Ben. It was ice cold going down his throat. His head was clear and he was enjoying himself. He found himself liking Sean's company; he was actually pretty funny. Before long, they had both finished their beers and Ben ordered another round of beers. He just felt like he should.

They drank the second beer almost as fast as the first and Sean ordered a third. By now Ben had forgotten the day completely. He had forgotten the police. He had forgotten Tamzin. He had forgotten Kim.

Ben ordered some bar snacks and a fourth beer. He and Sean both flirted with the new barmaid as they chatted to each other. The barmaid seemed to enjoy the attention and was happily flirting back. As much as Ben was enjoying himself, he still found Sean's habit of saying 'what's it' before most of his speech very annoying. He was thinking about asking Sean the reason why he did this, but decided against it. It did grate on him, though. Ben wondered if the barmaid had noticed it and if she hated it as much as he did.

By now, Ben was pretty drunk. He was revelling in the attention from both Sean and the barmaid, and started to feel confident that the barmaid liked him.

'Hey, Sean,' Ben said, when the barmaid was away from the bar. His voice was starting to slur a little now. 'What do you reckon about the barmaid? She's hot, isn't she?'

Sean smiled at Ben. 'What's it…er, she sure is, mate. It was worth coming here just for her, eh?'

'Yeah. I might ask her out, mate.'

'What's it…er, why not, mate? If she says no then I

will try my luck with her instead. Maybe she fancies a threesome!' Sean winked at Ben.

'No thanks, mate, I'm quite happy not seeing your dick!'

Sean laughed and then stopped suddenly. 'What's it…er, she's on her way back. Go for it!'

Ben looked towards the barmaid and smiled drunkenly at her.

'Can I get you another?' she asked.

'Yes, two more pints, please,' Ben replied. 'And a date, if you fancy it?'

'What?' the barmaid replied.

'A date? What do you say?'

The barmaid smiled back at Ben. 'Thanks for the offer, but I am spoken for.' She walked off to get the pints.

Sean started laughing loudly. 'What's it…er, gutted, mate! She blew you right out of the water!'

'Fuck you, Sean. You try.'

'What's it…er, no way, man — she said she's spoken for. I'm not asking her out now!'

'Fuck you!'

The barmaid came back with the pints and Ben paid her without looking at her or saying a word. His head started to hurt him again, but it was a different pain to earlier. It was one that he had felt before but he couldn't remember when.

Then it happened. That sound. The high-pitched screech. It hurt. Ben strained his eyes against the noise. The lights hurt his eyes now. The screech was piercing his head. It felt like an arrow scratching at his brain.

Sean noticed the change in Ben. 'What's it…er, you ok, man?'

Ben didn't answer at first. He hadn't heard him. Not right away. The voice was distant; it seemed miles away.

'What's it…er, hey, Ben, you alright?'

'My head hurts again, mate. I think I'll finish this and head home. I'll have to get a taxi or something.'

'What's it…er, ok, mate. After these we'll go.'

* * *

Hannah woke up with a scream, and the image of Ben's leering face stuck in her mind. It was dark and cold. She could feel a gentle breeze on her face. She touched something soft and damp underneath her hand: leaves. She was in the forest still; she must have fallen asleep after eating the nettles. She was shaking with cold and fear. Slowly, she calmed her breathing down. Two things then dawned on her. Firstly, what had just happened had been a dream; she hadn't been in the park with her mother, and Ben wasn't in her house. Secondly, and almost more frighteningly, *this* was not a dream; Ben attacking her and her being lost in the forest were both real.

Hannah's thoughts then went back to yesterday's decision: she was supposed to be spending one more night in the building before moving on to try to find…well, anything — anyone. She had planned on moving during the daylight but she had fallen asleep. She now had the choice to stay where she was, find her way back to the hut or head off in a direction in search of people or houses or whatever may be outside the forest. There had to be an end to the trees. There had to be a road to reach, a house to find nearby. Hannah was sick of the hut. She was sick of being alone. She was sick of eating disgusting things and drinking water that made her stomach hurt. She was sick of the pain she was in. Almost every part of her body now hurt at some point.

'That's it!' Hannah said aloud. 'I'm going to find people.' She turned around and looked up at the trees above her. 'Did you hear that? I'm getting out of here!' she shouted at the forest. She felt a little surge of adrenaline hit her and she ran. Hannah ran until her feet hurt. She jumped over branches that she saw in the dark and tripped over branches that she didn't. She pushed through bushes and brambles, ignoring the pain in her back, neck and feet. She wanted to keep a straight line. As straight as possible, in any case. After a while, she stopped. Her breathing was deafening in her ears. She bent down and put her hands on her knees, panting. She had no idea how long she had been running for. Maybe it was only a minute. Maybe it was an hour. Her feet were killing her. They were probably bleeding — she couldn't see. She could see scratches on her arms and legs, though.

Slowly, her breathing calmed and she decided that she had run enough in the dark. She may have missed important things. She sat down and leaned against a tree. Within moments, she was asleep again.

* * *

Ben was drunk. He knew it. His head was killing him. The terrible shrieking sound numbed his senses to anything else that was around him. He and Sean staggered out of the pub and the cold air hit them both like a slap in the face. It felt nice.

Sean smiled at Ben.

'What's it…er —'

Ben paid no attention to the rest of Sean's sentence; he had heard that annoying phrase, 'what's it…er', and that was enough. It grated on him. It almost made the screeching worse.

They started walking away from the pub and back towards the work car park. As they passed the gated main entrance to Sean's old workplace, Sean grabbed Ben's arm, making him jump.

'What's it…er, I've got to break in there, mate. I fucking hate the place so much. I need to get my own back on them. I'm going to take a shit on their front steps.'

Ben looked shocked. Despite being drunk and in agony from the sound smashing around inside his head, he felt the need to stop Sean from breaking into the car park.

'I don't think that's a good idea, Sean... How'll you get in, anyway?'

'What's it…er, I know a weakness in the fence. We can climb over it just down there.' He pointed about ten metres down the road. Ben could just about make out a small break in the fence. Sean was already walking towards it. Sean stopped and looked back at Ben. 'What's it…er, come on, Ben. Quick, or we'll be seen!'

Ben followed and saw Sean pull the fence down a little and climb over, carefully avoiding the barbed wire. Ben, who was not as nimble as he might have been when sober, tried to copy Sean and ended up tearing his shirt.

'Shit,' Ben whispered as he looked at the tear under his arm.

'What's it…er come on.' Sean said, running over to the main steps up to the front entrance. He clambered up the steps on his hands and knees in his drunkenness. When Sean reached the front door Ben saw him undo his trousers and pull them down to his ankles.

'What's it…er, Ben, come here and take a picture!'

'What's it…er' kept running through Ben's head. It hurt almost as much as the screeching. Ben winced against the mental pain.

SCREECH!

What's it…er…

Ben didn't know if Sean was even talking now or whether it was just in his head. Was Sean also making the screeching noise? He started to hate Sean. The hate brewed up inside him quickly. It is him. He is making both of the noises. He won't shut up. Why won't he shut up?!

Sean had his trousers and pants around his ankles now. He was squatting on the top step. He was loving it. Revenge! Sweet revenge! Best served cold! Yes! He could feel his bowel move and — slowly, gently — he started to squeeze out his revenge. He imagined the manager's face in the morning and smiled.

SMASH! Sean didn't even see it coming. He had been revelling in his revenge.

Ben, in his newfound hatred of Sean, had gone up the steps, picked up one of the plant pots that bordered the front door and smashed it down on Sean's head.

Sean lay motionless on the floor.

'What's it…er!' Ben shouted down at the body. He picked up the plant again and brought it down hard onto Sean's head. 'What's it…er, you fucking prick!'

Ben lifted up the plant a third time but it was broken. It would do no more damage as it was. The noise in his head had quietened a little, but it hadn't gone. Then Sean groaned quietly.

'Fuck,' Ben said as the screech cried out in his head again. 'Fuck, fuck!'

He looked around but saw nothing. The car park was empty. Then he remembered the damaged fence. Ben ran over to the fence and looked at the barbed wire. It was damaged where they had climbed over. Maybe he could rip a bit away from the fence posts…

Ben grabbed the damaged end of the barbed wire. It was quite loose in his hand. He pulled hard. Nothing. He pulled hard again, and this time the wire loosened more. Ben pulled again and again. Before too long, the damaged wire had come free from the fence post. He had a piece of wire about a metre long in his hands — enough to put an end to the noises.

Ben walked back to Sean's body. The place was a mess. Dark red blood flowed down the steps like a river. The plant pot was smashed over the body, and there was black soil mixing with the blood on the top step. As Ben got to the top step he saw something else: Sean's stinking revenge.

'You sick fucker!' Ben shouted. He stepped over the brown mess and lifted Sean's limp head. Ben pulled the barbed wire around the front of Sean's neck and let his head drop back to the floor. Thud! It made a dense, heavy sound as it hit the concrete step. Ben grabbed either end of the barbed wire and pulled. The sharp metal tore into Sean's neck. Ben pulled harder. The wire tore further and deeper into Sean's throat; it was cutting into his windpipe now. Ben held the wire tightly for a few minutes. The wire slowly cut through Sean's neck and then stopped when it reached Sean's spine. The noises and pain inside Ben's head subsided and he opened his eyes fully for the first time in a while.

Ben stood up straight and looked down at Sean's lifeless, almost decapitated body.

'What's it...er, fuck you!' he said through gritted teeth. He kicked Sean's body once and turned to leave the car park. He walked to the broken fence and climbed back over. Without looking behind him, Ben walked towards FanCorp. He felt amazing. The cold air was intoxicating. He breathed it in as he looked around.

'I need to get home,' he said, and went in search of a taxi.

Chapter 47

Kim was furious. She had been calling Ben for hours now. She had left him at least four voicemails and had sent a number of text messages, but Ben hadn't replied. Where was he? Was he ok? She had rung his direct work number. No answer. His mobile seemed like it was dead; it didn't even ring. How long do you leave it before reporting someone missing? A few hours? That's all it had really been. Overnight? This was the first time Ben had disappeared on her when they were supposed to be doing something together — today, of all days! She needed him. She wanted to get a takeaway and some wine and take her mind off her rough day.

How should she react when he came back? Should she scream and shout at him? That's what she wanted to do. Or would that mean she was a controlling girlfriend? Instead, should she play it cool — like she didn't care? Or would that leave the door open for more episodes like this? She hated the whole situation. She didn't like the way she felt right now. She was angry. She was worried. She felt scared. Something somewhere was playing on her mind. She searched her thoughts but found nothing.

Kim tried Ben's mobile one more time. Nothing. She didn't leave a voicemail this time. She got up from where she was sitting in front of the television and went to her computer; she would do a little online shopping to take her mind off of everything. She enjoyed online shopping. Something about buying something new gave her a little thrill. She wasn't a shopaholic, not by any means, but she did like to buy something new to wear every now and then.

The computer was in sleep mode and fired up very quickly. Kim moved the mouse over to the web browser icon and clicked. Her homepage came up.

She had personalised it to show her recent news, new emails and any social media messages. She had no new emails or social media messages. She looked at the newsfeed that was changing every few seconds. Some team had won some match. Some celebrity had been arrested for speeding, or drink-driving, or both. The third news item caught her eye. The picture had the Eiffel Tower in the background and in the foreground there was a park with a load of police tape around a tree with a white tent in the middle of it. 'MURDER IN PARIS' the headline read. Kim clicked on the picture. The link took her to a page on the BBC website. The headline was there again, with a smaller subheading underneath. 'Woman Found Brutally Murdered in Paris Park.' Kim read the entire article. The hairs on her neck stood on end. Her palms started to sweat. She could feel her heart race in her chest.

She read the article again. It explained that, over the weekend, a young woman in her twenties had been found brutally murdered in the Jardin Du Champ de Mars in Paris — directly in front of the Eiffel Tower. Her head had been completely smashed in. There were signs that sexual intercourse had taken place in the moments before — and possibly even after — she had died. The French police say witnesses have said that the victim was last seen leaving a bar near the park with a man. The man was described as being around six feet tall with thick, dark, possibly black hair. He had been smartly dressed in dark red chino style trousers and a dark shirt. Any further witnesses were encouraged to come forward quickly. The police were worried about another murder happening due to the brutality of this crime.

Kim sat back in her chair and stared blankly at the computer screen. A tear came to her eye and she wiped it away. Then she felt sick as a thought struck her. No, she told herself, there must have been other men dressed similarly to Ben in Paris, surely...

She got up and paced around the lounge for a minute. Then she went back to the computer and read the article again a third time. This time, Kim cried in earnest. It was as though they were describing Ben without having ever met him. But he had been with her the whole night. They had eaten and gone back to the hotel and slept. Hadn't they? She had been a little drunk that evening, so her recall wasn't as good as she wanted it to be. Again, something was biting at her thoughts, irritating her. Her mind was racing.

Then it hit her. The thing that had been irritating her for a while...it was about Ben. The news article had almost put the something into place. Although the thought of it was absurd... She shook her head to rid the outrageous thought from her mind. But it would not leave her alone. For a second, she allowed it to manifest inside her. Ben — Paris — murder. She had had a thought similar before. A much smaller thought, but a thought all the same: Ben — Birmingham — murder. He had been in both cities when someone had been brutally killed. Her mind raced forward again. Tamzin. She hadn't been seen since the Christmas party at Ben's work. Then the worst thought of all hit her, making her insides disappear. Her mind hurt like hell now. Why was she even thinking these thoughts? This was Ben. She loved him. He loved her. He was the best thing that had happened to her.

The thought that she had been trying to keep out of her head suddenly popped up again. Tom and Hannah. Ben had been there when they had disappeared. He had been there...

No. This was stupid. This was insane. The more she thought about it, the more it seemed possible. Could Ben have killed five people without anyone knowing? Could he have murdered two *children*? Could he have *slept* with other women?

Not Ben. No, not her Ben.

Kim was crying hard now. Her face was a mess.

She didn't know what to do with herself. She couldn't contact Ben — his phone was dead. Then her thoughts drifted again. What was he doing now? Was he murdering someone else? She shook her head. No, he wasn't, because he hasn't murdered anyone.

Kim sat back down on the sofa. She couldn't help thinking about what he was doing right now. She needed to speak to him. But what would she do when she saw him? Would she ask him about the murders? He would surely laugh at her. Would she think her so ridiculous that he would finish with her? She couldn't deal with that. She needed him. Would he hate her for not trusting him? What sort of girlfriend accused her boyfriend of murder? One who had good reason to, she supposed...

Kim lay down on the sofa and closed her eyes. Her mind showed her pictures of Ben. Then she was shown pictures of the murder scene in Paris. Her mind then continued the show by making up pictures of Ben killing the victims. Kim cried again. She was exhausted; her whole body and mind were now aching. She fell into a fitful sleep.

* * *

Hannah woke to some birds tweeting above her. She slowly opened her eyes. It was daylight. She stirred and winced. Her back ached. Her legs ached. Her head ached. She felt pain in her feet from the running she had done the night before.

She had no idea where she was. She remembered running for what seemed like hours last night. What she was sure of, however, was that she didn't recognise anything around her. She was definitely away from the hut that she had called home for the last few nights. Hannah suddenly felt afraid — had she made the right decision to leave the ruined building? Was she ever going to find anyone? Then a depressing thought hit her. Either way, if she had stayed or ran, she was probably going to die out here. If the weather got any colder, she would freeze to death. She had been lucky that the weather was quite warm for December. December…why, it must be nearly Christmas! She'd miss it!

Gently and carefully, Hannah got to her feet. They were tender when she tried to stand, and when she looked down at her toes she saw they were covered in dried blood. She must have hurt them badly last night during the run. Today, she would have to walk slowly and cautiously through the forest — there was no way she could run.

Hannah started walking. She hoped that she wasn't heading the way she had come last night. She would have cut her feet to shreds for no reason at all then. She looked in front of her; the bushes and undergrowth had not been disturbed in this direction. That probably meant that she hadn't come this way last night. She pushed onwards with what might be the last journey of her life.

***

Matthews woke with a jump as a thought hit him hard. Something was playing on his mind. It had been playing on his mind for hours. It was Ben. He didn't like him. He had a strange feeling that Ben was hiding something. No, not hiding something — more like he was not sure what he was actually saying. Was Ben lying to him? He didn't know. He had seemed to believe what he claimed. Matthews was very good at picking out lies or liars. He didn't think Ben was *lying*, exactly. He just thought that Ben was delusional.

Matthews scratched his head. He must have just fallen asleep without realising earlier. He looked at the clock on his bedside table. It read 3:32. Matthews sighed heavily. He swung his legs out from under the duvet, stood up and gave a little yawn as he stretched. He went downstairs and put the kettle on.

Christmas Eve. Up at half three on Christmas fucking Eve.

He yawned again and looked out of the kitchen window at the quiet residential street on which he lived. There was no one around. He didn't really expect there to be at this time in the morning. There was a light on in the upstairs window of the house opposite. Whatever time he finished work at night, that light was on. There were a few streetlights illuminating the cars below. He saw a fox dart out of one of the gardens opposite; it stopped in the middle of the street and looked around with an air of arrogance. It almost seemed to look directly at Matthews, then it ran off up the street and out of sight.

The kettle had boiled now and the click of the switch broke Matthews from his reverie. He turned and poured the hot water into a mug with a teabag in. He let it brew while he went to his computer and turned it on. He also turned on the TV. He didn't expect much to be on at that time in the morning, but it was a way to break the silence in the house.

* * *

Kim woke up around seven. Her neck was stiff and aching; she had slept awkwardly on the sofa all night. As she began to wake up fully, she remembered the events of last night.

Ben. What had happened to him last night? Where the hell was he? Was he even alive? And what about the murders?

Kim sat up abruptly. She had to go and see if he was home. If he wasn't there then she would call the police.

She got up off the sofa and went to the bathroom to have a shower. She made the water as hot as she could bear, and it felt amazing. She started to feel better. The pain in her neck eased. She ended up staying in the shower for half an hour; she simply didn't want to leave. She didn't want to have to face the day. It was Christmas Eve, and she felt miserable.

Kim dried herself off and got dressed. Her stomach started making noises, almost like a dog whimpering for its food. She had to have something to eat.

She went to the kitchen and made herself a cup of tea and some cereal. Kim glanced at the clock on the oven as she wolfed down the breakfast. It was ten to nine. Where had the time gone? She downed the rest of her tea; it was still a little too hot to drink comfortably, but she needed the caffeine. It burned her throat as it went down and she winced.

Kim picked up her coat from the hook behind the front door and headed for her car. So many thoughts were spiralling around her head. What was she going to say to Ben when she saw him? What would he say? Should she confront him about the murders?

She felt nervous. Incredibly nervous. She got into the car and started the engine.

Chapter 48

Hannah was physically and mentally exhausted. Her feet were not holding up very well, so she had to walk on tiptoes sometimes, and then on her heels. She had taken a number of breaks to sit down and rest. She looked down at her hands; they were black with dried mud and blood. Her feet were in a similar state. Her legs and arms were going the same way. She was feeling weak. She had cried a lot.

Every now and then, she thought about home. Would she ever see her house again? Would she ever see her friends and family again? At this point she had almost given up hope. Should she just let nature take over her and put her to sleep in the forest? She would become animal and bug food before long. She might die in her sleep. That would be the best way to go — just a peaceful sleep. Then the animals could eat all they wanted of her. She would be doing the forest a favour by feeding the animals.

Hannah shook her head, hard. What a ridiculous thing to be thinking! She had to keep going. There had to be an end to the forest. Then another thought came to her: what if she was already dead? How would she know? Maybe this was heaven or hell or wherever we go at the end of it all! If it was heaven or hell why was she alone? Maybe that was how it worked.

Hannah decided to keep going regardless. She would push on until she physically could not move any further. She gritted her teeth against the pain and started walking again.

* * *

The drive over to Ben's flat was a blur for Kim. Her mind was a mess. She couldn't concentrate on the road at all. She ran a red light without even noticing and stopped at green lights with her thoughts miles away. She tried to get her mind on the road but it kept drifting.

Could Ben do such things? Surely not. It was *Ben*. She loved him. He loved her. The thought of Ben murdering people was impossible.

Pictures of the scenes ran through her head. She saw him beating women. Beating children. Killing them. She was crying again — loud, heavy sobs this time. What was she going to say to him when she saw him? *If* she saw him. Where was he? What if he wasn't at home? Should she go to the police? Should she tell them her suspicions? They would think she was crazy, making up these assumptions based on Ben just being around the area at the time. But was it crazy? The more she thought about it, the less crazy it seemed and the more worried about seeing him she became. A chill went down her spine. How should she act when she saw him? Should she act as if nothing was on her mind, other than him not answering her phone calls? Should she come right out and say what she was thinking? She didn't think that would be wise. If he was a deranged killer...

Deranged killer — she couldn't believe she was thinking this!

If he *was* a deranged killer, she would need to be herself and talk to him as if nothing were wrong. Could she do that? Would he become suspicious?

BEEEEP! A horn sounded loudly as she turned into Ben's road without indicating or slowing down. The noise broke her thoughts and Kim came back to the driving in time to dodge an oncoming car. The driver looked at her angrily as he drove past and stuck his middle finger up at her. Kim lifted her hand up to apologise, but the driver was gone.

Slowly, Kim pulled up outside Ben's block. She looked out of the car window at the building. She was breathing heavily — not just from the thought of seeing Ben, but also because of the near miss she had just had. She needed time to relax and calm down. She needed to gather her emotions and think about what she was going to say.

***

Hannah resorted to crawling for some of the distance because her feet were in so much pain. It didn't help her much; it was slow, and it also meant that she was scraping her hands and arms. Her hands were getting torn to pieces and sharp stones were jabbing her as she moved. Her bare knees were wrecked. What was left of her dress was in tatters. Her hair was catching on branches and ripping out in clumps.

She had long since stopped crying; it did no good and only made it more difficult to see. Every now and then Hannah stopped to rest but the rest only made her body throb more intensely. It made her feel sleepy. She didn't want to sleep. She wanted to keep going until she reached civilisation or killed herself trying to get there. She was hungry and thirsty but tried not to think about that. Stopping also made her think about food and she didn't have any so there was no point in thinking about it. Slowly and painfully Hannah crawled onwards through the undergrowth. Her mind constantly thinking about being found. Seeing her family again. Seeing her friends again. She didn't want to die out in the forest.

***

Sergeant Matthews got the call around eight o'clock in the morning. A man's body had been discovered outside an office building by a jogger going for an early morning run. He had noticed an unusually large amount of gulls and crows gathered in front of one of the office buildings on his running route. The sight was so unusual that the jogger had stopped his run and looked over at the entrance to the building. After the jogger shouted at them, the birds all flew away, leaving a sight that made the jogger sick. He had immediately rung the police, who quickly arrived on the scene. That was when Matthews got the call.

Sergeant Matthews arrived after the first responding officers. He passed through the police tape that had been set up and went to the top step. What he saw made his stomach retch. He was usually pretty good with crime scenes, but this one was different. The skull was smashed in; he could see jagged white fragments sticking through the skin. The head itself was almost severed completely from the body. Sharp, barbed wire was sticking out of the man's throat; it had only stopped when it had hit the spinal cord. The lifeless eyes were glazed over, and one was nearly out of its socket. The body was a mess, but the strangest part of it all was the lack of blood. There was faeces between the man's legs — but no blood. There should have been lots at a scene like this...

As Sergeant Matthews was having a closer look at the body, an officer came over to him.

'Sarge, you are going to want to see this,' the officer gasped. 'We have some CCTV footage of the incident. It's pretty horrific, to be honest.'

'Ok, let's have a look.'

They walked around to the side of the building. The side entrance was open and there was a security guard standing at the door looking pale and nervous.

'I've never seen anything like it,' the guard told Matthews as he entered the building. 'It's the worst thing I have ever seen in my life...real life that is. It's almost like a film. I can't believe what I actually saw happen.'

The guard took the two men over to the security desk and started pressing some buttons on a computer. After a few seconds, the main screen on the desk showed a grainy black and white picture of the outside of the building they were in. It was pointed at the main entrance and showed the top step and the front door. The security guard tapped the 'Enter' key and the small trees either side of the doorway moved slightly.

'It'll start any second now...'

All of a sudden, a man entered the picture. He was on the top step. He had pulled his trousers down and started squatting with his back to the camera.

'Oh my God, gross,' Matthews said. 'Is he taking a shit?!'

A number of seconds passed, and then it happened. The three of them stood in silence as they watched the events of the previous night unfold in front of their eyes. They saw a second man smash the plant pot onto the head of the first man, who instantly fell to the floor. The second man hit the first man again and again with the pot, then left the scene for a while. The three onlookers said nothing. Matthews was just about to start saying something when the man reappeared in the shot. He had something in his hands. He stood over the first man and pulled something in front of the first man's throat. Matthews could see the second man pulling hard on what was now obviously the barbed wire he had seen earlier. The second man threw the head of the first man's body down to the ground. The scene was a mess of dark pools of what must have been blood. Interesting — the blood was no longer there. The second man got up, kicked the first man and appeared to be shouting at him. He then left the scene.

The security guard pressed the 'Enter' key again and the scene froze.

Silence engulfed the room. No one wanted to say anything. What they had seen would haunt them all for years to come. It was not every day you saw a real life snuff film. Shivers went down Matthews' spine. He wanted to see more of the second man. He needed to see another angle of the steps or the car park.

'Do you have any other footage of the area at that time last night? I need to see the man's face.'

'Just give me a few seconds and I can get the car park footage up for you,' the guard replied, and started tapping on the computer keyboard. The frozen image disappeared and was replaced with a new scene featuring the car park.

'I have moved the time back a bit because then you can see the men arrive,' the guard explained.

The three men watched the screen again and saw two men clamber over a gap in the fence. The second man was a few paces behind the first. They then disappeared from the scene. A few minutes later, the second man re-entered the scene; he was running towards the fence. He spent a little while wrestling with it, and then pulled the barbed wire free and ran back out of view. A few minutes later, he casually climbed the fence and walked out of the shot away from the car park.

'How good is the zoom on this thing?' Matthews asked the guard.

'It's pretty good, I think,' the guard replied.

'I need you to zoom in on the man's face when he is heading towards the fence.'

The guard rewound the footage a few minutes to when the man first came into view by himself. The camera zoomed in on the face of the man, but the shadow on the man's face made it impossible to see his features.

'Move to the point after he has garrotted the man,' Matthews ordered.

The officer looked at the sergeant in surprise. 'Do you know who it is?' he asked.

Matthews held up a finger to the officer, telling him to be quiet. He needed to concentrate on the scene. The second man came back into view, walking casually. He quickly glimpsed in the direction of the camera.

'There!' Matthews shouted. 'Zoom in there.'

The guard rewound the footage slightly and zoomed in on the face as it looked up at the camera for a split second.

Matthews smiled to himself. 'Ben,' he said under his breath. 'Ben, you sick bastard. I knew there was something about you...'

'Ben, sir?' The officer was confused.

'Follow me,' Matthews ordered. 'Find Miles and bring him to me. Get FanCorp on the phone. I need to find out where Ben lives.'

Matthews ran out of the building. The fresh air hit him like a sledgehammer. He was out of breath. Yesterday, he had interviewed someone who had now committed the sickest murder he had ever seen.

He needed to find Ben. He had to bring him in before he did this again.

Matthews' mind was all over the place. He felt sick. He needed to sit down. In the distance, he saw Miles running over to him. He shut his eyes and tried to get his breath back. His heartbeat returned to normal after a while. He opened his eyes and saw Miles looking at him.

'Ben,' Matthews said. 'It was that guy we spoke to yesterday — Ben. We need to find him.'

Chapter 49

Kim looked at her watch. She had been sitting in her car for over half an hour. She hadn't noticed. She must have fallen asleep. She couldn't remember thinking about anything. The last thing she did remember was pulling up to the kerb. Kim took a few deep breaths. She wiped her eyes and checked her face in the rear-view mirror. Her eyes were puffy but there was nothing she could do about that now.

Slowly, Kim opened the car door. She picked up her handbag and got out, gently shutting the door behind her. She didn't want to make her presence known until she was completely ready. She wanted the upper hand.

The upper hand for what?

Cautiously, she walked to the main door of the flats. The door was already open. She pushed the door and it creaked a little, so she stopped pushing and waited. It was unusual for the door to be unlocked and open. Nothing. She pushed the door again and looked into the hallway. Nothing. It was silent. She crept inside and walked up the small flight of stairs to Ben's front door, which was open. Not just unlocked, but ajar. Once again, Kim pushed the door open carefully and crept inside.

The smell hit her first. It was the pungent smell of stale booze. She looked around her. The place was a mess. She couldn't remember the last time she had been to Ben's flat, but it had always been neat and tidy. The scene that was in front of her now was disgusting; there were food cartons on the floor and on the sofa, empty cans of beer on the floor and glasses full of stale beer sitting on the table.

Kim walked into the kitchen. There were plates on the sideboards with food starting to rot. Flies were making themselves comfortable on the rancid food.

She could see vomit in the sink; she gagged and nearly added to it. She steadied herself and backed out of the kitchen, heading instead towards Ben's bedroom. The smell of putrid alcohol grew stronger the nearer she got to the closed bedroom door. Kim tried the handle and it turned easily; she took a deep breath and pushed the door open.

She peered inside. The room was dark and quiet. The stench was awful. She looked around before entering. There was a shadow on the bed. Kim squinted harder against the darkness. It was Ben. Was he alive or dead? She couldn't see him breathing. Carefully, Kim entered the bedroom and stood at the head of the bed. She looked down at Ben, and then she saw his back raise slightly as he breathed. Kim realised that she had been holding her breath and let it out. It made a thunderous noise in the silence. She looked down nervously.

Ben started to move.

* * *

Matthews was getting annoyed. There had been no answer at FanCorp. It kept going to voicemail, and there was no alternative number to call. He had called the station and told them that he needed them to find out where Ben lived. He had left it with them, but he had been waiting twenty minutes so far and that was twenty minutes too long.

By now, the sun had risen into the sky, and even though it was Christmas Eve it was unseasonably warm. He had drunk three cups of coffee and not only needed the toilet but he was also very hungry. He had to get a sandwich.

Matthews ran over to a large bush at the edge of the car park and relieved himself. On his way back to the crime scene, he saw Miles.

'Can you go and grab me a sandwich from

somewhere, please?' he asked Miles. 'I think I passed a place just on the edge of the industrial estate.'

'Yeah, no worries, boss,' Miles replied. 'Any luck on the address?'

'Nothing yet, and it's pissing me off. He may have left the country by now.'

Miles turned and went to one of the squad cars. He drove slowly out of the car park in the search of sustenance.

* * *

Kim felt a surge of adrenaline hit her like a locomotive. She didn't know if it was fear or anxiety affecting her most. She continued to stare at Ben. She thought about running out of the room and back to her car. She could drive back home and finish it with Ben.

Why was she thinking this? She had no proof that anything she was thinking about was true. What if none of it was true? She was being paranoid.

She felt her heart smashing inside her chest, trying to get out. It was beating so hard she thought that Ben would hear it. What should she do now? Should she wake him? She didn't know if she wanted to wake him. What if all of it was true? That changed everything. She had to find out, but how would she go about asking him? It was not the sort of thing one could just ask their boyfriend. Hey, how are you doing? By the way, did you brutally murder a load of people recently? She smiled to herself. It seemed ridiculous.

Ben stirred again and let out a tiny groan. In that moment, Kim decided she would do it. She would wake him up, and once he had come round and they had had the inevitable row about him disappearing last night, she would ask him. She would just ask him if he noticed anything when he was in the places where the murders occurred.

Kim sat on the edge of the bed. Gently, she touched

Ben's bare, sweaty shoulder.

'Ben,' she whispered, and gave his shoulder a little shake. 'Ben, wake up — it's me, Kim.'

Ben let out another groan and slowly rolled over. His eyes were puffy, his breath rancid. He finally opened his eyes and stared at Kim. It took a few seconds for him to focus properly on her. Then he smiled.

'Hey, Kim,' he groaned. 'What are you doing here?'

* * *

Hannah could hardly move. She was completely exhausted. She had all but given up now. This was where she would die. In the forest. Alone. She would be eaten by whatever animal found her first, and then the maggots would eat the rest of her. She might get found at some stage — maybe years from now. She would just be a skeleton. She might even become a legend or a ghost story that children her age told each other. The ghost of Hannah — the girl who got lost in the forest.

Hannah lay down among the dirt and moss on the floor. If she drifted off now, she might die in her sleep. No pain. She closed her eyes.

Hannah had been lying down for a few minutes when she heard a noise. A sort of whooshing noise. She opened her eyes quickly and sat up. It sounded almost like a car going by. She listened again but didn't hear anything else.

Hannah turned to face the direction the noise had come from, feeling a sudden rush of energy engulf her. She almost jumped up from the ground. Everything ached, but she ran. As she ran, she noticed the forest seemed to be getting lighter up ahead. There were not so many trees. It was a clearing. Hannah stumbled a few times, but she didn't slow down. Then all of a sudden the forest ended. There were no more trees. There was a small ditch in front of her that was home to a stream when it rained. Above the ditch, Hannah saw something that made her scream out. A road. Not a big road, but it was a road nevertheless, and a road meant cars. Cars meant people. People meant being saved. She hoped.

Hannah clambered up the side of the ditch on her hands and knees. She reached the top and her hand touched the tarmac. She smiled. She crawled up a little further and then collapsed. She could move no more.

Chapter 50

Matthews was annoyed at how slow the station was being at getting him Ben's address. However, he now found himself sitting in the accident and emergency room in the hospital, talking to a young girl. Matthews was amazed that this girl wasn't dead. He wasn't sure whether she would live, even now, but the fact that she had made it this far was a miracle.

The girl had been found unconscious by the side of the road, curled up in a ball. She was incredibly undernourished, dehydrated and covered in mud and blood. The elderly couple who found her had called for an ambulance, and the girl was taken to the hospital. She was put on a drip immediately and when she starting to come round she spoke deliriously of being lost and attacked in a forest. The hospital had called the police and the girl had relayed her story to them. The girl mentioned a name and description of a man called Ben, and this was the reason Matthews had been called.

From what Hannah — for that was the girl's name — had told them, she been violently attacked and almost murdered by Ben in the forest a number of days ago. She told Matthews that her friend Tom had saved her by kicking Ben. She had run away, but didn't see Tom again. Hannah then told Matthews about how she had survived the last few days. The story was amazing. The sergeant couldn't believe her resilience. She should be dead.

Matthews praised her and thanked her for the help she was giving the police. He said he would call her family and let them know she was safe and that they could come and see her.

Matthews' mind was in overdrive. In the past two days, Ben had gone from being a minor suspect to a violent killer. He asked Hannah what she knew about Ben.

Hannah told him that he was the boyfriend of her teacher, Miss Coombes.

He asked her about Miss Coombes but Hannah didn't know much about her. She described what she looked like, but that was it.

Matthews called the station again. He asked them to find out the phone number of Miss Coombes. Without her first name, though, he didn't think they would have much luck. He might have to try every number that came up under Coombes in the area.

Matthews started thinking. Was Coombes alive? Dead? Did she know about the murders?

* * *

'What am I doing here?!' Kim almost screamed at Ben. She tried to stay calm, but when he had looked at her blankly the emotions erupted inside of her. Rage was the emotion that exploded out of her first. 'Why the fuck do you think I am here?! Where the fuck were you last night? I've been worried sick! You haven't answered my texts or my phone calls. You just disappeared. I thought you might be dead in a ditch somewhere!'

Ben's head hurt. He was hungover; he didn't need this grief. He thought for a minute. He needed to calm Kim down.

'Oh my God, Kim, I'm so sorry. I completely forgot. I ended up going for drinks with the new receptionist in work. He's a bit of dick, to be honest. I'm such a prick. I'm so sorry, babe.'

Kim seemed to calm down a little. Ben shifted his position and sat up. He leaned in towards Kim, hoping she would lean in and hug him. She did. She was crying, but she hugged tightly.

They hugged without a word for a few minutes. Kim broke the hold first and looked straight into Ben's eyes. He smiled at her and melted her anger away. How could this man be a murderer? It was impossible. But she still needed to know.

She smiled back at him. 'Right, get your hungover, lazy backside out of bed and get in the shower. Then you can make me a cup of tea. You owe me that, to start with. You owe me a lot more, too.'

Ben got out of bed slowly and walked unsteadily towards the bathroom.

'Oh and brush your teeth — your breath stinks!' Kim shouted after him.

Ben raised a hand in acknowledgement and went into the bathroom.

Kim looked at Ben's bedside clock. Somehow it was almost midday. The time had flown this morning. Tomorrow was Christmas. She couldn't believe that. Where had the year gone? Just then, her phone started buzzing in her pocket. Kim took the phone out and looked at the screen.

Unknown Number.

Kim tutted and pressed decline. She never answered unknown numbers anymore. She hated cold callers.

***

'FUCK!' Sergeant Matthews shouted as the phone went to voicemail. 'FUCK, FUCK, FUCK!'

This was the third Coombes he had tried. The first two had answered but were not the right person. One was an old woman who was almost completely deaf, and the other was a very grumpy woman with a strong northern accent who told him not to call her again or she would call the police. Matthews left a message on the latest voicemail saying that if she was in fact the right Miss Coombes she needed to call him immediately. It was urgent. He left his number and hung up. He dialled the last number on his list and got another voicemail. This voicemail was self-recorded, and it was a male voice speaking. Matthews hung up without leaving a message.

* * *

Ben stood under the hot water for almost half an hour. His head felt like it was rotting away. His body ached. What had he done last night? He vaguely remembered drinking with that new receptionist. He remembered not liking him. He was weird. He kept saying something weird. It was almost like a nervous tick, but a vocal one. What did he say? Ben couldn't remember. What he did know, however, was that he was in trouble with Kim. He had to smooth that situation over quickly. He couldn't deal with too much stress today with his head feeling like there was a jackhammer inside it.

The water soothed his body. Ben washed himself carefully. He retched a few times while brushing his teeth and spat whatever came up into the drain. He felt hungry and thirsty. He needed food and caffeine, then he would feel better. His hangovers were usually cured by food. Although the thought of a greasy fry up didn't appeal to him at all right now; just some toast would do. And some coffee. He definitely needed coffee.

* * *

Ben had been in the shower for a long time. Kim thought she should check in on him to make sure that he hadn't passed out. Then she heard him retching, so she knew he was alive, at least.

Kim got up off the bed and looked around. The bedroom was a mess. It smelt of stale alcohol. There was a shard of light from the window scything its way across the room. Kim went and opened the curtains. Sunlight flooded the room. She had to squint until her eyes got used to the brightness. Kim moved from the window and walked towards the bedroom door.

Something caught her eye on the wall. The sunlight was reflecting off it sharply. She went over to it. It was the weird picture that Ben was given years ago. It was the same one that arrived in her post a few days ago — only it was different somehow. At first, Kim couldn't quite put her finger on it.

Then it hit her, sending a shiver down her spine: the boy in the picture…his face had changed. He still had a menacing smile, but she now recognised the face.

Ben's face was looking back at her.

Kim looked away, and then looked back. She was surer now than before. Ben was looking at her from inside the frame. She then noticed something else in the picture. A shadow. Very faint, true, but it was there, just behind the boy there — a shadow of a man, almost ghostly in appearance. You would hardly notice it unless you stared at the picture hard. Did hers look like that too? She couldn't remember.

Kim's eyes drifted back to the child's face. Ben's face. It scared her. She tried to look away, but was unable to. She was drawn to the face by some almost magnetic force. She couldn't take her eyes of the picture.

'Hey…'

The whisper jolted Kim out of her trance. She jumped as her heart smashed against her ribcage. It was Ben. He had finished in the shower and was looking over her shoulder.

'Oh my God, Ben! You scared the hell out of me!'

Ben hugged her from behind and put his chin on her shoulder. She smelt sweet. A coconut tropical smell. Ben started to feel better.

'Look at the picture, Ben,' Kim said without looking at him. 'Look at that boy.'

Ben looked at the picture. There didn't seem to be anything different. 'What about it?' he asked.

'The boy looks like you!'

'Only that he has the same colour hair.'

'No, Ben, he looks *exactly* like you. He has your face.' Kim couldn't believe that Ben hadn't noticed it.

'No, Kim, it's a little kid. He looks a bit cross, I guess, but he definitely doesn't look like me!'

Kim was silent. He couldn't see it. Maybe it was her imagination. Maybe he was lying. Maybe she was going a little crazy with all that had happened the night before.

That thought brought her back to this morning. Maybe Ben was a murderer. Her heart started pounding again. She could hear it in her ears. Was the murderer holding her in his arms right now? She felt a little sick. She didn't know what to do. Just then, Ben let go of her.

'Would you put the kettle on, babe, while I get dressed? I am desperate for a cup of coffee.'

He smiled at her and Kim smiled back. It was a difficult smile to make. She forced it through.

'Yes, of course,' she replied and went to the kitchen.

Ben started to get changed. His hangover was getting better but his head still throbbed. He looked around the room. It was a real mess. Clothes everywhere. Cups and plates on the floor. His mind wandered back to Kim. What was she on about with the picture? What did she mean it looked like him? It was a strange picture, that was true, but how could it possibly look like him? It must have been a hundred years old!

Ben finished changing and looked at the picture again as he left the bedroom. It definitely didn't look like him. Ben shook his head and went to the kitchen.

Kim had made the coffee and there was buttered toast on a plate.

'You are a star,' Ben said, and he went over to kiss Kim.

She let him kiss her neck but it felt wrong. It felt alien. She needed to confront him about the murders. But how?

Ben took the coffee and toast into the lounge. Kim followed with a cup of tea. They sat down on the sofa without saying anything. Ben turned on the TV. It was some sort of antiques show.

'Daytime TV really is shit! It makes me glad to be in work sometimes.'

Kim said nothing. Her nerves were motorcycling around her stomach. She was shaking. She tried desperately to keep her cup still, but she spilled some tea over the edge. She was going to ask him. She was going to ask her boyfriend if he was a murderer. She was building the courage to do so. It was making her shake harder and harder. At one point, she almost dropped her cup — and that's when she asked.

'Ben?'

It was almost a whisper. Ben didn't hear her. He was watching the TV and eating the toast. Kim tried again, a little louder this time.

'Ben?'

Ben turned to her and saw that she was completely white. She looked terrified.

'Kim? Oh my God, what's wrong?!'

'Ben,' Kim swallowed. 'I need to ask you something. It's important. It might seem weird but it's important and I have to know.'

Ben's face went from concern to worry. He was confused. What could she want to know that was making her so pale?

'Anything, Kim, what is it?'

Where would she start? What should she ask about first? The children? The Birmingham incident? The Paris killing?

'Did you see Tom and Hannah after the Christmas show the other day? You went outside. I was wondering if you had seen them at all. Did they walk passed you, or did you speak to them?'

Ben's head was already hurting, but now it screamed at him. His mind starting moving at an incredible speed.

He saw flashes in his head. Flashes of himself. Flashes of strangers. Scenes that he seemed to recognise but didn't know why. He saw blood. Lots of blood. The scenes were shockingly horrific. People died in front of him. He couldn't understand what was going on. What was he seeing?

'Ben?' Kim's voice came through the crowd of images. 'Ben?'

The images vanished and his vision focussed on Kim. She was staring at him. She looked scared.

'Sorry, Kim, my head hurts...I was miles away.'

'Did you hear what I asked? About Tom and Hannah?'

'Yes I heard you, I don't remember seeing... AAHHH!' Ben screamed as a vision of Hannah jumped into his head. He was on top of her. She was looking at him through terrified eyes. Then he saw Tom beneath him. He saw a rock smashing down on Tom's head again and again.

Ben felt a touch on his arm, which brought him back to the present. He looked at Kim again. She was saying something to him but he could not hear the words. All he could hear was a screech. An ear-piercing screech was coming out of her mouth. Just then it dawned on him. It was Kim! It had been Kim all along. *She* had been making the noises. *She* was the one who had been wreaking havoc inside his mind! After everything he had done — everyone he had silenced — it was her all along!

He couldn't believe it. He felt a sudden hatred for her. She had destroyed his life. Why did she make that sound? What did she want from him?

His head was killing him. His eyes hurt. The sunlight was painful. He looked at Kim again. She was still screeching at him. Why?

He had to stop her.

He had to silence her.

Chapter 51

Ben's face had changed. Not just his expression, but his actual face. There was a hatred in his eyes. An evil.

He was staring right at her. She had tried talking to him, but he wasn't listening. She had asked about the children but got nothing back from him. She thought about asking about the other suspicions she had, but after his reaction to the first question she was too afraid to.

Kim didn't know what to do. What was going on? Was this the person who had killed all those people? Right now, she could certainly believe it. This wasn't Ben standing in front of her. This was someone else. This person could definitely have killed people.

She couldn't look at him anymore. Not into his eyes, at least. There was something there that petrified her. She turned away from him. As she did so, she felt a force on the back of her neck. It was a hand. A powerful hand. Ben's hand. Kim let out a scream and the grip tightened on her neck. She screamed again as Ben pulled her backwards. His other arm went around her waist and he started dragging her back out of the lounge. Kim tried kicking out at him, but it was hopeless. She knocked the sofa as she passed by, but nothing more.

Ben dragged her into his dank bedroom. It seemed colder than before. He threw Kim down onto his bed, and she didn't move. She dared not move. She didn't know what was happening. Who was this man? What did he want? She started crying into the pillow. Still, she didn't move.

***

Ben looked down at Kim lying on his bed. She was still. Was she dead? No, she wasn't dead — she was still making that fucking noise! Even now, with her head in the pillow, she was screeching at him. It wasn't even muffled. How was she doing it? *Why* was she doing it? He had to stop her.

Ben bent down and grabbed Kim's shoulder, roughly turning her over. Her eyes were tightly shut but she still screeched at him. She screeched *through* him. It was burning through his head. He had to silence her.

'Shut up! Shut up!' Ben shouted down at her.

Nothing. The noise seemed to get worse. Forks scraping on a dinner plate. Chalk down a chalkboard.

The pain in his head had to stop.

Ben looked around and saw a dirty sock on the floor from the night before. He picked it up and forced it into Kim's mouth. The noise erupted, the sound pulsing in his head now.

* * *

The sock tasted vile and smelt of stale sweat. It hurt her mouth and throat. Kim tried to scream out again but she couldn't. She tried to sit up, but Ben was now sat over her with one leg either side of her and his hands pinning her arms down. He was shouting in her face, but it was silent. There was nothing coming out of his mouth except spit. She writhed under him. What was he going to do? Was he going to rape her? Was he going to kill her?

Ben looked away from her for a second. He quickly got up, so she tried to sit up. It hurt. She ripped the sock out of her mouth and gagged. She had to get out of the room. She had to get out of the flat. Kim got up off the bed. She couldn't see Ben. Slowly, she walked towards the bedroom door. It was quiet. Her senses were heightened. The whole flat seemed darker now. There was sunlight edging its way through the windows, but it didn't make much difference.

Whack! A hand crashed into Kim's face. She felt a

crack as her nose broke. There was a warm sensation on her upper lip. Blood.

Ben pushed her back into the bedroom and threw her against the wall. Kim's head smashed against the picture of the boy. She opened her eyes and saw the boy with Ben's face looking straight at her. Mocking her.

Ben pulled Kim away from the wall and threw her back onto the bed. He shouted at her again, but she heard nothing. He straddled her again and she saw something long in his hand. It was one of Ben's work ties. Ben grabbed her right arm roughly and forced it above her head. He began tying her wrist to the metal bedpost. He tied her so tight it hurt. She felt the blood pulsing through her veins, trying to push its way through the narrow space in her wrist. Ben did the same with her left wrist. Kim tried to move, but she was held fast by the ties.

Kim looked directly at Ben and screamed. Ben picked up another sock and pushed it hard into Kim's mouth again. Kim felt blood ooze down her throat. Her nose was hurting her. Her head was hurting her too. She felt a trickle of blood coming down her cheek.

Ben got off Kim and sat on the side of the bed, his head in his hands. It looked like he was trying to shut something out; his eyes were tightly shut and his teeth were gritted.

Ben raised his head, shook it and put it back in his hands. Kim tried to speak, but couldn't. She squirmed against the ties and Ben looked at her. He was crying. His eyes were red. Ben mouthed something at her but she couldn't work out what he had said. She could make out the word 'noise' but nothing else.

Ben stood and left the room without looking back. A few minutes later, Kim heard the front door shut with a bang. She thought she heard Ben's car start but that could have been anyone's car outside.

* * *

Ben slowly pulled out of the drive. He was almost blind with his hatred of Kim right now. She was taunting him with her screeches. Even now, in the car, he could hear her screeching at him. The pain was getting worse and worse. He had to end it.

Kim was secure in the flat. She wasn't going anywhere. He needed to get away for a few minutes. Maybe it would give Kim time to stop her noise — the noise that had haunted him for so long. The noise that had crippled him — that was crippling him right now. What if she didn't stop though? What if she kept taunting him? Hurting him? He had to do something.

Bing! The petrol light came on. A little petrol pump image showed on his dashboard. Ben hadn't realised how far he had driven. There was a petrol station at the end of the main road, just a few hundred metres ahead. He pulled into the station and got out of the car. Ben filled up the car with unleaded petrol and went inside to pay. As he went inside he saw a number of bright green cans. Ben picked one up and took it to the cash desk. There was a grubby looking teenager stood behind the desk. Ben took no notice of him; he just paid for the petrol and the can, then left.

The sound in his head was deafening. He shut his eyes to try to keep it out.

As Ben reached his car, he opened the can, lifted the petrol pump and filled the green can up. A little spilled out of the top. He closed the lid and put it in the car, then got in and started the engine. He slowly pulled out of the station. The young cashier looked out of the window and starting shouting something. Immediately, he picked up the telephone and dialled a number.

Oblivious, Ben drove back to his flat. He parked on the street outside instead of the drive and got out, taking the can of petrol with him. Ben opened his front door and went inside. The noise in his head intensified. Ben leaned on a wall for stability. He stayed there for a few seconds and then walked through the lounge and into the bedroom. Kim was lying motionless on the bed.

Chapter 52

Matthews had hit a wall. He had rung the three numbers again. Two answered but were not Kim Coombes. That left the third number. He rang it again, but there was no answer. He had a bad feeling in his stomach. He still hadn't heard anything about Ben's address. He was getting more and more frustrated. He was getting desperate. The next step was to break into FanCorp and find the staff files. If they were on computers, he would be wasting his time, but if they were old school and had paper copies, he might be able to dig out Ben's file from somewhere inside the building. He decided to wait a little longer. He tried the third phone number again.

* * *

As Ben entered the bedroom, he saw Kim's phone light up on the bedside table. The number on the screen said 'UNKNOWN'. He let it ring off.

Ben leaned over Kim. He put the petrol can down on the floor and Kim opened her eyes. She shook her head. Ben tried to smile at her. She was beautiful. Even though she was torturing him, she was beautiful.

He winced against the pain in his head. The sound was bouncing off the inner walls of his skull. He had to stop the noise. He had to stop Kim tormenting him.

Ben couldn't work out what was happening. He was seeing things. Things inside his head. Visions. Horrific visions of death. Why was he seeing these things? Was Kim somehow doing this to him too? Was she controlling his mind?

Wait...maybe he was dreaming... That could be it. An incredibly vivid, grotesque dream. A nightmare. Nothing more than a nightmare. How could he wake himself up? The nightmare was so real he actually felt like he was driving the car earlier. Maybe it wasn't a dream. Maybe it was something else. What could he do?

Ben got up and went out to the kitchen. Water might do the trick. Ben went to the sink and ran the cold water until it felt really icy cold. He put his hand under the water and felt the chill. He cupped his hand and lifted a small pool of water up to his face and splashed it on his cheeks and forehead. He shuddered and blinked a number of times, but nothing changed. Nothing happened. He didn't wake up in his bed. He didn't wake up anywhere else, either. That meant he was either already awake, in a very deep sleep or dead. Maybe this was what the other side was like. Surely not. But how would he know?

Ben's vision was blurry because of the intense pain inside his head. He slowly left the kitchen and traipsed back to the bedroom. He bumped into the doorframe as he entered. He almost felt drunk. He looked at Kim lying on the bed. He loved her.

He walked over to her and stubbed his toe on the can.

'Shit!' he cursed, and looked at the can. He was confused. What was that doing there? Why was there a green can of liquid in the bedroom? He looked from the can to Kim. Suddenly, rage hit him hard. Through the noise in his head and the mist that was now his vision, rage emerged.

Kim.

She was going to kill him.

That explained the noises in his head. That explained the visions he was getting. He didn't know how she was doing it, but somehow she was getting in his head. And now that wasn't enough; she was going to kill him. Burn him alive...or dead. He couldn't let that happen. He had to stop her. He had to stop what she was planning to do to him!

Ben jumped on top of Kim again, leaning close to her face and snarling, 'You bitch! You fucking bitch! I fucking loved you, and you want me dead!' Spit flew into Kim's face. She shut her eyes tightly and started crying. Ben was also crying from a mixture of rage and sadness. He shook Kim's arms, hard.

***

Kim opened her eyes again. Tears were streaming down Ben's face — but it wasn't Ben's face. Not the one she saw every day, at least. Something had changed. The features were different.

No, the face looking at her was the child's face, from the picture. Angry and screaming at her.

Kim tried to shout but she gagged on the sock in her mouth. She was helpless. There was nothing she could do. She looked directly into Ben's eyes to try to communicate with him. Whatever was happening, the real Ben must be in there somewhere. If she could connect to that Ben, maybe she could calm down the monster that was now holding her captive.

She was trying not to cry. She didn't want to seem weak. She wanted to be strong, but the tears kept coming. Ben was shaking her wrists hard. Then she heard it.

Crack!

Her right wrist broke under the strain from Ben. A new pain shot into Kim's head. She bit down hard on the sock and writhed in agony. Ben didn't even notice. He shook her arms some more.

Just then, the weight lifted as Ben got off of her.

A few seconds later, Kim knew it was the end. This was it. She was going to die here in Ben's flat.

The smell hit her first. A strong smell that anyone would recognise.

Petrol.

Under normal circumstances, she quite liked

the smell of petrol. Right now, though, the smell terrified her. Suddenly, she felt something drop onto her stomach. Her t-shirt felt wet. The smell of petrol became intense; it started to burn her nostrils. The fumes were getting through her closed eyelids and stinging her eyes.

Kim quickly opened her eyes to see what was happening. The petrol fumes scorched her eyes and they immediately started watering. Through the tears, she could see Ben standing at the side of the bed with a green can in his hand. His face was bright red. He poured petrol from the can onto her stomach. Ben then caught Kim's gaze and he turned towards her. He lifted the can again. Kim shut her eyes as tightly as she could. The liquid hit her face. It felt almost warm. At first she could taste it. Then she felt it in her throat. The petrol had gone up her nose and into her throat. It burned. A few seconds later, she tasted it in her mouth. The sock had soaked up the petrol and what had started off as a barrier was now wicking petrol into her open mouth. It tasted metallic, repulsive. Her tongue started tingling, but the numbness didn't last long. The petrol was torture.

She thrashed against the pain. Ben stopped pouring the liquid. She still couldn't breathe properly. Every breath tasted horrendous. She was breathing petrol into her lungs now. Kim couldn't open her eyes. He lids must be giving her some protection; if she opened them, raw petrol would seep into her eyes.

Kim stopped moving and listened. She couldn't hear Ben anymore. Where had he gone? What was he doing? Was this it? Was he leaving her here to die?

* * *

Ben couldn't take it anymore. He had to end it. The noise. The torture. The visions. He had decided to use Kim's plan against her.

He would burn her.

He had poured some petrol onto her, and now he was pouring the petrol on the floor of the bedroom and out in the lounge. He threw some of it onto the walls. The smell was intoxicating. He could hardly see at all now; the mix of fumes, tears and pain had seen to that.

Ben emptied the last of the petrol onto the floor and sat back on the bed. He looked at Kim, hating and loving her at the same time. Why was she doing this to him? Even now, she was tormenting him. His head was ready to explode with the screeching noises.

'Fuck you, Kim,' he whispered at her. 'Why are you doing this? You can stop this, Kim. You can stop this.'

Nothing. She didn't respond, and the noise inside his head seemed to get worse.

Ben got up from the bed. He needed fire. He didn't have a lighter — both he and Kim didn't smoke. If they were at her place there would be lighters and matches because Kim liked to have candles from time to time. Ben didn't have candles. He didn't remember having matches, either.

He walked out to the lounge. There was nothing there that could make a spark. He went into the kitchen. The hob. It was gas. He could use that to light some paper. He didn't have any newspapers — he hadn't read any for years. Ben got his news from the internet. He went back into the lounge. There were a couple of books on a shelf in the corner of the room. Some books that he had read and enjoyed over the years. They had saved him from boredom, and now one of them was going to save him from the intense agony in his head.

Ben picked up a James Patterson novel. He liked reading Patterson; the stories moved fast. Slow-paced stories bored him. He found himself looking at page numbers and how long chapters were if the stories weren't fast-paced.

With the novel in hand, he went back to the kitchen.

He tore out a couple of pages and turned on the stove. It clicked a few times before igniting, but then the blue flame burned brightly. The heat was warm against his face. Ben held the ripped pages up to the flame and they caught alight quickly. He ran into the lounge and held the burning bunch of pages to the damp area on the wall, setting it ablaze almost immediately.

The pages were almost black and burned out now. Ben picked up a cushion from the sofa and held it into the fire. The fabric took some time to catch. A little while later, however, the entire wall of the lounge was in flames. The sofa was almost melting in the heat. Ben picked up a fiery sofa cushion and moved it into the bedroom. The room caught fire without much effort. The fumes caught and the room burst into flames. The walls were alight. The floor was alight. The bed was ablaze. Kim started to writhe and shake, straining against the ties around her wrists. She looked like she was screaming but Ben couldn't tell.

The room was hot. Flames brushed Ben's face, but he didn't notice. He was staring at Kim. The sound in his head did not subside. His vision was narrow and foggy. He went over to the bed and sat down next to Kim. He stroked her face gently.

'I'm sorry, Kim,' he whispered. 'But you wouldn't stop. You had chances. It was too much, babe.'

The room was filling up with smoke. The heat was melting everything in the bedroom. Kim was choking. Ben started coughing. The smoke was infiltrating his lungs. He didn't notice. He lay on top of Kim and slid his arms under her body. He squeezed her tightly in an embrace. He could feel her breathing gently, faintly.

The flames had caught Ben's clothes. He was on fire, but he didn't notice. The noise was burning his mind. The flames were burning his flesh. Ben kept hold of Kim.

Chapter 53

The call had finally come through and Matthews had etched the address in his mind. Ben's address. The station had found it. It was almost twenty-five minutes away. He needed to have the lights going. Hopefully, with it being Christmas Eve, the roads would be quiet. He wasn't going near any shopping centres.

Matthews took Miles in the car with him and had called for other officers to get over to the address as soon as possible.

Matthews sped through what little traffic there was. The rush of driving fast through traffic never died. He lived for these moments. He didn't like the idea of a desk job. He belonged out where the action was. He enjoyed his job, but this case was different. There was something weird going on.

Matthews reached the end of Ben's road and he stopped sharply. He saw the smoke in the distance. Instantly, he knew that it was coming from Ben's flat.

Matthews sped down the road and pulled up outside the flat. Dark black smoke was spewing out of the windows. He could see flames licking the walls of the building. Miles got out of the car and started to run up the drive.

'Miles, stop!' Matthews shouted after him. 'Don't go in! We need the fire service for that. It looks like an inferno in there.'

Matthews took his phone out and called the fire service.

'Ben! Ben! Are you in there?' Miles was shouting at the window nearest him. Black smoke was the only reply he got from the building.

***

Somewhere in the distance, Ben thought he heard someone calling his name. He didn't pay it any attention. His head was pounding. The noise was breaking him. The bedroom was completely engulfed in flames now. Kim had long since stopped squirming beneath him. He had calmed her down.

He lay on top of her. He couldn't feel anything now. The heat from the fire was relaxing. It was the first time that he had felt relaxed all day. Ben was comfortable where he was. This is where he belonged. This is where Kim belonged.

He hated having to do this to Kim, but it was her fault. She had been messing with his head.

Ben lay his head gently on top of Kim's face and closed his eyes. As he did so, he thought he heard his name being called again. He smiled to himself.

The screeching noise was subsiding. The pulsating, agonising pain was weakening. Kim's power over him was fading.

Slowly, gently he felt he was able to sleep. Ben felt the noise disappear altogether.

* * *

The story hit the papers. There were numerous reports about Ben and Kim, lots of interviews with people who were 'saddened' at the news of Kim and 'horrified' at the news about Ben. People couldn't believe Ben could have committed the crimes he was accused of. 'He seemed such a nice guy,' was the usual response.

The fire had been so intense that it had taken many hours and a lot of firefighters to put it out. The chief firefighter had not seen such an intense fire in such a small space burn for so long. The firefighters had pulled two charred bodies out of one room in the ground-floor flat. There was no one else in the building. The bedroom and lounge were completely destroyed in the blaze. The other rooms in the flat were not so badly damaged. There was a lot of smoke damage but the fire itself seemed to be concentrated mainly in the bedroom. The building itself may well have to be condemned. The damage to the two rooms was severe and it may eventually cause the top flat to come crashing down.

There was very little salvageable in the ground floor flat. When the police were finally able to enter the building, there was nothing left. And since Ben was dead, there wasn't much else they could do with regards to their investigations.

Matthews had gone round the flat one last time before he let the rest of the authorities deal with the scene and clean it all up. He found nothing of interest. He didn't like being in the flat. It felt cold and it had a dark, sinister feel to it. Each time he entered the flat, he felt as though he was being watched by something, or someone. It was eerie. He decided it was time to go.

As he started to leave the flat, something crunched loudly under his foot. He bent down to see what it was. He expected it to be some glass from the window that blew out during the blaze, but instead he'd picked up a broken picture frame. Three sides of the frame remained. The last shard of glass slid out of the frame as he brought it up to take a closer look. There was a picture in the frame. The picture was completely intact and undamaged by the fire.

Matthews stared closely at the picture. It was weird — quite an unusual picture for someone like Ben to have in his home. The picture was around ten inches square and had a kind of sepia tone to it. It must have been an old photograph. The picture was of a woman and a man who both had an eastern European look about them. A young boy sat on the woman's lap.

Matthews stared at the picture for some time. He almost thought he recognised the young boy's face, but didn't know where from.

Matthews smiled to himself. And for reasons he

couldn't himself explain, Matthews took the picture out of the broken frame, folded it up and put it in his pocket. He didn't know why he did it. It was strange.

The picture... He just liked it.

Author Profile

Matthew Gilbert was born in Southampton but grew up in Swansea, South Wales. Matthew was an avid reader from an early age; Enid Blyton, Richmal Crompton and Malorie Blackman were his favourite authors as a child. Growing up, Matthew's influences were Stephen King and Dean Koontz. He also enjoys reading John Saul and James Patterson.

Matthew liked creative writing in school and enjoyed writing stories. After university (where he earned an undergraduate degree in French and Italian and a postgraduate degree in Early Childhood Studies), Matthew went travelling. Whilst in Australia, Matthew came up with the idea for his first novel, *Ben*. However, this project took a back seat when Matthew returned to Wales and started writing children's books. Over time, Matthew found that he really wanted to finish his thriller novel, so he decided to stop writing children's books and concentrate on *Ben*. He found it refreshing to write for a different audience, and especially enjoyed developing the characters.

Aside from writing, Matthew enjoys playing football, travelling and running. He is still an avid reader. In 2013, Matthew married Laura, whom he had first met when he was nine years old. They had their first child, Ellie, in 2015.

Publisher Information

Rowanvale Books provides publishing services to independent authors, writers and poets all over the globe. We deliver a personal, honest and efficient service that allows authors to see their work published, while remaining in control of the process and retaining their creativity. By making publishing services available to authors in a cost-effective and ethical way, we at Rowanvale Books hope to ensure that the local, national and international community benefits from a steady stream of good quality literature.

For more information about us, our authors or our publications, please get in touch.

www.rowanvalebooks.com
info@rowanvalebooks.com

Lightning Source UK Ltd.
Milton Keynes UK
UKOW04f0611141217
314453UK00001B/350/P